A War For Truth

Legacy of Light Book 2

M. Lynn and Michelle Bryan

A War For Truth © 2018 Michelle Bryan and Michelle Lynn

All rights reserved under the International and Pan-American Copyright Conventions. No part of this book may be reproduced or transmitted in any form or by any means, electronic or mechanical, including photocopying, recording, or by any information storage and retrieval system, without permission in writing from the publisher. This is a work of fiction. Names, places, characters and incidents are either the product of the authors' imagination or are used fictitiously, and any resemblance to any actual persons, living or dead, organizations, events or locales is entirely coincidental. Warning: the unauthorized reproduction or distribution of this copyrighted work is illegal. Criminal copyright infringement, including infringement without monetary gain, is investigated by the FBI and is punishable by up to 5 years in prison and a fine of $250,000.

Edited by Melissa Craven
Proof-edited by Angela Caldwell
Cover by Melissa A Craven

This one is for our characters who allow us to test them and strengthen them. For Davion and Rissa who break our hearts. For Alixa who makes us stronger. And for Trystan who makes us believe we can do anything. We held the pens in our hands. They told us what to do with them.

GLOSSARY

The world of Dreach-Sciene and Dreach-Dhoun was created using a combination of words from Old English and Gaelic. In these two languages, words didn't only have one meaning. They had many. They became ideas rather than just singular objects. That's why we chose to blend the two. Deep meanings can be conveyed in a single beat. Even our location names can hold more power.

Aldor – (All-door) Old English for life. 'Aldorwood' means the wood of life.

Bràthair – (Brah-thair) Gaelic word for brother.

Dhoun – (Doon) Old English for dark. 'Dreach-Dhoun' means dark magic.

Dreach – (Dray-ach) A simplified spelling of the Gaelic term 'draiocht' meaning magic.

Isenore – (Eesen-oar) Old English for iron mine.

Scíene – (Scene) Old English for beautiful, brilliant, light. 'Dreach-Sciene' means light magic.

Sona – (So-na) Old English for hope. The Isle of Sona means the Isle of Hope.

Tá sé in am – Gaelic for 'it is time'.

Tenalach – (Ten-eh-lahct) – An Irish term for a deep connection with the earth.

Toha – (Toe-Ha) An old English term meaning the leader of an army, but also a leader of people.

Tri-Gard – Gaelic for the three guards.

Trúwa – (True-wah) Old English word for trust, fidelity, promise.

Uisce – (Ish-ka) Gaelic for water.

Breach-Sciene

Palace of Sciene

Whitecap

The Sea of Wisce

Isle of Sona

CHAPTER 1

Darkness consumed the world, swallowing up every path that lay before Dreach-Sciene's prince. He represented everything they hoped for. He'd bring back their light.

Trystan Renauld stood alone. Always alone. The pitch-black night surrounded him. Was it night? Or had he already lost?

A light appeared farther along the road, the small blaze from a ball of fire. It grew and hovered in the air, illuminating the palm that held it aloft. As it moved closer, the face behind the flame became clear. The seer. Lorelai.

Why didn't it burn her?

"Someone you love will die by your hand." Her deep voice vibrated from the heavens. "Someone you love will sacrifice their life for yours." She raised her palm and curled her fingers. The fireball pulsed. "Someone you love will forsake your name."

Sweat poured down Trystan's face. He wanted to run from her words, from the obvious magic she held, but his feet stuck in the quicksand of her power.

"The curse of kings," he breathed. His body shook. "Death. Sacrifice. Betrayal."

The seer raised her arm, the light from the fire shining in her pale hair. She threw her head back as her magic shot forward and flames danced along Trystan's skin. He screamed as they rose toward the sky and swirled around him.

An image appeared among the flames.

"Davi." Trystan choked as his best friend's eyes lifted to meet his.

"Trystan." The voice didn't come from right in front of him, but from the very air that infused life into the flames. "You promised!"

He shook his head violently as the scene played out before him. As Davi clutched the sword that would crush them all, Trystan fell to his knees. His friend screamed as the blade pierced his flesh and the light in his fierce eyes went out.

Trystan covered his face with his hands, only lifting his eyes when the flames released him and shot past his huddled form. He watched helplessly as they threaded through a village.

"Toha," someone screamed. "You're supposed to protect us."

"Trystan." Another voice cut through the noise, this one kinder. "My Prince, wake up."

Trystan jolted awake, sweat soaking through his hair. "Davi," he said.

The eyes that met his swirled with sadness.

"Lonara," Trystan said when he finally realized where he was. "Is everyone okay? Have they found us?"

"No, but we should move on soon. It won't be long before they track Briggs' magic here."

He nodded, pushing himself up, so he was sitting. His back ached with the movement and he scanned his body for burns as the dream came back to him.

Why was Lorelai important? Surely she was still at the Dreach-Sciene palace with his father. He stretched his arms out in front of him. Pain was good. It meant he was still alive. That was the one thing the loss of Davi couldn't take from him.

He glanced around the cave they'd arrived at yesterday. With a shiver, he huffed out a breath. It was cold enough to see the air linger in front of his face. He rubbed his hands along his arms. "I think it'd be better if we stayed here until the cold passes. Knowing Dreach-Sciene, we'll have a heat wave tomorrow."

"No." Lonara looked wholly unaffected by the cold. "It has only been a week since Briggs used magic to pull down the side of the mountain." She pursed her lips in disapproval. "His magic will remain traceable to those with seer blood for a while yet, but the thread will grow weaker with a little more time. Until then, we must keep moving."

He nodded. Disappointment shot through him, but he understood. He rubbed his eyes, fighting the exhaustion brought on by the constant danger.

He climbed to his feet and held his hand out to her. Lonara was a small woman with russet, reddish-brown skin and dark wiry hair. She turned golden eyes on him as if to say something and only nodded as she took his hand and pulled herself up.

Trystan watched her hug her furs tighter around her shoulders, wishing he had some as well. She wore traditional mountain dress as she'd been living in hiding in the mountains for many years.

As he stepped to the edge of the cave, his eyes roamed over the snowy landscape. The white powder must have fallen while he'd been sleeping. It gave a false sense of peace.

"Before the magic was gone from these lands," Lonara began wistfully. "There was a time of year for this. Winter. For months, the cold would encompass the land and dust it with snow. We always knew it was coming and prepared."

Trystan grunted, resentment stinging his thoughts. Along with the other two members of the Tri-Gard, she'd had a hand in changing Dreach-Sciene forever.

Snow crunched beneath his boots as he walked out. Edric sat near the mouth of the cave deep in thought. He nodded to Trystan.

"Ladies," Trystan said as he walked up to Avery and Alixa. "Are you healing well, Avery?"

She looked up from where she was sharpening her sword. "Almost good as new."

She was lying, but none of them had healed well from their battle. Trystan dreamed of Davi every night. He hadn't taken an arrow like Avery, but he was in no better shape.

"Good of you to finally wake, your Highness." Alixa's tone didn't hold as much of a bite as it had before. The corner of her mouth lifted in a tentative smile. At least she was trying to return to some form of normalcy.

She placed her freezing hand over his.

None of them could be the same after that day. His hand grew slick, and he snatched it back just in time to see deep red blood oozing between his fingers. He squeezed his eyes shut as his breath came out in short gasps.

He hadn't loosed the arrow that killed Davi. His friend died by his own hand. But he'd done it to save Trystan. He was the sacrifice. Maybe Lorelai's curse was true.

A hand landed on his arm and he opened his eyes to find Alixa staring at him. He calmed his breathing as her bright eyes held his.

"He may be gone, Trystan, but our mission is still alive. We'll do it for him."

He swallowed hard and nodded. With a glance from Alixa to Avery to Lonara, he sighed. "Where's my sister?"

"The princess went into the woods at the end of the path." Avery pointed with her sword.

Trystan turned to trudge through the snow to the trees. He should have known. Rissa had an affinity for trees or any kind of life that grew from the earth. She had the Tenelach, a deep connection to the earth, that he used to think was a fairytale. For most of his life, he'd thought that was all magic was. Fancy stories and unrealistic dreams.

Lonara followed him into the trees. He wanted to ask her to give him some time with Rissa, but she looked determined.

Rissa had barely spoken to anyone since Davi's death. A constant scowl lined her face, marking the anger brewing just below the surface.

They heard Briggs before they saw him. The Tri-Gard member was bent over, drawing something on the ground and mumbling to himself.

"We're so close," he said. "Only one more."

Rissa leaned against the base of a large tree, one leg propped up behind her. Her pale skin seemed paler still against the snowy backdrop, and her fire-red hair blazed bright. As Trystan and Lonara neared, she turned her once bright eyes on them. They'd dulled considerably and Trystan imagined they now matched his own.

For most of their lives, it'd been the three of them—Trystan, Rissa, and Davion. Now they were the only ones left, and it felt as if they didn't even have each other to hold on to anymore.

She turned her head so she no longer had to meet his eyes. "Are we moving on soon?" Her voice was as listless as he felt.

"Yes." He stepped forward cautiously. "I'm glad you didn't go off alone today."

She shrugged. "Briggs doesn't expect me to talk to him. He just talks to himself."

The accusation was plain in her voice, but he didn't address it. Instead, he walked to look at what Briggs was drawing. Carved into the snow were two symbols. Each was a triangle in a circle, but one was upside down.

"What are these?" he asked, scanning the detailed depictions.

Briggs looked up as if noticing he had company for the first time. "I already explained the first one."

Rissa kicked off the tree and strode forward. "To me, old man. You didn't tell my brother."

Briggs looked confused for a moment before pushing up the sleeve of his shirt to reveal the symbol tattooed on the inside of his wrist. "There are three of them, sigils, that must work together to balance the magic. We need all three to bring it back."

"Each represents a member of the Tri-Gard," Lonara explained. "The mark Briggs wears means dark magic." She pointed to the second symbol he'd drawn. "Mine is light magic." She pointed to each symbol inside her sigil in turn. "Light. Harmony. Fate. Magic."

Briggs looked to her in alarm. "We're missing earth."

She put a hand on his arm to calm him. "We will get to him."

He shook his head violently. "Ramsey was in league with the dark king."

She smiled weakly. "We can't completely blame him. We too, stole the magic. In the end, it did not matter that we were saving Dreach-Sciene from destruction or that we were forced. Ramsey was protecting his daughter. Love is the greatest force in the world. Greater than hate. More influential than fear. With it, we are flawed. Without it, we are nothing."

Trystan met Rissa's eyes. His love for Davi prevented him from fulfilling his promise. If Davi hadn't taken his own life, it would've put the people of Dreach-Sciene in jeopardy. There was no doubt in his mind he would've saved his friend at the expense of his kingdom.

Rissa's cold eyes were too much. Too real. Too painful. He turned on his heel and walked back the way he'd come, his footsteps fading away as fresh powder filled in the evidence that he'd been there, the proof that he'd cared.

Rissa's grief threatened to pull him under the current of his own despair. Hardening himself, he climbed to the surface until all he felt was an emptiness and a fierce determination.

Because all he had now was this mission. He couldn't save his friend, his brother. He refused to let his people suffer the same fate. For he was Toha. He was their protector, their light in the darkness. When he had no hope himself, at least he could give some to them.

That's what he was born to do.

THE LIGHT BLINDED Rissa as it pushed through the clouds and bounced off the clean white snow in front of her. She shielded her eyes with a hand and glared across the landscape before them.

"We should stop here to rest." Trystan's teeth chattered as he spoke.

Steam drifted in front of her face as Rissa huffed out a breath. They were getting nowhere. They'd been trudging along in the mountains for almost two weeks. She'd thought they'd have left for Dreach-Dhoun by now, but they had to wait long enough so Briggs wasn't traceable to every seer.

He'd used his magic twelve days ago and Lona still said the traces clung to them.

Rissa didn't care. All she wanted was a Dreach-Dhoun soldier to hit.

It didn't help that it'd been so cold for days. They couldn't travel far without stopping, lest they freeze to death.

"I'll get to work on a fire," Alixa said.

"I'll help." Trystan shot a look at Rissa and she averted her eyes.

How could Trystan act like everything was normal? She saw the way he followed Alixa. Davion was dead and Trystan continued to flirt.

Edric dug in his pack as Avery tied up the horses. After the fight, they'd only found three of the horses that had ridden off—meaning Rissa's feet screamed with every step. But she didn't stop. She passed Lona and Briggs, who paid her no mind as she continued up the path.

Snow drifted from the sky, catching in her eyelashes. She blinked, and the snowflakes fell to her cheeks where they melted instantly, almost as if they were tears. She hadn't cried since it happened. Crying meant it was real. It would serve as the final dagger twisting in her gut.

It had happened. Of that, there was no doubt. But there was a difference between knowing someone died and the crushing realization that they were truly gone.

The road bent around the corner before moving farther up the mountain. Rissa stopped and stepped off the side of the road onto the narrow strip between the well-trod path and where it dropped off.

It could've been the edge of the world.

The air was hazy with falling snow, obscuring the long drop off the cliff. She imagined there was a road down there or something of the sort. She shuffled forward so her toes hit the cliff. Fear surged through her, but she didn't move back because it proved she could still feel something.

It was better than the emptiness inside her. She'd tried to fill it with anger. That worked when she didn't think about it too much.

She closed her eyes as a frosty blast blew her hair from where it stuck to the damp skin of her neck. Her fingers rubbed the pendant at her throat.

"Tell me how to get through this, Mom," she whispered.

As soon as the words were out of her mouth, she jumped back and whipped around. After pulling her knife free, she threw it at the bank of snow on the other side of the road. Leaping towards where it dug in, she tore it free before plunging it in again. The tip hit ice, the impact reverberating up her arm.

She stabbed it again.

She'd never known her mother, and she focused her anger on that. For so long, Davi had been the sole recipient.

But she couldn't maintain an ire towards someone she didn't know. Before long, it came back to Davi as it always did. He'd left her.

She collapsed into the snow, letting the cold freeze her heart.

She didn't know how long she stared into the swirling sky before Alixa blocked her vision. Her coat was pulled up to cover the bottom half of her face, but her eyes shone with disapproval.

When she spoke, the fabric muffled her voice. "You're going to freeze out here." She planted her hands on her hips and narrowed her eyes.

"Go play keeper to someone else." Rissa's lips trembled with the cold.

Alixa never listened to anyone. She sat down. "I've lived in these mountains most of my life, Ri."

"Don't call me Ri." Only two people ever had—Trystan and Davion—and she couldn't bear to hear it anymore.

Alixa kept going. "You don't want to be caught too far from your fire when the sun goes down during a snowstorm."

Rissa shrugged.

"I'm serious. You'll die of cold."

"I don't care."

Alixa jumped to her feet. "Rissa Renauld. Get your princess butt out of that snow right now. I know you're hurting. We all are. That doesn't mean we can forget why we're here."

"Haven't we already forgotten? All we're doing is wandering around these mountains."

Alixa crossed her arms. "I won't ask you again. Stand up. You will come back to the fire that Trystan and I have put our every effort into starting. I, for one, don't want to die before we take that bastard in Dreach-Dhoun with us." She reached a hand down.

Rissa had no more fight in her. She took the hand and pulled herself to her feet before following Alixa back down the path.

Before they reached the others, Alixa stopped. "Rissa, you know I'm here, right? We didn't exactly start on the best of terms, but I know what it's like to lose your best friend. My maid—"

"Davi wasn't my best friend," Rissa cut in. "Most of the time we couldn't stand each other. He was annoying."

"But you loved him."

Rissa looked away.

Alixa sighed. "If you won't talk to me, you should at least talk to your brother. You've both done your best to avoid each other, but maybe you need him. I know for a fact he needs you."

Rissa pushed past her. "I don't need anyone."

She rejoined the others before Alixa could respond. Avery handed her a tin mug of tea as she sat. The flames warmed her face, but that heat didn't permeate the skin. On the inside, she was just as cold as she'd been before.

As night descended, a silence stretched between them, broken only by the roar of a mountain cat in the distance. Lona's sad eyes burned into her as Briggs tried to goad her into conversation. She ignored him and leaned against her pack. As she closed her eyes, she imagined Davi's laughter cutting through the tension of the night.

THE CRUNCH of snow had Trystan shooting up from where he half dozed beside the fire. He rolled sideways to grab his sword and sprang to his feet just as the sound of clashing swords reached his ears. After running towards the commotion, he came to a stop, the sight before him sending a shock through his system.

Two Isenore soldiers had found their camp, but Lonara fought them fervently. Her magic wasn't the weapon she chose. Instead, she blocked and parried with a long, thin sword that gleamed in the early morning light.

Her movements were swift, sure, as she moved gracefully.

"Help would be appreciated," she called to Trystan.

He snapped out of his momentary daze and jumped into the fray.

"King Calis is going to gut all Dreach-Sciene scum," one of the soldiers snarled.

Trystan grunted as he shuffled his feet and pushed his opponent so his back was against a tree. "All I hear is blah blah, I'm a bloody traitor."

It was something Davi would have said and Trystan found his smirk dropping.

Lonara knocked her soldier's sword away and swept his legs out from under him. He landed with a thud, the tip of her sword pressed to the hollow of his throat.

"Are there others?" she asked.

Trystan forced his opponent to drop his weapon and kept him pinned to the tree. After a few moments, the soldier stopped struggling.

"We won't tell you anything," he growled before spitting in Trystan's face.

With his hands occupied, Trystan couldn't wipe the spittle away, and it dripped down his face as the Isenore traitor grinned.

Trystan slammed his knee into the man's gut, eliciting a grunt of pain. "How many know where we are?"

The man shouted curses at Trystan rather than giving him any answers.

Suddenly, he went quiet and jerked before he slumped in Trystan's arms. An arrow protruded from the side of his head.

Trystan let him fall to the ground and wiped his face as the twang of another loosed arrow sliced through the air. He turned slowly, knowing what he'd find but hoping he was wrong.

"Rissa Renauld," Lonara shrieked as she stood over the dead soldier at her feet. "What is the matter with you?"

Rissa stepped from where the trees hid her and shrugged as she fingered her bow. "They wouldn't have told you anything."

Trystan marched over to confront his sister. "What if we have a whole troop of soldiers after us?"

She met his glare unflinchingly. "They were traitors. They deserved to die." Her voice was devoid of any sign of life and Trystan shrank away from her. That was not his sister. She wasn't cold, heartless. Not Rissa.

Lonara shook her head. "I would expect a daughter of Marissa Kane to have something inside her head besides air and anger."

The sorceress trudged by them without another word.

How was Trystan supposed to help his sister when every part of his soul was broken as well?

Rissa wasn't the one who'd broken the promise to prevent Davi's capture. Trystan put a hand on the nearby tree to steady himself and closed his eyes, trying to rid his mind of the images that plagued him every day. Davi knocking the soldiers away from Trystan. Davi struggling to break free. The acceptance entering his eyes. His pleas for Trystan to fulfill his promise.

"Ri..." He opened his eyes but stopped when he saw her standing over the dead men, not a flicker of emotion on her face.

"We're going to kill them all." She plucked at the string of her bow. "Dreach-Dhoun is going to run red."

He opened his mouth to speak, but no words came. There was nothing he could say to fill the hole inside of her.

"We need to get moving." He turned and walked back towards the others, leaving behind the girl he no longer recognized.

Where was his sister?

They packed up their few supplies and hit the road once again. The day was slightly warmer than the one before, but the world was still bathed in white.

Trystan blew on his hands and sped up to match Lonara's stride. Her long-sword was strapped across her back.

"So," he began. "You can fight."

She nodded shortly. "How do you think your mother learned?"

"I wasn't aware my mother knew any of the Tri-Gard."

"Dear boy, there is so much you don't know." She paused almost as if considering how much she should tell him. "Your mother was like a daughter to me. Her death was the greatest tragedy of my long life."

He scrunched his brow. How could a member of the Tri-Gard think one person's death was worse than the tragedy she'd forced on the rest of the kingdom? "If you loved her so much, why did you choose a different side in the war?"

It was her turn to look confused. "I fought for Dreach-Sciene. For your mother. I forsook my sacred vow of neutrality to protect her. What happened later—draining the magic—that was forced upon me."

He was quiet for a moment. "Can you tell me about her? My father rarely speaks of her… almost as if he wants to forget."

A smile warmed her dark face. "Marcus Renauld would never forget. A love that strong would not fade. I've never seen anyone else like Marissa and Marcus. I helped raise the girl, but your father brought her to life. Even though it was for too short a time. They were beautiful."

He didn't ask any more questions after that. Trystan had never completely understood his father. There was a part of the man that had always been closed off, held back. Now he realized that maybe that part died with his mother.

Trystan had very few memories of her. Just the occasional image of a woman who looked very much like Rissa.

Having someone with him who'd known her was almost like having his mother with them, watching them.

As soon as they stopped traipsing across the mountains and found a village, he'd send word to his father. The news about Davi would hurt him as well. He'd loved him as a son from the moment he'd brought him home. But knowing Trystan and Rissa were still okay might bring him some comfort.

That night as the fire thawed the icicles that had grown along his cloak, he sat silently beside his sister. She didn't speak, but she didn't move away either.

They'd get through it. Together. And then they'd get their revenge.

CHAPTER 2

Someone was coming.

Trystan swore under his breath as he tried to conceal himself behind the snow-laden tree stump he'd been resting on.

They were almost on top of him. He'd been wallowing so much in his worry over Ri, and his need to be alone for a few minutes to pull his head together that he hadn't heard them until now. After the attack days before, he should have been on high alert and wanted to kick himself for letting them be found. Again.

Whoever was approaching wasn't any of his people. He'd left their Eastern camp before sunrise, his dreams still too haunting to allow sleep. These sounds came from the West. Someone else was making their way through the Isenore mountains, and with the way lady luck had been taunting them lately, it was more likely foe than friend.

The sun rose at his back. That was in his favor at least. The shadow cast by the background of trees would hopefully keep him hidden while he observed the newcomers. A few soldiers he could handle if he took them by surprise. Even without Lonara's help. A regiment was a whole other story.

The quiet neighing of horses and the occasional snapping of a twig were the only signs of their approach, but Trystan's fingers tapped silently against the hilt of his sword, readying for battle. His heart thumped against his ribs, and he tried to calm his frazzled energy. If Davi were here, he would have made some stupid joke by now to break the tension. But Davi wasn't here. Ri's accusatory glare reminded him of that every time she looked his way. His stupid desire for solitude had left him alone in the woods against the unknown, imminent threat. He no longer had his brother to watch his back. That harsh realization only fueled his anger instead of his fright, and he began to hope it was enemy soldiers. Nothing like a battle to take the edge off one's anger.

It didn't take long for the horses to make their way through the sea of dead trees. The sun's rays highlighted the steel blades of two men flanking the women on horseback. The men were soldiers, their uniforms hidden under snow speckled furs, but Trystan swore he caught a glimpse of the Isenore colors and his grip tightened on his blade. The last group of Isenore soldiers had tried to kill them. This was not looking so good.

He would have attacked already if it weren't for the women. The young girl and the older matron were no soldiers. He could tell that, even from afar. Their postures in the saddle were perfect, and their furs of the finest quality, despite the well-worn look. *Nobles.* Trystan stayed hidden a bit longer, his curiosity piqued. What the hell were nobles doing this far up in the mountains?

"Are you sure we are going the right way, Anna?" The older lady's voice floated through the quiet, the refined tone bringing with it the familiarity of court. No, she definitely was not a soldier.

"Yes, Mother. The aura of magic is waning, no doubt, but it still shows me the way. We are getting closer to the magic wielder. May we stop so I can concentrate?"

The older lady motioned to the soldiers and all four horses came to a halt.

Trystan could hardly believe his eyes as the young girl lowered her cloak and breathed deeply as if she were trying to draw in the magic's very essence. Understanding set in. This girl was a seer, drawn here by Briggs' magic. Alarm stiffened his spine. Who was she?

Before he could react, a stealthy form shifted quietly from the shadows at his back and crouched by his side.

"Toha." Avery's use of his title was a mere whisper, but Trystan heard the underlining reprimand. She was mad at him for wandering off by himself.

No time to worry about her anger. He pointed to the left flanking soldier, and she nodded, readying her bow. At his urging, Avery let loose an arrow that missed the soldier on purpose and embedded in the tree inches above his head. They reacted quickly, he'd give them that. In the blink of an eye, the soldiers yanked the woman from their horses and boxed them in between themselves and their beasts.

"Show yourselves," the right soldier growled as he held his blade in Trystan's direction. The prince had no intention of doing any such thing.

"We are the ones with a bow trained on your women. You don't make demands on us."

To his surprise, the older woman stood upright and pushed her way past the soldier's restraining hand.

"I am Lady Yaro, wife of Hendry Yaro, and mistress of Cullenspire Manor. How dare you take a shot at one of my guards?"

Trystan was more than a little taken aback at her demanding tone. There was no mistaking the sincerity of her words.

"Cullenspire Manor? If memory serves me correctly, that is a vassal in Isenore territory, is it not? And last I heard, Lord Eisner was a traitor to the king. Do you follow the same path, Lady Yaro? For if so, my archers surrounding you at the moment are excellent shots and will not miss."

"You take me for a fool, boy? That arrow came from where you hide. There are no archers in the trees, just like there are no coins in our purse if you're aiming to rob us. If you wish for me to answer your question, then stop being a coward and show yourself."

Trystan scowled but stood upright even as Avery shook her head in disagreement. He motioned for her to stay hidden as he stepped from the shadows, his sword loose in his grip in what he hoped was an unthreatening gesture.

"I'm no bandit, my lady," he said. "But to reiterate my question, do you follow in Lord Eisner's footsteps? Are you a traitor to King Marcus Renauld?"

She narrowed her eyes his way. "I don't know if that's a trick question or not, boy, for how am I to know if you yourself aren't an Eisner follower? You have not revealed your identity. But regardless of where your loyalties lie, I have no qualms with telling you where mine do. I am no follower of *Lord Eisner.*" She spat his name in contempt. "Not only is he a traitor to the king I follow with the deepest of loyalty, but he is also why I stand before you a grieving widow. The reason why my children are left fatherless. The reason my eldest son has already died in the Dreach-Dhoun dungeons and my second son has left home to fight in a war we have little chance of winning. And the reason why I am traipsing through these god-forsaken mountains searching for the few people who may offer us a sliver of hope. Now, if you are indeed a man of Isenore, then step forward and accept your fate. For while I live, I'll order the execution of every single follower of his that has the misfortune to cross my path."

Surprise coursed through Trystan, but before he could respond, a disbelieving, "Dona Yaro," echoed through the trees. Their exchange had drawn the rest of Trystan's party. Alixa, Edric, and Rissa followed behind Lonara, their weapons drawn and ready, eyeballing the Isenore soldiers with distrust.

"Mistress Lonara?" Shock painted the older lady's voice as her face paled to match the falling snow. She forgot about Trystan as she stumbled toward the Tri-Gard member, her hand held to her heart like she feared it would jump from her chest and splatter at her feet. "It is really you. When my dearest Anna said she felt a magical disturbance, I knew it had to be one of the Tri-Gard, back to save us. I told my people you would not abandon us forever. Oh my, what a glorious day to have found you. I thought we'd never meet again."

The old lady fell to her knees as she grabbed Lonara's hands and raised them to her lips, dropping a kiss on each knuckle. Tears ran down the wrinkled cheeks as Lonara gently pulled the woman back to standing and wiped her tears away. The Tri-Gard's familiarity and fond smile put Trystan at ease and he sheathed his weapon.

"It is good to see you as well, old friend. It has been far too long. But your words raise concern. The trail left by the magic is still traceable? I'd feared as much, but hoped it was growing too faint to follow."

Lady Yaro called to her daughter over her shoulder and the young girl approached, wide-eyed and pale. "Anna, answer the Mistress's question."

"It is still traceable, yes, but is growing weaker. We've been following it for a few days. It's why we came. We needed to find you."

Lonara's troubled eyes met Trystan's. "You must pack up camp and make a swift departure."

Lady Yaro glanced back and forth between the two in puzzlement. "This arrogant bandit is traveling with you?"

Trystan ignored Alixa's slight snort at the lady's assumption. Even Lonara's lips twitched despite her concern. "He is no bandit, Lady Yaro. Let me introduce you to Prince Trystan Renauld and his sister, Princess Rissa." She waved a hand Rissa's way, and the girl nodded her head in greeting.

The look of horror on the lady's face would have been funny if it weren't for the worrisome news she'd just imparted.

"Prince? Oh, my goodness. Your Highness, I am so sorry." Her curtsy was awkward with embarrassment. "Please forgive my impertinence. I did not recognize you."

"No need to apologize, my lady. Your answer to my allegiance question is the most reassuring I've heard in quite some time. But Lona is right. We don't have time to stand here talking. We need to make haste and you need to remove yourselves from our company. It won't end well for either of you if you are found with us."

The older lady pulled herself back to full height, regaining her composure once again. "Thank you for your concern, your Highness, but we aren't going anywhere. Not without what we came here to find. Anna was not only able to feel the magic but also your distress. We came here looking for the Tri-Gard member, but we also came to offer our aid. More will be looking for you. We need to get you back to Cullenspire. It will be the perfect place to hide you, right in the belly of the beast."

"Why do you offer your help?" Rissa's unexpected words were as frigid as the mountain air as she stepped out of the shadows of the forest. "You are from Isenore. Why should we trust you?"

"Rissa," Trystan admonished, and his sister's icy gaze fell on him.

"What?" she questioned. "It's not like you aren't all thinking the same. Alixa, Avery, Edric, do you not all feel the same?"

"I understand your distrust, Princess." Lady Yaro was the one to answer Rissa. "Yes, I am from Isenore, but my allegiance does not lie with Lord Eisner. On the contrary, there's nothing more I wish to see than that man's head rotting on a stake on my manor wall." Trystan winced at the harsh comment and glanced Alixa's way, but she seemed impervious to Lady Yaro's words. "I can feel your sorrow from here. You've lost much. So have I, but we can't let that impede us from doing what we can to fight back. Protecting the Tri-Gard is the first step. Although I'm surprised you slipped up, Lona, and used your magic. You of all people know how dangerous that can be."

"It wasn't Lonara," Trystan supplied, suddenly taking a liking to the straight-shooting Lady Yaro. "It was Briggs who used magic. Although in his defense, he was trying to protect us."

"Briggs? Briggs Villard?" Lady Yaro's face lit up. "He is with you as well? Oh my heavens, two Tri-Gard members united? This is glorious news indeed." She stared around in confusion. "Where is he?"

Trystan groaned as he and the others all realized the same thing. Briggs wasn't anywhere in sight. "Good Lord, you left Briggs behind? We need to get back to camp right away before he does something moronic like wander off or use magic again."

Lady Yaro's eyes sparked in amusement. "Briggs Villard and

moronic used together in the same sentence? Glad to see some things never change."

"Briggs?" Trystan crouched down beside his still sleeping form. "Wake up, you old fool."

Alixa walked around to the other side of him and met Trystan's eye. They'd all had enough of Briggs' antics on their journey.

"This isn't funny, Briggs," she snapped.

"Wish we could just leave him," Rissa mumbled under her breath.

She wasn't the first to express the same thought. They didn't trust the Tri-Gard and for good reason. They were only in this mess because of them.

Trystan reached forward to press his frozen hand against Briggs' cheek, hoping it'd shock him awake.

"Briggs." His eyes darted around as he moved his hand from the old man's cheek to his forehead. "He's burning up."

Trystan cast a worried glanced back to Lonara, and the woman ran forward.

"Something's wrong." He backed away to make room for Lonara.

Lonara looked her fellow Tri-Gard member over. "You need to get him to the healer at Cullenspire. Now." She gestured to the two guards, and they lifted Briggs onto one of the horses.

Fear spiked in the prince as he took in the pale skin of the man who could help them save the kingdom. What if he didn't wake?

"Where are you going?" Trystan gripped Lonara's arm to stop her as she began readying her own horse.

She glanced at Briggs draped across the saddle then shifted her eyes to the prince. "I am going to give you time, my prince. One week should be sufficient for Briggs' magic to fade away. You will be protected at Cullenspire. I will use my magic to create a new trail that veers off from this one. Hopefully the stronger one will lead any followers away while you all regain your strength." Her eyes flicked to Rissa. "And deal with your new circumstances."

"Don't let Briggs die or we will all follow soon after."

"Is it wise to use magic again? They will come after you in droves."

Lonara's mouth thinned to a grim line. "I'm aware, but we have no choice. You need to get to Cullenspire undetected. Trust me, I can look after myself. I will rejoin you when the time is right."

Before anyone said another word, she was gone.

There was nothing left to do but follow her directives. Trystan wasn't convinced it was the right choice, but Lonara was right. It was the only choice.

They rode hard, doubling up on the few horses they had. By the time they finally exited the mountains, Alixa could barely manage to stay balanced in the saddle in front of Trystan. His frozen hands steadied her, and she threw a tiny smile of gratitude back over her shoulder. Traveling through the heart of Isenore had not been easy on any of them, but Trystan could only imagine the torturous memories Isenore had dredged up for Alixa. In response to her smile, his arm tightened on her waist and she stiffened in surprise under his touch but didn't pull away. Instead she glanced back at him with worried eyes.

"Do you think Lona's plan will work?"

His mind drifted to Lonara. He truly hoped it did. He worried for her but if he were being honest with himself, his worry was more so for the rest of them. Lonara had survived in the mountains for years without their help. She could do so again. He just felt they were safer when she was around. If he had to choose to be left alone with her or Briggs, well, the choice was obvious.

"It will." He answered back. "Lonara's right, we need the week to rest and heal. We need to keep the old man alive for this plan to work. Lady Yaro's healer will know what to do."

Trystan hoped he sounded far more convincing to Alixa than he felt.

The snow fell heavily as the smoke-spewing chimneys of Cullenspire finally came into view. The manor spread below them on a sea of pristine white, the tidy gables of its rooftop making a dark silhouette against the gray evening sky. Lantern light spilled from every window, a welcoming glow against the frigid wind. The stone walls and gates surrounding it offered a sense of security, unlike the barren mountains and forests they'd left behind. Trystan sighed in relief and commented softly over Alixa's shoulder.

"After all we've been through, is it trivial of me to say I cannot wait to sleep in a real bed again?"

He heard the laughter in her voice. "Not at all. Know what I'm looking forward to the most? A nice, hot, long leisurely bath."

A flushed of heat stained Trystan's cheeks as the image of Alixa relaxing in a steaming tub filled his mind. This was not the time or place for such foolish thoughts. To cover his unease, he lifted his chin Rissa's way. His sister rode ahead, her back stiff with anger, ignoring Edric's attempts to talk to her. Ignoring everyone.

"Maybe that's what she needs. A bit of normalcy to bring her back around."

Alixa's gaze shifted to Rissa and her voice filled with sadness. "Give her time to overcome her grief, Trystan."

Alixa was right. But time was not a luxury any of them could afford right now. He needed his sister back. But she was nowhere to be found, and Trystan was deathly afraid she might be gone forever.

A pair of burly soldiers met them as the gates opened, toothless grins indicative of how relieved they were to see their mistress again. Lady Yaro called down to them as they rode by. "We need the healer immediately. If he's in his bed, wake him." They moved instantly to do her bidding.

More servants exited the manor to greet them as they pulled up in front of the oversized, grand doors. Lady Yaro turned to the guard riding with Briggs' unconscious form. "Take him to the healer's workshop right away. We will check on him as soon as we are settled."

The guard slid down and two other men ran forward to help carry Briggs away.

Trystan dismounted and helped Alixa do the same before turning to follow the guards and Briggs, but a servant's message to Lady Yaro stopped him.

"I'm glad to see you back, Mistress. A visitor arrived from Whitecap this morning. A messenger of Lord Coille. He says it's important but refused to speak to anyone but you, so he awaits inside under watch."

Lord Coille sent a messenger? A cold shiver passed over Trystan and it didn't have anything to do with the icy wind at their backs. Lady Yaro must have felt the same, for she jumped down and strode anxiously toward the grand house.

Trystan handed his reins to one of the waiting young stable hands and followed Lady Yaro up the marble steps to the double oak doors without hesitation. She threw them open and swept into the massive hall, pinning a terrified maid with her demanding stare.

"The messenger who arrived this morning. Where is he?"

"In… in the study, my lady."

With no consideration for their snow-covered boots, Lady Yaro marched over the fine floors and around the corner to the end of the hall. A guard standing outside the door at the end of the corridor came to attention at her presence and opened the door. Lady Yaro paused and glanced back at Trystan.

"I would appreciate it if you would accompany me, your Highness, as this is surely news of the kingdom, but perhaps we should do this alone?"

Trystan shook his head. "I hide nothing from my companions, my lady. They are privy to everything. No room for secrets."

She tilted her head in acknowledgment of his decision. "As you wish."

The young man shot to his feet as soon as they piled into the room, his weary face a testament to his arduous journey. His eyes darted over all of them in puzzlement before finally settling on the older woman. She stepped his way.

"I am Lady Yaro. My guards tell me you've come with a message?"

"Yes, my lady. But Lord Coille said it was meant for your ears alone...." He trailed off as his attention flitted about the room.

"No worries, young sir. You are free to speak in front of everyone here."

He swallowed hard before nodding and stepping out from behind his chair. He held a wool cap in his hands, which he twisted into a knot of nervousness. Trystan's stomach knotted in the exact same manner.

"Something has happened, my lady. Something bad. Lord Coille has received word that King Marcus is dead. Murdered in his own bedchamber by an agent of King Calis."

It took Trystan only a moment to track the whispered *NO* to his pale-faced sister. Her eyes met his, oozing pain and disbelief. Proof of what his mind refused to consider as truth. Trystan should have moved towards her. He should have offered her his strength, but in that moment, he wasn't sure he had an ounce of strength left. The words ricocheted through his mind, refusing to grab hold.

His head shook of its own accord. His father was the grandest man he'd ever known. He couldn't be dead. It wasn't possible.

Rissa turned and ran from the room, from him, the silence left behind echoing with her footsteps.

"Ri," he whispered in dismay as the pain stabbed into him. His father was gone. The man he'd looked up to his entire life. The man who'd felt like he'd always be there to guide him, to protect him, to love him.

You are to be a symbol of hope.

He'd said those words, changing Trystan's entire world. He wasn't just a protector of his people's lives, but of their very souls. But who would protect his now that his father was gone?

Dead.

Forever.

Just like Davion.

Just like his mother.

A single tear tracked down his face as he lifted his eyes to the grieving subjects who waited in anticipation for his reaction. Avery stepped up beside him, her head bowed and her face damp.

"Murdered in his bedroom." Anger tainted her words. "He deserved better."

Trystan didn't look at her. He didn't look at anyone as he paced further into the room. "He deserved to die of old age with my mother still by his side. But none of us get what we deserve. We take what Calis Bearne gives us." An unexpected wave of rage exploded in his heart, ripping through his body like jagged lightning. He lashed out at the nearest object, a footstool that careened into the wall and shattered into a thousand splinters. "I'm going to kill that bastard."

Running his hands over his face, he breathed deeply through his nose, trying to calm himself down. The others didn't need to see this loss of control. Reining in his anger, he dropped his hands, expecting to be met with gazes of shock or fear. Instead, he watched in puzzlement as Avery went down on one knee.

"And I will be by your side, your Majesty. For King Marcus and the people he loved."

Your Majesty. The title sounded foreign. It wasn't supposed to be his. Not yet.

When Edric, Lady Yaro, and Alixa also kneeled, he wanted to tell them to rise, but the gesture rooted him in place. As much as his heart craved revenge, as much as he desired to spill Calis' blood, he realized one thing. It wasn't only about him and the dark king anymore. It was about each and every person who'd been affected.

And he was now their king.

A chilling chant fell from their lips.

"The King is dead. Long live King Trystan."

CHAPTER 3

Lost. There was no other word to describe the feeling brewing inside Davion. He was utterly lost. It wasn't just the empty spaces in his mind where the memories from the last fifteen years should reside; it was his very soul. Nothing was right.

He looked around at the stone halls that were supposed to be his home, but he felt nothing but the cold. He kept his head down as he hurried along the corridor, realizing he wasn't just lost in spirit. He was actually physically lost.

"Dammit," he groaned. "Not again." Losing his way had become a daily occurrence. He refused to be confined to his rooms as his father suggested. His father. He shook his head. He barely knew the man. They had a blood bond, surely that should be enough. Memories returned in pieces. Every time he met with his father, the sorcerer was with him. But then again, they were all sorcerers in Dreach-Dhoun. Had Davi ever used magic before losing his memories? As a prisoner in Dreach-Sciene, he wouldn't have been able to. Ramsey, the man who seemed to enjoy rooting around in his mind, told him stories of his time in captivity. They'd been watching him somehow. Blood magic. He didn't understand any of it.

As he ran his fingers along the smooth stone of the wall, he released a sigh. How long would it be until he remembered? Why had he forgotten? That had never been fully explained, and it only deepened his confusion. He knew the prince of Dreach-Sciene had something to do with it.

His legs collided with something soft and a rough bark rang in the air. When he looked down, the wide snout of a very large dog confronted him. He jumped back instinctively, but the dog followed his movement and lunged for him. He sidestepped him, preparing for the teeth still coming his way.

"Hey," he yelled at the dog. "Hey, stop. Do you hear me? I don't taste nearly as good as you think I do."

The dog didn't listen and soft laughter joined the dog's aggressive growls. Davi jerked his eyes up to find his cousin, Lorelai, standing in a doorway. She held a hand over her mouth to stifle her laughs.

"I'm about to die and you find it funny?" He looked back to the dog that had gotten closer. The dog lunged again and Davi wasn't quick enough. Before he knew what was happening, a warm tongue slid across his hand. "What the…?"

"Cousin." Lorelai was still laughing. "Meet Deor." She gestured to the dog that was jumping to put his paws on Davi's chest. Davi stumbled back from the sheer weight as the wet tongue slid across his face.

"Ugh." Davi turned his head. "I know it's hard to resist my good looks, but I think he's trying to kiss me." He laughed and pushed the dog away.

Lorelai stepped forward and for the first time, he noticed she wasn't alone. A slightly older woman stood next to her with the same white-blonde hair. Instead of Lorelai's bright eyes, the other woman's were vacant. She didn't look at him.

"I think that's the first smile I've seen from you, Davi." Lorelai reached out her hand to scratch Deor behind the ears.

His lips turned down. For just a moment, he'd forgotten he didn't even know who he was. "You haven't exactly been a ray of sunshine either."

She crouched down to pet Deor, but he suspected it was so she didn't have to meet his eyes.

Something haunted her, but she was a stranger to him. What right did he have to ask?

Footsteps echoed across the high ceilings as a young girl sprinted toward them. The boys clothing she wore hung off her skinny frame. Her face was dirty and red hair hung down her back. Something sparked in Davi's mind. A memory? He couldn't pull it forth, but warmth filled him.

The girl skidded to a stop in front of him and dipped into an awkward curtsy. "Your Highness." She couldn't have been more than ten.

It took him a moment to realize she meant him. The girl looked in uncertainty at Lorelai. Davi was the Prince of Dreach-Dhoun. He had to remind himself of that every time someone bowed. The title was hollow, but the people were so happy to have their lost prince returned, he couldn't ask them to stop.

"Hello," he said slowly.

"I'm so sorry, milord," the girl said. "One of the boys was playing with Deor and left the door open. The king says he isn't supposed to be inside the palace, but I swear it ain't my fault. And he ain't even that dirty." Her voice wavered, the fear showing on her face.

Lorelai stepped forward to whisper in his ear. "If your father finds out, he'll give her a lashing with his magic."

Davi crouched down to look into her face. He put a hand on each shoulder. "What's your name, sweetheart?"

Her lip quivered. "Tessa."

"Tessa, how about we keep Deor's little trip as our secret?"

Her eyes lit up and Davi winked.

Her mouth curved into a smirk. "Okay, Prince. I won't tell a soul that *you* let the dog into the palace."

She flashed him a smile as she wrapped her little fingers around Deor's collar and tugged him after her. He followed willingly, clearly in love with his little friend.

Davi shook his head.

"It's nice to have you in the palace, Davi." Lorelai gripped his arm. "I know it's hard for you after everything you've been through." Her eyes shifted away as they'd been doing every time his memory was brought up in her presence. What was she thinking?

Dark thoughts once again worked their way into his mind.

She wasn't finished. "You're kind. It's… a nice change."

Was he kind? How could he remain kind or even sane after fifteen years as a prisoner? The answer: there was no possible way. The sudden urge to hit something had him turning away. Lorelai touched his arm again. The sad thing was, he didn't want her to release him. It was the only affection he could remember in the empty brain of his, and it made him feel slightly less adrift.

Why couldn't he remember any of his time away? His father told him he'd been injured, but it would return.

He turned back to face her once again.

"You're home now," she said softly. "It's going to be okay."

"Is it? Because you've been home, cousin, and I still see the shadows in your eyes."

She released his arm and ran a hand over the pale skin of her face.

"Shadows," the woman beside her mumbled. "That's right. Dangers in the dark."

"Ma," Lorelai whispered. "It's all right."

The woman turned her vacant eyes on Davi. "Nothing is all right."

"Davi," Lorelai said. "This is my mother."

The woman smiled and released a sigh. "Nephew. Where have you been?"

Davi looked to Lorelai who only shrugged.

He lowered his voice. "I was kidnapped."

"That's right." She stepped forward and patted the side of his face. "Our lost prince has returned to us." She held her palm against his cheek. "Hmmm, it seems not all of you has returned."

"Ma," Lorelai snapped, brushing her mother's hand away. "Quit it." She looked apologetically at her cousin. "She has the sight as well and…" She glanced at her mother. The older woman was no longer paying attention to them as she started to walk down the hall. Lorelai lowered her voice. "It's taken a lot from her. I'm sorry, I have to go."

"Wait," Davi called after her.

She turned.

"I have no idea how to get back to my rooms."

Her lips stretched into a smile. "Take this corridor until it dead ends at the door to the training yard. Turn right and go straight until you see something familiar." Her eyes dipped sadly. "I will help you, Davion. This is your home now. You have a family. And we have awaited your return for too long. Just give us time."

With that, she turned on her heel and chased after her mother, leaving Davi to his empty mind. Images flashed in the blank spaces, but he couldn't figure them out. The only thing left to do was trust in what he knew. His father saved his life. Dreach-Dhoun was his realm. And he had to do whatever he must to earn the title of prince, the designation as son. If he couldn't remember who he'd been, he must decide who he would become.

DAVI MANAGED to find his way back to the rooms he'd been given without much trouble. The palace was surprisingly easy to navigate once he found his bearings. The halls ran continuous in a square around the main hall and throne room that sat in the very center.

Stone and steel statues marked each corner, guiding the way. There was very little adorning the walls of the corridors, but his rooms were another story. He ran his hand along the soft tapestry near the door. It depicted three symbols he couldn't decipher. His fingers traced the inverted triangle of the first one. Was it important?

He moved on, walking towards the fire to warm his chilled hands near the wolves carved into the wood on the mantle. Everywhere he looked reminded him of the generosity of his father. He'd provided the best linens, plush rugs, and clothing fit for a prince.

He sat on the corner of the bed and unbuttoned the collar of his jacket before removing the tie from his hair and shaking it down over his shoulders. Solitude brought peace to his addled mind, but it didn't last long. A knock sounded at his door.

He stood slowly and crossed the room to greet the servant who stood on the other side. The older woman curtsied. "His Majesty requests your presence."

Davi refastened the loose buttons and followed her out the door. "Where are we going?"

"He's in the South tower, your Highness."

"Did he demand you escort me?"

She smiled sympathetically. "He did not, but servants talk, your Highness. We couldn't have you getting lost again, could we?"

He reached up to rub the tension from the back of his neck. Losing his way had been a daily occurrence. Heat crept up his neck, and he lowered his gaze to the ground. "Thank you."

She touched his arm. "It's okay, your Highness. What happened to you was horrible and we will help you as much as we can."

He finally met her gaze. "What's your name?"

"Clara."

"Okay, Clara, you can call me Davi."

She gasped. "That is not the proper way of things."

"Just in private, then. My father won't have to know." Desperation for some sort of normalcy clung to him. But what was normal? He didn't think of himself as a prince. His name was the only thing he had that was still truly his.

"The king knows all." They'd reach the door to the passage that would take him into the tower, but she stopped walking. "You'd do well to remember that, your Highness. I think you can find your way from here."

He sighed and pushed through the door. A staircase spiraled up into the darkness. Torches hung along the wall of the bottom landing so he took one from its bracket and began to climb the stairs. Each landing of the stark tower had multiple rooms, but none of them contained his father so he continued upward. His steps echoed through the narrow space, foretelling of his coming.

"Davion," his father's voice boomed from above. "Is that you?"

"It is," Davi answered.

"We're up at the top, my boy. I have much to share with you."

By the time Davi reached the room at the top of the tower, his thighs burned. His father turned from his place at the window and beamed at him. Ramsey stepped into Davi's line of sight, but something lay beneath his smile that Davi couldn't decipher.

The king's smiled dropped. "Davion, when I summon you, I expect you to make yourself presentable."

Confusion flashed on Davi's face.

"Tie your darn hair," his father burst out.

"I'm... I'm sorry, father. I don't..."

Before he could finish, his hair flew back from his face and was tied with a knot. His eyes widened as he tentatively reached towards the top of his head.

Ramsey cleared his throat. "Sire, the boy has no experience with magic. Maybe it's best if we go slow."

"Come to the window, Davion," his father said. "And put that torch out."

Ramsey took the torch and diffused the flame with a wave of his hand.

A light formed in the room and Davi jerked his head around to find the source. Ramsey placed a hand on his arm. "It's okay, my prince. It's only magic."

Only magic. Only magic? If he hadn't seen it with his eyes, he wouldn't believe.

Ramsey guided him gently to the window where Davi's father peered out on his kingdom. The palace was a sprawling structure surrounded by barren land. A garden stood along one wall, but as his father pushed the light out onto the land, the garden's twisting branches and dead grasses were on full display.

"This will one day be yours, my boy." His father put a heavy hand on his back. "Dreach-Dhoun has survived despite our enemies trying to destroy us. We have overcome great odds and will do so again."

He pointed into the distance. "The nearest village is there. Soon, you and I will be calling on our people to fight."

"To fight, sire?" Davi looked up into the dark eyes of his father. Eyes that swirled with something dangerous. He took a step to put space between them.

"Yes, Davi. You may not remember the past fifteen years, but some of us will never forget. Or forgive. You and I are going to take everything from the Renaulds. We're going to destroy their kingdom. Your dear cousin already began the fight when she killed their king."

He jerked away. Lorelai killed a king? The sweet, helpful cousin he'd come to rely on?

"I didn't know that," he whispered.

"Oh, yes." Pride coated his father's voice. "Lorelai is my sharpest blade."

Was this what haunted her eyes? Davi turned. He had to go to her. Something wasn't right.

"Enough about war." His father clapped his hands. "Ramsey is going to attempt to bring some of your memories back."

He looked to the sorcerer sharply. "Can you do that?"

Ramsey nodded. "I believe so." He held out his hand palm up and the king dropped a clear crystal into it. "Your Highness, I need you to kneel."

Davi obeyed, eager to regain pieces of himself.

Ramsey stepped forward and held the crystal against Davion's forehead. It warmed when it touched his skin, sending jolts of power straight through him. Ramsey placed his other hand on the crown of Davi's head and closed his eyes.

Davi's eyes slid shut as well and images flooded forth. At first he was just a boy with a mop of dark hair riding atop a horse in front of a guard. Rain pounded down around them. The scene played out until a hand yanked him from the horse and shoved him into a bare room. The image changed, and he was much older. It must have been recent.

He fought a lighter man with a grim expression. "Cede or I will run you through," the man growled.

The memories came so quickly he couldn't hold on to just one. Many featured a beautiful girl with fire-red hair and an unpleasant scowl directed his way. She hated him. He was below her. Her prisoner. Pain stabbed through his mind and the images disappeared, leaving behind the memories and feelings attached to them.

For fifteen years, the Renaulds imprisoned him. They were the enemy. A scream escaped his lips, but it sounded far away.

His eyes rolled up into his head and Ramsey jerked his hands away.

Immediately, the pain stopped. Davi hunched over, panting.

"That's all he can handle tonight, sire." Ramsey wiped his brow.

Davi clutched at his head as the empty spaces of his mind filled. His father walked towards him and bent down. He hooked one finger under Davi's chin and turned his face so their eyes met.

"Do you remember, my son?" he asked, hope thickening his voice.

Davi tried to speak, but the words didn't come. He cleared his throat and began again. "It's all in pieces, fragments. I don't…" His eyes darkened. "Are we going to get our revenge, father?"

His father's face filled with pride. "Yes, Davion. They will pay for what they've done to you."

CHAPTER 4

"Trystan." Why was Alixa's voice so soft? There was nothing about her that was supposed to be soft. She was hardened. Angry.

He stared wordlessly at the assembly before him. Cullenspire was in mourning for their king, and Lady Yaro wanted to put Trystan on full display. She believed he was the only one that could prevent the weight of despair from crushing all of Dreach-Sciene. The news would have been winding its way through every village and across the countryside over the past week. Marcus Renauld had been their hero king. He'd been crowned on a battlefield and never once stopped fighting for his people.

When Trystan was a child, he had badgered his father relentlessly to regale him with stories of their warrior mother. Now he couldn't recall much of what he'd been told, and he wished more than anything he could. Both of his parents were gone.

Trystan was raised to be the king, but it always seemed like a far-off destiny. Now it was here. Everyone looked to him to lead, but he had nothing. He opened his mouth to speak, but then closed it again. These people arrived in the hall for the noonday meal hoping to hear something from their new king.

He wasn't crowned yet, but in the ways of Dreach-Sciene, that didn't matter. Upon his father's death, he held the rank of king and would be treated as such.

It was a new world from what it had been only days ago when he was the Toha with a singular mission.

Much to everyone's dismay, Trystan gave up trying to speak and sat down. He took a generous gulp of wine.

"Trystan." Alixa rested her hand on his arm and tightened her grip.

He shook his head. "Please don't."

She smiled at him sadly and he hated it. There wasn't a sympathetic bone in that woman's body, yet something akin to pity shone in her eyes.

"Where's my sister?" he asked, scanning the long table for her bright hair.

It was Avery who answered. "She's been scarce, sire."

He scowled at Avery, wishing she'd drop the formality. It wasn't exactly new for her, but it had intensified. Avery was close to his father and his mother before that, but she was as unruffled as ever.

Avery stood abruptly. "I think it's time the princess joins us."

"I agree." Trystan nodded as Avery left to find his sister.

He'd spent the entire day before searching the grounds for her, but she was a ghost. As hard as losing Davi and his father was for Trystan, he knew he'd get through it. There would always be holes in his life now, but he had to be strong.

Rissa was different and her sudden change scared him. The holes in her life threatened to swallow her with their darkness.

Alixa's hand still rested on his arm and he stared at it for a moment before raising his eyes to meet hers, letting the familiarity comfort him. He'd had to talk to so many strangers offering condolences that her presence soothed him.

She jerked back suddenly, staring at her hand as if it betrayed her by touching him. She cleared her throat. "Briggs should be well enough to travel soon."

"We won't leave a moment before then."

She sighed. It was an argument he'd been having with Alixa and

Rissa both. They thought they should be returning to the palace as soon as they could, but they were daft if they thought he'd leave Briggs behind. The Tri-Gard was still their best hope of restoring the kingdom and as much as his father's death hurt, he refused to let it derail the mission.

His uncle and Lord Coille would handle things until he returned. Drake had taken over every time his father had to leave the palace. The king was never alone.

Trystan finished eating and left without another word to return to the solitude of his rooms for just a moment of respite. He sat on the edge of his bed and let the events of the past days enter his mind, taking over every thought, every emotion. Exhaustion had him slumping forward.

Davi.

His father.

Who would be next?

He rubbed his eyes, fighting back the tears. He was king now. He had to be stronger than everyone else.

But in that moment, he didn't want to be strong. He wanted to break down. To plead with the earth to give him back the people he loved. To take him instead.

A tear fell, followed by more he couldn't hold back. His back shook. He was so lost in his own grief, he didn't hear the door open and shut. Before he saw her, two arms came around him. Alixa stepped between his legs and he buried his face in her neck without shame. Her dark skin glistened with the evidence of his weakness.

She didn't say a word as she held a king and let him weep.

He didn't know how long they stayed there—him sitting, her standing in front of him—but after a while he reined himself in and pulled back.

She watched him intently and brushed the wetness from his cheeks. After giving him a short nod, she stepped back. "Lady Yaro wishes to speak with you. Are you ready to go be king?"

"Yes." He breathed out slowly.

"Okay, good. Just know, if you tell anyone I hugged you, your title won't stop me from coming after you."

He smiled, despite the weight in his heart, and raised a brow. "Treason already? My reign is only days old."

She tugged on his arm. "Come on. Let's go."

"Can you go back to being mean to me? I kind of miss it."

"Shut up."

THE WIND HOWLED through the tree tops, bringing with it tiny pebbles of hail. The past two days the weather had grown harsher, but Rissa felt none of the stinging cold that bit at her cheeks and nose, turning them a most unbecoming red. She was oblivious to the frost nipping at her fingers or the ice dulling her red hair. The weather matched her soul, barren and frigid. There was no distinction.

She'd made the small grove of trees at the back end of Cullenspire estate her escape from the others and had spent most of the past week and a half hiding out here. Fog lay low over the ground, damp and swirling around her ankles, only adding to the eeriness of the dead forest. She paid it no mind. In fact, she welcomed the quiet it seemed to bring with it. It was much preferable to Alixa's incessant mumblings of sympathy and Trystan's worried glances. She hated the way they were treating her. Like she was some fragile china doll about to crack from the tiniest pressure. Then again, she hated everything lately. Hate filled every crevice of her heart. Hate and revenge. There was no room for any other feelings. She preferred it that way.

She studied the thick tree trunk in front of her. The numerous gouges in the sickly, gray bark were a testament to how many times she'd struck it over the past few days. Ability to hit a mark while in motion was a useful thing to learn and since she had nothing else to occupy her time while they stupidly sat around waiting to move out, she might as well do something useful. Keeping her body in motion occupied her mind.

Waiting. She didn't understand the why. What the hell was Trystan waiting for? They needed to get back to Dreach-Sciene, to the castle. They needed to make haste. Instead, her brother kept insisting Briggs needed more time to recover. More time for him to make googly eyes at Alixa was more like it. That was all he did lately, stare after the girl with desire in his eyes. Pining after some traitor's daughter while Davi was gone and their father laid stiff and cold on his funeral pyre. Even just thinking about it fueled the anger burning hot in her gut.

She detested having to stay behind these walls, but since Trystan was the king now, he called the shots. King Trystan. King because their father had been murdered in his own home by some cowardly soldier of Dreach-Dhoun. The hatred won out over sorrow as she refused to let free the tears blocking her throat. Swallowing hard, she twirled and lunged at the tree trunk again with her sword, trying to hit the mark she'd placed there earlier. But like a hundred times before, she missed, and the blade stuck good and deep in an existing groove.

"Dammit," she muttered as she placed her boot against the tree and tried to pull the blade free. It refused to let go. Wrapping both hands around the hilt, she tugged harder, only to have it tear loose. Stumbling back, she landed on her backside on the marshy ground. Icy water splattered over her neck and ran down her back, but she ignored it as she stared up at her tree nemesis, narrowing her eyes with determination.

"I will not be beaten by a stupid tree. You will pay for that," she growled at it like it could hear her angry threat.

"And I'm sure the tree is cowering in its own tree-like way, Princess."

Avery's shadow fell over her as the sword master reached down with a gloved hand, offering assistance. Rissa glared up at her. She hadn't even heard her approach. Had she been watching her the whole time? And was that an actual smile threatening to break the grim line she called her lips? Not quite sure if Avery was laughing at her or not, Rissa accepted the gloved hand with a sigh.

Avery pulled her to her feet and Rissa hid her embarrassment by fussing with her tunic and cloak, wiping in vain at the muddy streaks on her clothes. Only once the color faded from her cheeks, did she lift her eyes to meet the sword master's gaze.

"Why are you here, Avery? Did Trystan send you to watch over me like some child?"

"The king worries about you, Princess."

The king. For a moment Rissa thought she was referring to her father, and her heart shrank a tiny bit more when she realized Avery meant Trystan. That sharp reminder made her response a bit harsher than she meant it to be. "Yes well, if Trystan worried more about our quest to save our realm than he did the old man back there pretending to be ill just so he can get out of traveling, then I'd be much happier."

"Our new king has much on his shoulders, Princess. You of all people know this. He will make the decisions in all of our best interests."

"Our best interest is to head back to the palace of Dreach-Sciene as soon as possible. This waiting is unnecessary and uncalled for."

"We do as the king wishes." Avery's dutiful monotone response irritated Rissa to no end.

"But of course," she hissed, her tone filled with venom. "We dare not disobey the king. After all, it isn't as if he's just some naïve, silly boy who had the title fall into his lap because of his father's murder. The *king* knows what's best for us all."

"Princess…"

Rissa cut short whatever Avery was about to say. She didn't want to hear the sword master's defense of her brother. She didn't want to hear any more talk. Talking was useless. Action was what made a difference. Turning her back to the other woman, she walked to the sword standing upright in the mud and yanked it out with a strong grip. She studied the dull blade and flipped it around a couple of times with her wrist, testing its weight in her hand.

"What am I doing wrong, Avery?" She glanced over her shoulder.

"I am sorry, my lady, I don't understand the question."

She turned to face the older woman. "With this? No matter how I try, I can't seem to hit my target. I must admit, it is quite a bit more cumbersome than my bow."

Avery crossed her arms and raised a brow Rissa's way. "Why the sudden interest in sword fighting? You're more than competent with your bow. Swords need not concern you."

"Oh?" Rissa's tone was deceivingly quiet. "And you think you know better of where my concerns should lie?"

Avery dropped her eyes and gave the girl a slight nod of deference. "Sorry, Princess. I did not mean that to come out the way it sounded. What I meant was, you are a skilled archer. The king needs you most where you are the strongest."

"Doesn't matter where the king needs me. I wish to learn the basics of sword fighting. Everyone in our group is adept with a sword. Even Alixa. I, too, wish to wield one with skill. The soldiers always say there is nothing more rewarding than cutting one's enemy down while you look them straight in the eye. And we have a lot of enemies now, do we not?"

The sword master studied Rissa in silence, but Ri could see the vein throbbing in her temple.

"Your father would not be pleased to see you wielding a sword. He never wanted you to be a fighter."

"My father is dead, Avery." Rissa's words were as cold as the northern wind blowing through the barren branches above their heads. "It matters not what he wants, or does not want me to be. Not anymore."

"Please, my lady. I ask you to reconsider…"

"You are in no position to ask me anything, sword master. I am the Princess of Dreach-Sciene and I command you to teach me."

Avery swallowed her next words at Rissa's challenging stare, choosing to stay quiet on the matter. Instead, she sighed and pointed down.

"As you wish, Princess. It's all in your stance. Your footing and proper foot placement is key for balance. Always have your feet shoulder width apart. When you move, move so your legs spread apart. Never have your feet close to each other. Like so." She demonstrated, and Rissa followed her movements.

"Like this?"

"Yes. Now hold your sword so you can handle it with ease. Keep your stance firm. The more grounded you are, the greater strength in your attacks. To keep your balance in battle, try to slide your feet rather than lift them up to take a step. Even a slight lifting of your heel reduces your grounding, so be cautious with how your feet are placed and used during each strike, otherwise you'll give your opponent a chance to knock you over."

Rissa followed the command, concentrating on her stance and slowly swinging with the blade in front of her. "I see what you mean, Avery."

"Well done, Princess. But stand up straighter. Keeping your posture erect and torso forward will also keep you from losing your balance during your swings. It also allows you to avoid any blows from your opponent with a simple twist rather than forcing yourself to turn sideways, which will only allow you to evade an attack in one direction. You need to be able to move away from an attacker effortlessly, and in either direction."

Rissa swung the sword, sliding her feet across the wet ground and evading her pretend enemy as Avery looked on. Finally satisfied with her footwork, she raised a brow Avery's way.

"What else?"

"Your sword, my lady. It's not just a weapon, it's your best protection. Missing just one block or parry can be fatal, so you need to protect yourself at all times. Maintain your sword in a position that runs from the bottom of your torso to the top of your head. Like so." Avery moved Rissa's hands, so the sword centered the middle of her body. "This will enable you to respond to an attack with speed and give you the best angles for your own strikes."

Avery stepped back as Rissa slashed at the air, time after time. Sparring with the enemy in her head with a viciousness only she could feel.

"Bend your elbows," Avery instructed. "Keep your sword closer to your body. That allows you to thrust and parry quickly. Extend your sword toward your opponent, not your arms."

Rissa did as told. Sweat beaded her brow as she moved and followed through on the commands Avery called to her. Over and over she repeated the moves, practicing until her uncertain actions evolved into the smooth flow of precise movement.

"Well done, Princess," Avery gave Rissa a slight smile of approval. "You learn quickly."

Rissa stopped, breathing deeply and wiping the sweat from her brow. "Yes, well any idiot can learn how to move with a sword. I want to learn to fight. Fight me, Avery."

"Princess, there is no need to duel with me. I can teach you to wield your blade well enough without actual sparring."

Rissa arched a brow. "And where is the fun in that? You didn't train Trystan or Davi that way. As a matter of fact, I remember them spending a lot more times knocked over on their behinds than they spent standing on their own two feet when sparring with you. Train me like that."

"That was different."

"Different? How so? And don't you dare tell me because they were boys. I will be sorely disappointed if that's the case. You, of all people, Avery, should not let a person's gender determine how good of a warrior they can be."

The sword master's lips compressed even tighter in disapproval. "That is not what I meant at all, Princess. You very well know many of my best soldiers are women. I meant it was different because the Prince and Davion were expected to be protectors of the realm. They were expected to train and fight. Your father did not wish that for you. He knew you were meant for greater things. Where Trystan was meant to be the sword and might of Dreach-Sciene, you were meant to be its heart and soul. It's what your father wanted."

"Why must you make me repeat myself, Avery?" Rissa's emerald gaze flashed with a mixture of anger and sorrow. "What my father wanted is a moot point since he is dead. Now pull your weapon." She pointed the tip of her sword toward Avery's throat, emphasizing her order.

The sword master crossed her arms stubbornly over her armor-plated chest. "I will not."

"I command you, sword master, to fight with me." Rissa's eyes narrowed in threat. "Do not make me tell the king that you disobeyed a direct command."

With an audible grunt of disapproval, Avery unsheathed her blade, raising it just in time for Rissa's attack. The echoing clang of blades roused the crows nesting in the trees above their heads and the birds flew off with an irritated squawking.

The two women paid no attention. Rissa was too intent on throwing attack after angry attack Avery's way, but Avery simply side stepped and parried every thrust, refusing to strike back.

"Fight!" Rissa screamed as her blade descended once more, only to be intercepted by Avery's. The jarring contact vibrated deep into Rissa's shoulder. Avery shoved at the crossed blades, sending Rissa stumbling backward.

"I said fight me, dammit!" Rissa ran at Avery, her sword extended in front of her. Avery calmly waited, sword held against her body in protection, until Rissa was close enough to thrust. The sword master deflected the wild slash and yanked the swords upward, sending Rissa's blade sailing over their heads. In the same motion she kicked Rissa's feet out from under her, landing the princess in a very undignified position on her backside in the mud.

Stunned, Rissa glared up at the older woman as the watery mud trickled down her face, but she ignored its icy touch. They both kept staring, Rissa breathing heavy from her exertion while Avery regarded her in cool silence, not winded in the least. Finally, Rissa grunted 'darn you' as she grabbed a handful of mud and threw it Avery's way. It splashed up the older woman's trousers, but Avery paid it no mind as she sheathed her sword.

"I warned you not to lift your feet. Never run at your opponent in anger. When you're in a frazzled state of mind you cannot act with speed or clarity, understand?"

Rissa wanted to scream in humiliation and frustration, but instead she gave a curt nod.

"Good. Now, I know you wish to train for battle but it's not something that can be done in a day. I will train you, Princess, since that is your wish, but it will be done on my terms. You will listen and learn, and you will not order me to rush it, agreed?"

Again, Rissa nodded in agreement.

Avery sighed as she shook her head. "After all the times you watched me set the boys on their asses, I'm so disillusioned you fell for it as well. I always thought you smarter than that."

A tiny smile tugged at Rissa's lips as her fury ebbed away. "Sorry to disappoint you, Avery."

The sword master leaned down and held out a hand. Rissa took it, appreciating the help.

"You could never disappoint me, Princess. Just remember, you do not stand by yourself in your grief."

For the first time Rissa saw the sadness in Avery's eyes as well, and for a moment she forgot what it was like to be alone in her solitude.

"Avery, I'm—"

The apology died on her lips as the sound of a horn pierced the air. The long blast was soon followed by two quick bursts and the alarm on Avery's face intensified Rissa's unease.

"What is it?" she asked, but Avery's answer was interrupted by shouting. Cullenspire guards appeared from everywhere, rushing toward the front of the estate. Avery, still holding Rissa's hand, started running as well, dragging Ri toward the manor.

"Everyone take arms and man your positions," a guard yelled as he led the others. His eyes fell on Avery and Rissa and he drew up short. "Sword master, we will appreciate your aid in this matter, but you must get the princess inside and hidden. We have enemies at the gate. Lord Eisner and his army are here."

CHAPTER 5

The horn resonated through the library, startling Trystan from his seat. The book he'd been focusing on—to drive all troubling thoughts of his father and Alixa from his head—fell from his lap and to the floor unnoticed. The horn faded away, only to be replaced by footsteps pounding along the marble halls. Outside the window shouting erupted, and though he couldn't make out any words, he knew it wasn't anything good.

He crossed the library in long strides and jerked the oak doors open, stepping into the hallway and right into the path of a running stable boy. The boy collided with him, but Trystan grabbed his shoulders to keep the slight child from falling on his rear.

"What's happening?" Trystan demanded, and the boy stared up at him with terrified eyes.

"That's the warning horn, sire. It means there are enemies at the gate."

"Enemies? What enemies?" He nearly shook the boy in his impatience.

The child looked like he was about to pass out. "I... I don't know, Your Majesty. Please... I gotta go find my ma."

Trystan let the boy go without another word and hurried through the marble hall.

"Your Majesty." Trystan paused as Lady Yaro appeared at the landing atop the spiral staircase dominating the hallway. Bunching her gown in both hands, she descended the stairs in her typical ladylike manner, the horn seemingly not affecting her poised demeanor at all.

"Do you know what's happening?" Trystan demanded of as soon as she hit the bottom step. A spark of fear in her eyes belied her calm facade.

"No, but we're about to find out."

In his mad rush, the young boy had left the main doors wide open. An icy gust whipped through the hall and the hair on Trystan's arms stood on end. They hurried outside to the sight of Cullenspire's guards rushing toward the closed gate. Without another word, Trystan headed in that direction as well; Lady Yaro tight on his heels.

Alixa and Edric appeared from around the stables, hurrying to join them. Trystan gave her a sidelong glance as Alixa fell in step with him. Her worried, light eyes questioned his. "What's happening?"

"Enemy at the gate, but not certain who. Have you seen Rissa?"

Alixa pointed with her chin and Trystan glanced over his shoulder at his approaching sister and Avery. Rissa's gaze met his, and he sent her a tiny nod of reassurance. She reciprocated with a hard, emotionless stare.

The Captain of the guard broke off from his men and headed their way, the grim expression on his face foreshadowing the bad news he was about to impart.

"Giles, what's happening?" Lady Yaro demanded. "Who is at the gate? Is it Dreach-Dhoun soldiers?"

"No, My Lady. Although, I do believe it's worse. Lord Eisner and his soldiers are here demanding entrance, or they will fight their way in."

"Eisner," she spat in cold contempt. "How dare that bastard show his face here again?" She glanced over at Alixa's slight gasp of fear, even as the young woman's face turned to stone, hiding any emotions churning inside. Lady Yaro knew who Alixa was, of course. Nothing had been hidden from their benefactor, but she had not informed anyone that Eisner's own daughter was residing under her roof. The mistress of Cullenspire kept the secret still as she questioned the captain. "Has he said what he wants? Does he know the rest of the royal family is here? Is that what he's after?"

"I don't know, my Lady."

"Then go inquire," she ordered.

The captain gave a sharp nod, turned on his heel and hurried off. They didn't have to wait to find out. Before the captain made it to the gate, a much despised voiced echoed through the air. It carried strong on the wind, like Eisner was already standing on this side of the stone walls. He used a speaking trumpet no doubt, but its effect on Alixa was obvious as a slight tremor shook her thin frame.

"Dona Yaro, I am sorely disappointed. I thought you and your family had already learned your lesson about defying me. Now I hear you are helping and harboring fugitives. Open the gate and allow us entrance, and I promise no harm will come to you or your family. I am here merely to converse with your royal guests."

Lady Yaro's cool facade finally cracked as her panicked gaze fell on Trystan. "He knows you're here. How is that possible?"

"Did he manage to track us through Briggs' magic?" Alixa asked, the slight quiver in her voice detectable only to Trystan.

"I doubt that. I don't think he has a seer in his grasp, plus Lonara is far too skilled to not have covered our trail successfully."

"Then how?" Edric questioned as his hand fell on the sword at his hip. Trystan cursed himself under his breath for having not worn his own weapon. A king should be prepared at all times, yet he'd foolishly left his sword in the library.

Trystan's shrug belied the fear reverberating through his chest. "I'm not sure."

"Only one way to know," Rissa interjected as she gripped the sword she carried more firmly. "Open the gate and let them in."

"No! We can't do that," Alixa yelled, before bringing herself back under control. "I mean, no. He can't be trusted, no matter what he promises."

"The girl's right." Lady Yaro nodded Alixa's way. "The last time he entered those gates, I lost my husband. I will not lose more today."

Trystan ignored both women as he turned his focus to the captain of the guards. "How many men do you have here, captain?"

"Just shy of a dozen, sire."

"And outside the gate?"

"Fifty or more."

"Then it appears we don't have a say in the matter. They will enter one way or another. Boy!" He called to the one of the young guards standing on the fringe of soldiers awaiting orders. The young man looked up in fear. "Fetch my sword from the library. The rest of you, prepare for battle. Captain, do you have archers?"

"Aye, your Majesty. I have a couple of men that can handle a bow with decency."

Trystan's gaze swept the courtyard. "Good. Get them in position. One atop the stables and one in the guard tower. Rissa, replace that rusted piece of junk in your hand with your own bow and take a position on the top balcony of the manor. You'll be of more use doing what you do best."

He recognized the stubborn look that crossed her face, so he added, "That's an order," even as he prayed silently, *Don't argue with me, Ri. Now is not the time.*

The prayer seemed to work. Even as her brows cinched together in a scowl, and he knew every bone in her body was screaming to disagree with his order, Rissa gave a shrug of resignation and hurried off to take up position. Trystan let out a quiet sigh of relief as he watched her go. At least she would be out of immediate danger.

"Alixa, go with…"

"Don't even suggest it," Alixa growled at Trystan as she flicked her cloak and grabbed the base of her own sword. As if suddenly realizing her insolence in front of the others, she bowed her in head in deference and added, "My place is by your side, your Majesty."

"Are you certain?" Trystan asked, his words low and meant for her ears only. "It won't be easy facing your father."

Alixa gave a noncommittal shrug, but Trystan detected determination in her eyes along with fear. He stepped toward her, to give reassurance, but Edric beat him too it as he placed his hand over Alixa's on the sword.

"I'll be by your side as well, my lady. I'll watch your back."

Trystan stepped back, swallowing his irritation and averting his eyes from the entwined hands as the young guard ran up to him with his sword. Trystan didn't bother to strap the sheath around his waist. Instead, he pulled the blade and tossed the sheath aside as a resounding volley of thumps on the wooden gates informed them of their enemy's lack of patience. Eisner's voice filled the air once more.

"Lady Yaro, this is your last warning. I am a man of honor but even I only have so much patience. Open the gate and allow us in and no one will get hurt. I wish to speak with Trystan Renauld, and I know very well you are hiding him, along with my traitorous daughter."

Alixa could no longer hide her fear. Her terrified gaze collided with Trystan's and even from a distance, he could see the effort it was taking for her to keep herself together.

"Alixa," he began, but she squared her shoulders and waved a dismissive hand his way.

"I'm okay," she said through clenched teeth. "There's nothing else he can do to hurt me. It's good he knows I'm here. I need to do this. I want to face him… and hopefully watch him die."

Trystan fumbled for an appropriate response, but none was forthcoming. It was hard for him to grasp the hatred she harbored for her father when he had loved his so much. Instead, he met her gaze with a deep, calming breath.

"Okay. If you're sure. Let them in. Let's hear what he has to say."

"I hope you know what you're doing," Lady Yaro whispered as she shouted the command, "Open the gate!"

The young guards standing at both sides of the massive wooden doors started in terror at the command, but still they did as told.

Silence fell over the courtyard as the heavy bolts were pulled back and dropped, the metal clang echoing in the quiet. Trystan swallowed the lump of dread in his throat and took a deep breath as the gates groaned in protest, like they didn't want to admit entrance to whoever was waiting on the other side. He drummed his fingers along the sword's hilt and planted his feet, expecting any moment for Eisner's army to break their way through and attack.

His dread was unnecessary. Instead, the waiting mob on the other side stayed rooted in place. Even as the opening grew allowing the army easy access, no one made a move. The only movement was from Eisner himself, as the squat man ambled casually into the courtyard, a smile on his face and a hint of laughter in his voice.

"Finally. It was extremely rude to keep us waiting so long." His eyes skimmed the small crowd waiting in the courtyard, stopping on Alixa. "Hello, daughter. Don't you at least have a hug for your dear father?"

"What do you want here?" Alixa snarled, showing much more teeth than necessary.

"I see your manners, or lack of, haven't improved any since we last saw each other. Can't say that surprises me much." His eyes flitted from his daughter to Lady Yaro. "Ah, Mistress Dona. You look well. So much better than you did when we last met. When was that again? Oh yes. When I killed your traitorous husband."

"Trust me, Eisner, I haven't forgotten a moment of our last meeting." Lady Yaro's expression remained unruffled even as her cheeks flushed bright with anger. "It's all I think of these days. You'd be wise to remember no one escapes the consequences of their actions."

Eisner's laughter grated along Trystan's spine and curdled his gut.

"Why if I didn't know better, dear lady, I'd say that was a threat." Eisner's laughter stopped abruptly as he narrowed his black eyes. "Are you threatening me?"

"Take from it what you will," Lady Yaro replied.

"So be it. I take it as the ramblings of a soured, old woman whose husband was stupid enough to put his faith in the wrong man and earned himself a traitor's death."

"My husband was no traitor. He was loyal to one king and one king only. Marcus Renauld, his friend and rightful king."

Eisner barked more laughter. He truly seemed to be enjoying himself.

"And please tell me. What did Yaro's loyalty to Renauld earn him? Death. And a painful one at that. You think you would have learned a lesson from that, Dona. But no. Instead, I find out from an intercepted messenger boy that you not only still serve the Renaulds, but you've given them sanctuary in your home along with this treacherous little witch," he motioned to Alixa.

"Enough," Trystan growled as he stepped forward and raised his sword, pointing it Eisner's way. "We all know who the traitor is here, there's no need to argue the truth. Why are you here, Eisner? I know you're aware of my father's murder. Have you come here to gloat about having a hand in my father's death?"

The swarthy, little man appeared truly surprised. "You think I had a hand in Renauld's murder? Oh no. I wish. I mean, it would have been an honor to knock that pompous airbag off his pedestal. But sadly, that honor did not go to me. Calis had another do that for him. You should know by now that his people are everywhere." He enhanced his comment by wiggling his stubby fingers into the air.

"Then why are you here, you turncoat piece of crap? And speak true or else I'll cut your blasphemous tongue from your mouth." Trystan ignored the little voice in his head telling him to stay calm and instead allowed the anger to take control.

"Oh my, brave words, boy, for someone far outnumbered." Eisner laughed again as he rocked back on his heels. "I didn't think you had that sort of gall. I always thought you a cowardly idiot. A pretty boy, soft little prince too scared to get his hands dirty."

"How dare you speak to King Trystan that way." Avery's voice filled with fury as she drew her sword and aimed it toward Eisner. In retaliation, Eisner's soldiers drew their own swords in unison, rushing to his aid. Trystan stopped the sword master in her tracks with a restraining hand on her forearm.

"Avery, no."

"Don't stop her, boy. Please, let your rabid dog loose. My soldiers are getting bored just standing here." Eisner stared at Avery in distaste. "You're as stupid as you are big. King Trystan, indeed. This silly boy is not king. That title has already been claimed."

Trystan tried hard to cover his confusion, but Eisner noticed and cawed in laughter again.

"Oh my. You don't even know, do you? Well, I suppose not since I've had every messenger on the roads killed of late. Let me fill you in on the news. While you've all been hiding out here, licking your wounds and crying over your father's death, someone else has claimed the title. Marcus Renauld's body wasn't even cold when his brother Drake crowned himself king. There is no throne waiting for you, boy. Only a cold dark prison. I'm here to take you all to Calis."

CHAPTER 6

Rissa wasn't sure if she believed her own ears. Did that hateful little man just announce that Drake had claimed himself king? Their uncle wouldn't do such a dishonorable thing… would he? Of course, he would. Rissa's lips thinned to a grim line as she answered her own question. Drake was a slimy snake, always undermining their father's decisions and hating having to follow his orders. Anyone with half a brain could see how much Drake resented his brother and his title. Everyone but her father. No matter how disrespectful Lord Drake was, Marcus always overlooked it. *He's family*, was his answer to everything his brother did wrong. She'd overlooked a lot of Drake's faults at her father's request. He had trusted way too easily. And look where it had gotten him.

Shaking her head, she trained her bow on Eisner directly below her and squinted her eye. She could take him out. Right now. What was Trystan waiting for? Give her the signal and Eisner was a dead man. His soldiers as well. Didn't matter they were outnumbered. She'd take pleasure in killing them all. They'd already chosen their path. They deserved no mercy.

"You truly believe you can take us to Calis without a fight?" Rissa heard the steel in her brother's voice and a tiny smile lifted the corner of her lips. Now we're getting somewhere. Maybe Trystan did have some fight left in him after all. She had begun to believe otherwise since Davi's death. No. Not going there. Not now. The enemy below was the focus right now.

Dammit, Trystan. Enough with the talking already.

"Oh, dear me, no." Eisner's voice settled over her with an oiliness that she could practically feel on her skin. "I'm hoping for a fight, to be honest. Like I said, my men here are getting bored. But take you to Calis I will, one way or another. King Calis always gets his way. You should know that by now. Before we commence, however, I must ask you to order your archers to step down."

"I have no archers," Trystan growled, but Eisner responded by clucking his tongue and pointing a finger toward the younger man.

"Please, don't bother to lie. You have archers trained on us as we speak. One of them your sister, no doubt, since I don't see her around. I've studied you all on my visits to the palace. The girl is more than adequate with a bow and arrow. Princess, please come out and join us. I'd feel much better knowing you weren't planning to shoot me in the head."

"Ri, stay where you are," Trystan ordered over his shoulder, not taking his eyes off Eisner. He really didn't need to say so. Rissa had no plans to do otherwise. She leveled her bow on her forearm once more and caught Eisner in the crosshairs.

"Anytime now, brother," she whispered.

"I wouldn't say that if I were you, *Prince Trystan*. For you see, I didn't come without a backup plan. Bring her to me."

Rissa lowered the bow once more and watched in puzzlement as a guard made his way through the throng from outside the gate. He dragged a girl behind him. With no regard to the cold, the girl was dressed in nothing but rags, her blonde hair hung loose and wild about her shoulders and one side of her face was swollen and bruised. She stumbled to a stop next to Eisner, her hands tied in front of her, as the soldier yanked her head back and settled a knife at her throat. Rissa had no idea who it was until Alixa's cry of "Ella" pierced the air.

Ella? Rissa pulled the name from her memory. This was Alixa's maid and Edric's sister? But she was supposed to be dead.

"Release her," Edric's tortured voice elicited a small whimper from the girl.

"Now why would I do that? After I gave you two ingrates a home and fed you as well as my family, you both turned around and helped this treacherous little wasp run straight to Marcus Renauld with news of my loyalty to King Calis. Calis was not happy with that breach. My rations suffered greatly because of the three of you. I was punished. Withheld my rightful share *and* no wine. Do you know how much I love wine?"

"What have you done to her?"

Rissa almost didn't recognize Alixa's voice, it was so ragged and strained. It didn't seem right to hear the usually snarky Alixa sound so broken.

Eisner spread his hands wide in fake innocence. "Me? I've done nothing. You caused this, my dear. All of it. Ella's suffering falls entirely on you and her brother."

"Ella…" Alixa stepped toward her friend but was met with numerous sword points as her father's soldiers cut her off, allowing her no access to the other girl.

"Uh, uh. No comforting allowed. This is my time, remember?"

"What do you hope to achieve by bringing the girl here, Eisner?" Trystan demanded, and Rissa rolled her eyes at the question. *Who cares what he's doing, brother. Give me the signal to shoot.*

"What I hope to achieve, boy, is to take you all prisoner. Calis requires you and your sister, and Briggs Villard. I'm just here to fetch you all and get back into his good graces. Now if you cooperate and come along quietly, I'll let the girl and everyone else go free, including my back-stabbing daughter."

"And if we don't come willingly?"

"Then the girl and everyone else here dies and I still capture you. So, what do you say? Call off your archers and I'll command the knife to be taken from the girl's throat. Tit for tat."

Don't do it, Trystan. Rissa yelled silently at her brother's back. Quiet stretched out for what felt like an eternity. Rissa was almost convinced Trystan was going to give up without a fight and her fingers tightened on her bow. She sure as hell wasn't about to. Finally, Trystan's steely tone floated up to her.

"My father was the bravest, smartest man I've ever known. He would never let Calis win that easily. Not without a fight. And neither will we. Today we will honor King Marcus Renauld by claiming victory. Stop hiding behind the girl and fight justly like the nobleman you claim to be."

Trystan took a stance and held his sword in front of his body, ready to fight. Pride competed with the fear coursing through Rissa's heart as she did the same with her bow.

"So be it." Eisner's tone was nonchalant with no indication of what was about to occur. Crimson blood splattered the young girl's rags, her scream cut short, as the soldier carried out his threat and sliced his knife across her throat. She crumpled to the ground in a heap as Alixa's agonized shriek pierced the air.

The girl's death and Alixa's scream were like sparks to a powder keg. Chaos broke out as Rissa loosed an arrow in retaliation. It sailed through the air and buried deeply into the murderous soldier's thick neck. He grabbed at the arrow in shock as he fell to his knees and disappeared under the horde of soldiers at his back.

The roar of the attack was deafening, but Rissa exhaled, pushing all her emotions out and settled her stance. No time to be afraid. She nocked the next arrow and aimed straight for Eisner. Feeling for the wind. She could not miss. Calm settled over her as she zoned in on her target, but as if he sensed his impending death, Eisner ducked in amongst his men, hidden from her view.

Cursing with frustration, Rissa targeted the next in line. No time to pick and choose. She needed to take out as many of Eisner's men as possible. The arrow sailed true, and the soldier Edric was battling screamed as the barb pierced him straight through the heart.

Again and again she volleyed shots into the crowd below, taking down their enemies, until she had no more arrows to spend. She threw her bow aside in impatience and grabbed the rusty sword she'd left leaning against the balcony rail. It wasn't the best blade, but Trystan needed her help.

Terror thrummed through her veins in time to the pounding of her footsteps on the marble stairs. She refused to let it overwhelm her. Trystan was right. Her father would never give up without a fight. Calis could not get his hands on another member of the Tri-Gard. She would protect the senile old man with all she had, or die trying.

Taking the stairs two at a time, Rissa hit the main floor and skidded to a stop as she caught movement out of the corner of her eye. A pale young girl emerged from the library at the bottom of the stairs, her face a mask of panic. Anna. Lady Yaro's seer daughter.

"Wha-what's happening?" the girl stuttered as she wrapped her arms around her thin frame.

"We're under attack. Lord Eisner and his men," Rissa responded as a shadow fell over the marble hallway. "Go. Hide," she whispered. The terrified girl ran past her and up the stairs as fast as her legs could carry her. Moments later, a soldier barreled through the open doors, his hulking frame covered in a tunic of Isenore's colors rather than Cullenspire's plainer garb. One of Eisner's men.

His cold, mud colored eyes fell on her and he actually smiled as Rissa held her sword in defense in front of her body like Avery had shown her. His smile widened as he took a couple of steps her way and she backed up from his approach.

"What do we have here now? Did they really leave a little girl in charge of protecting the old man?"

He was looking for Briggs.

"Don't come any closer," Rissa growled, hoping she sounded far more threatening than she felt.

"Or what?" he questioned as he took a few more steps.

"Or I kill you," she answered bluntly. It didn't seem to scare him at all. He actually laughed as he pointed to her blade.

"I hope you aren't trying to scare me with that?"

Rissa held the sword in out in front of her, holding on tight with both hands, trying to keep the blade from shaking. "I said that's far enough!"

"Get out of my way, girl." The soldier sprinted across the distance separating them, swinging his massive broadsword and connecting with Rissa's. The shock reverberated up her arm and into her shoulder. She grimaced in pain. For a moment they stared, hatred in each other's eyes, blades intertwined before the man looped his blade low and jerked upward, tearing Rissa's sword from her hands and sending it clanging down the hall.

Weaponless, Rissa turned to run, but a huge hand settled on her shoulder with a vise-like grip and pushed her straight into the wall. Her head bounced off the wood with a hollow sound as black spots filled her vision, the threat of passing out all too real. Her knees wobbled, and she nearly sank to the floor, but the meaty hand grabbed the front of her tunic and pushed her back into the wall, her toes dangling just above the marble floor and his sword at her chest. She yanked in vain at the hands holding her, trying to loosen his grip.

"Where is the old man?" the soldier growled in her face, his breath enveloping her with its rotted meat stench. She gagged in reflex. "Answer me before I slice you open," he spat as he shook her a bit more.

Rissa fought to control her panic as Avery's words popped into her head. *When you are in a frazzled state of mind, you cannot act with speed or clarity.*

Her eyes fell on the knife sheath at his side and a spark of hope bloomed.

"Please," she begged as she stared up at him. "Don't hurt me. You need me alive. I'm Princess Rissa. Eisner and Calis would want me alive. You can't hurt me."

His muddy eyes opened wider in recognition, and the black toothed smile crossed his face again as he realized what her confession meant. He had the princess in his possession. Eisner would be pleased. His grip loosened as he dropped her back on her feet and lowered his blade. Rissa made her move. Before he could react, she ducked, evading his grasping hands and yanked the knife from his belt. She dodged around him, so she was at his back. She kicked at his knee with all her might, connecting solidly and sending him stumbling off balance. He growled as he tried to catch himself against the wall, and spun with his sword out, not seeming to care that she needed to be taken alive. Rissa evaded the wildly swinging blade and caught him in his side with the knife. It sank deep, up to the hilt and she ripped down on it, slicing him open from his side to his gut. He died with a silent scream still on his lips.

Rissa stumbled back as he collapsed, his flowing blood staining the white marble floor. That same blood covered her hands, and she stared in horror as they started to tremble. This wasn't the first time she'd killed, but it was the first time her hands had directly taken a life. This was different. Shooting an arrow was by far easier than staring into someone's eyes as the light left them. She clasped her hands to stop the trembling and closed her eyes, breathing in deep through her nose.

The sounds of the outside battle finally registered. Trystan and the others were still fighting Eisner.

Pull yourself together. Trystan needs you.

Wiping her bloody hands on her thighs in disgust, she leaned over the soldier and grabbed the heavy sword from his lifeless fingers. She pushed what she'd just done to the back of her mind and turned to run for the entrance, hoping against hope that her people were still alive.

She hit the cold air expecting to see the worst, but a miraculous sight met her eyes. Whereas Cullenspire's soldiers had first been outnumbered by Eisner's men, the grounds were now crawling with what looked like villagers—women and men dressed in peasant garb-overrunning the enemy soldiers with pitchforks and axes and homemade spears. Rissa paused in disbelief, even as her frantic eyes searched for her brother.

"Princess!" Lady Yaro sprinted across the distance separating her from Rissa, the fear evident in her voice. "Are you injured? You're bleeding."

"It's not my blood," Rissa answered, distracted as she continued to search for Trystan. Her panic mounted as he was nowhere to be seen. "I need to find my brother."

"No, you can't go into battle." Lady Yaro stopped her headlong flight by grabbing Rissa's wrist holding the sword. "The land owners still loyal to your family have come to aid us. Let them and my men handle this. You must stay safe."

"Let me go." Even as Rissa yanked on her arm a horn sounded, startling both women.

"Retreat!"

The yell echoed on the wind. Rissa met Lady Yaro's gaze, the older woman's expression as confused as her own. Was the enemy truly retreating? She prayed to the earth it was so.

And is if answering Rissa's unspoken prayers, the Isenore soldiers began to dissipate in realization that they were now outnumbered and losing ground. They turned tail and ran through the gates, leaving behind their injured comrades without a second thought. Some land owners chased after them, screaming obscenities and ordering the cowards back, but it did no good. They disappeared into the evening shadows, leaving silence in their wake.

Rissa stood for a moment, her breath wheezing in her chest, before realization struck her and she went running into the courtyard. Avery was the first one she saw, and she almost collided with the woman.

"Trystan." His name stumbled out of her mouth. "I need to find Trystan."

Avery shook her head, her eyes scanning their surroundings. Cullenspire's soldiers picked themselves up in a daze. Some bent over bodies on the ground. Some wept.

Lady Yaro appeared at Rissa's side again. "The last battle we had here…" She paused and wiped a tired hand over her face. "Your father and Adrian Coille fought alongside my husband." Her expression turned dark. "That was the last time any of us had any hope." She turned away from them. "My daughter's inside. I need to go to her."

Rissa's eyes found Alixa and Edric next, huddled over the body of the girl Eisner had brought with him. If her heart wasn't already cracked beyond repair, it would break for them. They'd thought she was dead and then for one moment they'd had her back.

Rissa ran a shaky hand through her hair. Would losing Davi again be worth looking him in the eye once more? No. She didn't think she'd survive seeing the light fade from him again.

Turning from Alixa, she wiped her bloody hands on her shirt. *Where are you, brother?* Her heart beat painfully in her chest. She had to know he was okay.

She lifted her eyes at a commotion up ahead as a man pushed through the crowd of injured and tired people. When his gaze found her, relief flooded his face.

Rissa sucked in a breath. "Trystan." She ran the short distance between them and fell against him. "Thank the earth you're okay."

His arms came around her and he held on tightly. "I lost sight of you. You weren't supposed to leave your post, especially not to join the fight down here."

"You can't tell me what to do." His shirt muffled her words.

He released her and met her eyes sternly. "I'm glad you're okay."

"Yeah, yeah. If you'd have died and left me as the only heir, I'd have killed you. I'm no queen."

Her words pushed them both into silence for a moment as the aftermath of the failed attack swirled around them.

"Eisner got away." Trystan sighed and rubbed the back of his neck. "He ordered the retreat and I just… let him go."

"No one else needed to die," she said quietly.

"Do you think he was telling the truth?"

Rissa's eyes hardened. "Eisner wouldn't know the truth if it cut off his balls and shoved them down his throat."

Trystan snorted but there was no humor in it, only disgust because they both knew. Despite their feelings about Eisner, he hadn't been lying.

Rissa sighed. "Uncle Drake stole our father's throne, didn't he?"

"I think that's a fair assumption."

"He can't get away with it."

"He won't." Trystan raised his face to the falling snow.

"What are we going to do about it?"

"Think about it, Ri. If Drake had taken control of the palace, do you really think he has allies among the nobles? Among Father's nobles? Where would our friends gather?"

"I quite enjoy Whitecap," she said, finally catching on. "I think we'll find many friendly faces there."

"Briggs should be well enough to travel." He glanced back towards where Briggs was being kept safe inside. "Dammit, we're supposed to be heading into Dreach-Dhoun."

"Trystan." She gripped his arm firmly. "What's the point of going into Dreach-Dhoun to save our kingdom if we don't have a kingdom any longer?"

"I thought all you wanted to do was run towards Dreach-Dhoun to take your revenge?"

She released a long breath. "Davi is gone, Trystan. Nothing I do will change that. Father is gone as well. I don't want to lose Dreach-Sciene too."

He nodded. "We'll leave tomorrow for Duke Coille's estate at Whitecap. If we have allies, that's where they'll be."

She offered him a grim smile and turned to head back inside.

"Ri," he called after her. She paused but didn't turn to face him. "You know you still have me, right?"

Her lips twitched, and she started walking again. She had a journey to prepare for. It wasn't the trek she'd been expecting, but it was the one she needed. After feeling helpless to save so many people in her life, it bolstered her knowing she could do this. They would save their home.

CHAPTER 7

Someone screamed, and the sound bounced around the room. A sharp slice of pain dug deeper into Davi's chest until it was all that existed.

He didn't understand the jumbled images in his dreams. A battle. There'd been a battle.

The scream sounded again, a high-pitched keening that settled in a heavy cloak around him. His eyes popped open, and the screaming cut off abruptly, the pain vanishing in an instant.

It had been him. His chest rose and fell with rapid succession as he tried to breathe air that was laden with grief.

Grief? What did he have to grieve? He'd returned home from his prison to a father who loved him and a people who revered him.

He was the triumphant prince.

But not in his dreams.

He ran a hand through his sweaty hair as he tried to recall the images from the night. Nothing.

Memories had been returning rapidly with each of Ramsey Kane's sessions and the information was almost too much to process.

Maybe he'd been dreaming of what they did to him in Dreach-Sciene. His time there hadn't been pleasant. The cruel King Marcus deserved the death his cousin served him, and his children would soon face the same.

He sat up and climbed from the bed on shaking limbs when a scratching noise sounded at his door. Pulling a robe around his shoulders as he went, he yanked the heavy door open and jumped back to avoid being mauled by the dog who barged his way in.

Davi's heart finally returned to a steady rhythm and he couldn't even think of sending the beast away. Shutting the door, he turned to find Deor making himself at home on the middle of the bed.

"I thought you weren't allowed inside the palace?" He shook his head, surprisingly glad for the company.

Deor lowered his head, his large brown eyes studying the prince.

Davi walked past the canopied bed to a table that sat in front of a large window. Golden morning light streamed through, catching on the silver ewer Davi used to pour himself a glass of water. He studied the grounds outside with their dead and twisted trees. The grass was a dusty brown wherever it managed to sprout up at all. Had it been beautiful once?

He'd been told his father drained much of the magic surrounding the palace in order to have the power to bring him back.

But was he worth it? Was he worth turning his kingdom into a graveyard?

A sharp yap rang out behind him and he took a long gulp of water before setting it aside and approaching the bed.

"Lorelai tells me you're harmless." He narrowed his eyes. "But nothing is ever truly harmless."

As if to tell him how wrong he was, Deor shifted forward and lowered his head onto his paws while meeting Davi's eyes.

"Darn dog." Davi reached forward and dug his fingers into Deor's fur, massaging him between the eyes.

Unable to face the prospect of another day as a prince who didn't know how to be a prince, he climbed back in bed. As he laid back, Deor scooted up and nuzzled against his chest.

Davi turned his head away from the dog's smell, but let him

remain, his warmth providing the prince with the peace he needed to close his eyes once again and fall asleep.

The heavy rap of a fist on wood woke Davi. Deor jumped from his arms and ran to the door, barking like mad. Davi was slower to follow as he scrubbed a hand across his tired eyes.

He didn't bother with a robe this time as he yanked open the door, suddenly irritated at whoever was beyond it.

Lorelai stood with a fist still raised as if planning to knock again.

Her usually sad smile turned into a smirk as she took in his disheveled state and the dog who tried to push past him to greet Lorelai.

"Put some clothes on, cousin. Today, you're with me."

His eyes flicked down over his bare chest and linen pants and he sighed. He didn't have a choice. He'd had no control over his days since coming to the palace. And a day with Lorelai was infinitely better than another one spent under the magical powers of Ramsey.

"Give me a moment." He closed the door, noting Deor opted to stay in the hall with Lorelai.

After pulling on an ensemble more suitable for a prince, he flattened his hair with his fingers and met Lorelai out in the hall. Deor walked at Davi's side, his large frame occasionally bumping into Davi's legs.

"Where are we going?" he asked as she led him into the courtyard. Two horses stood saddled and riderless among a handful of guardsmen atop their mounts.

"Davi, you've lived most of your life in a land that holds no magic. It's time you learned of your birthright."

She swung up gracefully. He pulled himself into his own saddle. In his spotty mind, he didn't remember doing much riding, but his muscles seemed to remember what his brain failed to recognize as familiar.

They took off through the gates, the guards following at a distance. To Davi's surprise, Deor loped along next to the horses.

Lorelai looked down at the dog, the hint of a genuine smile on her lips. "Don't worry, Davi, Deor is a hunting dog. He can keep up."

Davi hadn't been worried, but he looked sideways at his cousin. Her smile was gone as she focused on the road ahead. It was as if she fought against every urge to smile or laugh.

He recognized it because he knew the feeling.

The scarred and twisted surroundings soon gave way to rolling hills that grew greener the farther from the palace they rode.

A village came into view, stacks of smoke stretching from rows of chimneys and children's laughter floating on the breeze. But they didn't enter. Instead, they skirted around the edges until they came upon a meadow on the far side that screamed of life.

Davi sucked in a breath. The memories that were returning of life in Dreach-Sciene featured a land so devoid of life that he was sure this was the most beautiful sight he'd ever seen.

Their guards put the horses to grazing and then gave them space as Davi walked forward. Freedom existed outside the palace walls and he soaked it in.

"This is what I love about Dreach-Dhoun." Lorelai smiled, the joy touching her eyes for once. "I spent so long in Dreach-Sciene that I forgot what it felt like to be surrounded by magic."

"Magic?" He cocked his head as the buzz of energy slithered along his skin.

Amusement flashed across her face at his ignorance. "It's in the earth, Davi." She crossed her arms across her small body. "What's it like to… not remember?"

He shrugged as a weight settled in his chest. What could he say to the cousin he barely knew? But he wanted to know her. If only to have a friend.

How did it feel? Confusing. Painful. Terrifying.

"I can feel them missing," he finally admitted. "You'd think you wouldn't know something wasn't there if you don't remember it, but you do. I just want it all back."

Lorelai's smile dropped, and she shifted her eyes away. It wasn't the first time he'd sensed there was something she wasn't telling him. But he never pressed. Something inside him told him he didn't want to know, whatever it was.

She cleared her throat. "We didn't come out here to talk. Your father wants me to show you how to control your magic."

"My magic?" He looked down at his hands but they didn't look like they were meant for power.

She laughed. "Sometimes, Davi, you get this look on your face that turns you back into the little boy who…"

When she trailed off, he met her eye. "Was kidnapped?"

"Yeah. Kidnapped." Her shoulders shook as if shivering and he pressed his lips together, trying to read her thoughts.

"We were close when I was a child?"

That brought her smile back. "You used to follow me everywhere. Even as a teenager, I never got annoyed. It was impossible to be mad at you."

"I wish I remembered."

The sadness returned to her face. "That isn't a result of your lost memories, cousin. Even if they were fully intact, you wouldn't remember those years. It's the greatest tragedy of childhood."

His lips curved into a smirk. "I'd say my childhood tragedy was being stolen by an enemy king and held prisoner."

A laugh burst from her lips and she shook her head. He liked that he could make her smile. Everything inside the palace–his father included–was so very cold. Lorelai's sadness echoed through the great halls, a tragedy in its own right.

He felt connected to her as if his earliest years tied them together in the most unbreakable of bonds. Family. They were family.

Something the Renaulds had taken from him.

It was another thing they would have to answer for.

Deor pranced across the meadow, pulling Davi from his own thoughts. Could the dog feel the magic?

Lorelai lowered herself to the ground, fanning her skirts around her, not worried about dirtying them. She glanced up, imploring him to join her.

He knelt in front of her.

"I am a seer," she began. "That is the only kind of magic that does not come directly from the earth. It lives inside of me. But the greater power lives in the very ground beneath our feet. It is not ours to own, only to use. We draw upon it, fighting for control." She nodded towards the ground in front of her. "Place your hands directly on the earth."

As soon as he did, all surrounding sounds faded away as warmth flooded through him.

Lorelai continued to speak, and it took a moment for her words to break through. "Some people can actually hear the earth. It's called the Tenelach. Their power is infinite. Yours will have its limits. Now, don't think about it. I just want you to release any barrier in your mind, let yourself go."

He closed his eyes, breathing deeply, and opened himself up. It was easier than he expected—as if his mind already knew what to do.

Energy surged through him, filling him.

"Slowly," Lorelai said softly. "You can control the flow. Your body should instinctively know when to stop. Listen to it. If you don't, you'll draw more power than you can handle and you could die."

She was right. It struggling to squeeze more into him. The flow grew weak. He could have taken more if he pulled, but he heeded Lorelai's warning and slammed up a wall in his mind while pulling his hands free of the soft grass.

"How do you feel?" Lorelai asked tentatively.

Davi raised his eyes to the clear blue sky, a grin forming on his lips as the power swirled inside of him. "Like I can do anything."

It was the truth. Invincibility. Nothing could touch him.

Lorelai stood and turned to face him, satisfaction bright in her eyes. "That was the easy part." She gestured to a patch of trees nearby. "Try it out."

His shoulders cocked with confidence, Davi faced his target. He didn't need to think about the first thing he'd do with the magic. He knew. He could do this. He could do it all. Feeling more like himself than any time since he'd arrived in Dreach-Dhoun, he lifted his hands and pressed them forward, expected the trees to burst into flames.

But nothing happened.

The power inside him fought for dominance, but it wouldn't come out. He tried again. It crackled on his fingertips and died.

Lorelai muffled a laugh with her fist. "You can't just draw on magic and expect to have it mastered. The use of magic is a battle within oneself. The power wants control. You need to fight it and take that control for yourself. Everyone has varying levels of magic. Most people can only use it for small things. The strength of one's power depends on their body's tolerance of it."

The longer he stood there not using it, the more he felt the magic seeping out of him. He was unable to keep it in. He tried again, but nothing happened and he growled.

"It'll take practice, Davi."

His mind suddenly focused on the palace and the barren lands that surrounded it. They'd been drained of magic to save him—although he didn't know what that meant.

"My father," he started. "He's… powerful?"

"The second most powerful man I've ever heard of. Don't you dare tell him I said that."

"Who was the first?"

She turned away from him and for a moment, he thought she wasn't going to answer. Then her sad words reached him almost as if carried on a breeze.

"Before Dreach-Sciene lost their magic, it was Marcus Renauld."

LORELAI TOOK comfort in being out among the fields that were humming with magic as Davi practiced using his power. He'd managed to create a tiny blast of air and she'd never been more proud of anyone. Magic worked like a muscle one had only to use to know how. They called it magic memory. Instinct. Evolution. A connection to the earth.

When Davi was a child, Lorelai had taken care of him. He'd first used magic as a young boy. He may not remember it, but his body did. It already knew what to do. It only needed to be reminded.

When they'd journeyed into Dreach-Sciene together and she had to hand him over to the king, it nearly killed her. But it was her uncle's orders. Through Davi and blood magic, they'd kept a close watch on Marcus Renauld and his household.

Marcus. Every time she thought of him, her heart squeezed. Everyone thought she'd killed the man. Thom hadn't told that secret, but she knew he had his reasons. He held it over her head each night when he came to her rooms and put his disgusting paws on her.

But if Calis found out she'd chosen not to carry out her mission, the punishment would be great.

A boyish grin formed on Davi's face, creating two adorable dimples. At least she had him back in her life even if she had to lie to him every day.

He sent a bolt of energy towards a tree and the crack of the bark sounded loud as he let out a whoop of glee. Lorelai hid a smirk behind her hand. Davi's pride at something children could normally do was endearing.

Would he be as powerful as his father? If he was, she hoped it wouldn't destroy him too.

Power didn't have to ruin everything. She'd only been a girl during the war, but she heard stories of Marcus Renauld and how he used his abilities to protect his people. To protect his family.

Marissa Kane had been more mother to Lorelai than her own, but then she'd switched sides. Lorelai had barely been able to look at Rissa without memories flooding back. She looked so like her mother.

These thoughts would get her nowhere. She refocused on Davi, noticing his movements growing sluggish. He'd drawn more magic from the earth twice, but it was wearing on him.

"Davion," she said, putting a hand on his arm. "You're exhausted. We should stop."

"No way."

She leveled him with a stare. "There'll be plenty enough time to practice in the future. Right now, I need a drink."

That stopped him and his mouth hung open in shock for just a moment before a gleam shone in his eyes. He released the rest of the magic stored inside him and surprised her by dropping a sweaty arm over her shoulders. "We really are related, aren't we?"

She reveled in the feel of any kind of human contact. She'd never had family who hugged or showed affection. It felt... nice. Like someone cared about her.

Guilt ate away at her. She'd been there when Davi's memories were erased. She knew the truth of his time in Dreach-Sciene. But telling him would ruin everything, and she wasn't ready to lose the one person who'd always been able to make her smile. The one person she hoped could eventually love her for the simple fact that they were family.

It was selfish, but in that moment, she didn't care.

Deor ran up and bumped into their legs.

"There's a tavern in the village," she said. "But we need to ditch our guards."

He smirked. "Done." As he walked up to the guards, he stood as tall as he could and squared his shoulders. "Your presence is no longer needed."

"I'm sorry, your Highness, but we have orders." The man who spoke truly did look apologetic.

"Now you have new orders." The arrogance was new to Davi, and he found he liked it. "I am the Prince of Dreach-Dhoun." He cocked his head. "And I am not someone you want to disobey." He narrowed his eyes and waited.

The guard sighed. "Yes, your Highness. Just be warned, your father will not be happy about this."

The guards mounted up and rode away.

Lorelai watched them in stunned fascination. "That was way too easy."

Davi shrugged. "Let's go."

The ride to the village was short and people watched as they made their way along the cobblestone street. It all felt very familiar to Davi. Had he been in villages like this in Dreach-Sciene?

"They're staring," he whispered to Lorelai.

She ran a hand over her white hair, her lips turning down. "They always stare. I'm not exactly unrecognizable. I doubt they know who you are though."

They dismounted outside a squat building and tied their horses up before opening the door. Boisterous sounds poured out. A heavy laugh soared through the air among the clattering of cups and plates. Deor was made to stay outside.

Lines of wooden benches sat around tables that had seen better days. A long bar stood on one end of the room with the kitchen behind it.

As soon as they stepped inside, all sound stopped. Patrons turned to stare, open-mouthed. A few rose to their feet and scurried out the door, but others sat frozen.

Lorelai was used to the feeling of distrust that hung in the air. Calis made a habit of raiding the villages for any sign of unrest. He didn't realize he only created more unrest in doing so. He ruled his people harshly and without mercy. If there were even a rumor of rebellious leanings, the dungeons would fill.

But she'd been coming into the village since she was a girl. As a child, she'd played with the village children. Over the years, she'd continued her trips. Calis didn't approve, but he didn't stop her either. As long as it didn't interfere with her missions for the crown, he ignored it.

Davi sat down heavily at one of the tables and rested his head in his hands. "Does magic always do this?"

"Do what?" She joined him.

"Is it always so exhausting?"

She patted his arm in sympathy. "Yes."

He groaned and a small laugh escaped her. She was still smiling when a dark-haired man walked over carrying two tankards of ale. He slammed them on the table, the golden liquid sloshing over the sides.

"See the destruction of any kingdoms lately in that seer mind of yours?" he asked harshly.

Davi lifted his head and opened his mouth, but Lorelai shot him a look.

"Yeah," she finally answered. "And your tavern was right in the middle of it." She waved her hands in front of her face. "Poof."

He stared at her for a moment before a smile broke out across his face.

Lorelai picked up her ale. "Thanks, Garon."

He winked and left to greet another customer. Lorelai busied herself drinking and when she finally stopped, she met Davi's curious eyes.

"I've known him since I was young. Before my mission to Dreach-Sciene."

"How long were you there?" he asked, wiping foam from his upper lip.

Warning bells rang in her head. They were getting too close to the secrets she had no choice but to keep. "Too long."

He studied her over the rim of her glass and she couldn't help but think his eyes saw too much. Swirling in the depths of his gaze was the boy she'd loved as her family, the young man she'd met who had an undying loyalty to Trystan Renauld, and the son his father was shaping all rolled into one.

He was all of them and none of them.

Could you be yourself if your memories were either lost or twisted?

"Tell me about killing the king," he said. The thrill in his voice was all Calis Bearne. He leaned forward with an eagerness she couldn't hate him for. For all he knew, Marcus had only ever been his captor.

As he waited, something else shone through on his face. A hint of compassion.

Her lips turned down, and she studied the table. Could she trust him? He sure couldn't trust her. He just didn't know it. But losing his memories had stripped him of all walls. He pulled her in because he didn't know how to distrust her. Not yet.

And the earth knew, she needed to trust someone.

Setting her tankard down, she met his gaze unflinchingly, and leaned in to drop her voice. "I didn't kill him."

There, the words were out. They no longer belonged just to her. She waited for realization to strike Davi, but he seemed to only grow more confused. Her voice shook as the memories rushed in and she tried to explain. "I had the knife in my hand, ready to do my duty." She covered her face. "And then I realized why."

"Why what?"

"Why she switched sides. Marissa. Ramsey's daughter. She was like a sister to me until she chose Dreach-Sciene over her own people. For so many years, I hated her for betraying us, but what I truly hated was her leaving me. But then I met Marcus Renauld and knew instantly how she could choose him. Love him. I almost made the same choice."

Tears blurred her vision, and she waited for Davi to call for someone to help him get her back to the palace. To the dungeons. She'd admitted to wanting to betray his father. It was Davion's moment. His time to decide if he would be Calis Bearne.

The tears came faster as she thought of her mother and what would happen to her without Lorelai to take care of her.

Of Marcus and the pain in his eyes at her betrayal. He hadn't loved her as he'd loved Marissa. It had been different. But it could have been good.

If they were different people.

Her back trembled with silent sobs.

Her head jerked up when the bench shook as Davi slid in next to her and put an arm around her shoulders. She sank into him, relief rushing through her.

"But he's dead?" He couldn't mask the hope in his voice even as he comforted her.

"Yes, Davi. Someone else finished my mission."

He rested his chin atop her head. "Good."

The coldness in his voice didn't match the tenderness of his touch and she knew only one of those things would win in the end. He'd either be cold and cruel. Or he'd remain soft and caring. A friend.

The palace of Dreach-Dhoun and the king that resided there would shape him, rule him.

A sigh escaped her lips. The cousin she was beginning to know again, wouldn't be around much longer.

Just as hers had many years ago, soon his soul would disappear.

CHAPTER 8

The fear in the servant's eyes every time they were in the king's presence didn't escape Davi's notice. His father was not a man you wanted to cross. During his short time at the palace that was the only thing he'd really learned about his father.

When his heavy hand clamped down around Davi's shoulder, the son did his best not to flinch. He wasn't scared of Calis, but he still lived with caution.

"Son," the king began. "I hear your aptitude for magic is coming along."

Davi nodded his head slowly. "Lorelai is a good teacher."

"I'm glad she's helping you grow accustomed to Dreach-Dhoun. She is my most prized asset, other than yourself."

Asset. Not family. He liked to hope his father meant well, but there wasn't a warm bone in his body.

Despite the coldness that still existed in his father's presence, Davi had begun to enjoy his time at the palace. Using magic. Spending time with Lorelai. If he never regained all of his memories, he'd be okay.

"I've been told you and Lorelai have been going into the village?" the king said slowly as he showed Davi to a rack of practice swords.

When his father had asked him to spar, shock kept him from saying anything at all.

Davi picked up a sword and swung it loosely between his hands. How did his body know what to do? Surely in his captivity, he wouldn't have been allowed to learn to fight?

It was instinct. Nothing else could describe it. And with a sword in his hand, he felt better than he had in a long time. It returned something to him, a part of himself that couldn't be recovered by magic or any kind of family bonding.

He felt strong.

He turned to face his father. "We've gone once or twice."

To his surprise, a laugh burst past his father's lips. "Come now, my boy, I'd like to think I know you better than that. And I definitely know Lorelai. Nothing in this palace escapes my eyes." He leaned forward conspiratorially. "She thinks I am unaware of her journeys to play with the village children when she was young." He tapped the side of his nose with one long finger. "I see everything."

Backing away, the king bent his knees and held his sword aloft, preparing to spar. Davi narrowed his eyes thinking of his cousin's secret. Had she truly been able to keep it from the king? What would happen when he found out?

Davi didn't have long to consider the notion because his father lunged. Almost instinctively, he blocked the jab, knocking the sword away and shifting his feet back to avoid the next move.

In between attacks, his father huffed and continued the conversation. "Lorelai had a role to play. While she was rollicking with the children, she was also picking up important information she didn't even know she had. Her maids reported everything she said about her time in the village and we found quite a few rebels that way."

Davi arced his sword through the air, his father blocked it at the last moment and pushed him back.

Scrunching his brow, Davi thought about a young Lorelai. Had she looked as fragile as she did now? He felt fiercely protective of her, but even so, could he fault his father for using her? He couldn't let unrest stir in the villages.

Maybe that was what it meant to be king. Being forced to use even the ones you loved for the good of the kingdom.

Thoughts of another king entered his mind, and he spun on one foot, kicking the other up to catch his father in the stomach. He grunted and fell back against the wall.

Davi didn't want to think about Marcus Renauld. Every time he did, white-hot anger sliced through him. He hated the man. And he couldn't hate him. It was like a wall built up inside of him, splitting him in two. He wanted to kill him, but his gut churned at the thought of him dying. And then a small voice invaded every part of him, evaporating his anger. When that was gone, there was nothing left. Only a shell. Half of a man.

His father wheezed against the wall and Davi hung his sword back on the rack.

He turned his back on his father, his king.

"Davion," his father said softly.

Davi shook his head. "I'm sorry, Father."

A sigh blasted out from the silence behind him. "Coming home has not been easy on you, son."

Shame had Davi's chin sinking to his chest.

"Son, with you and Lorelai in Dreach-Sciene, this palace was empty. You were with my enemy and I was sitting here just waiting for a chance. Now I have you both returned, but neither of you are fully intact and I blame myself."

Davi turned to face him. He'd never seen much emotion in his father. Before, he'd almost thought his return had no effect on the man. Running a hand through his dark hair, Davi took a step forward.

His father's eyes widened in terror as if the thought of a hug was his worst nightmare. The corner of Davi's mouth twitched up. He patted his father's arm. "The only people who are at fault are across the border."

A grim expression settled over the king's features. "Soon, son. Soon, you will have your revenge. When I deem you to be ready, you're going back to Dreach-Sciene."

Fire. Blood. Death. It was all going to come true. Lorelai rubbed her eyes, cursing the day she learned she was a seer. It had been a joyous day with her uncle celebrating as if it was the greatest news. As if he hadn't seen what the sight had done to her mother.

But she was stronger than that crazy old woman. No matter how many images of burning villages and rotting corpses she saw, she would not stop fighting.

More than fifteen years had passed since the night she first met Marcus Renauld. The rain should've been an omen. Nothing she said had been false, but she hadn't told him everything she knew.

Her prophecy told of a man would rise to save them all. But save who? That was still a mystery, even to her. He'd been so sure it was his own son, but she'd seen Davi in the vision along with Trystan. Both princes—although one of them hadn't known it at the time.

But Trystan was cursed. Death. Sacrifice. Betrayal. Davi was the sacrifice, giving his life for Trystan's. He could also serve as the betrayer once he came face to face with his old friend once again.

But death.

Someone you love will die by your hand.

If the first two were Davi, did that mean the third would be as well?

Lorelai had little experience seeing curses or prophecies come to pass. She didn't know if they could be broken or overcome. One thing was for certain, she'd do anything to keep Davi safe.

She walked aimlessly through the halls, desperate for a distraction to keep her from having to return to her rooms before her maids scrubbed every trace of Thom away. It didn't matter. Not when he'd just return again at night.

It shouldn't bother her. Her body had never been hers. It had always belonged to her uncle to give to whoever he deemed worthy or in need of a lesson. She'd used it to lure men in before slitting their throats. It helped her get information for the crown. It rewarded those loyal.

And this life was all she knew.

So, why did it bother her to use the skills she had for her own means? To keep her own secrets?

Because it wouldn't go on forever. Her uncle would learn the truth.

She stilled her shaking hands by running them through the pale hair hanging over her shoulder.

The click of nails on stone had her twisting around until she found Deor running toward her. Planting her hands on her hips, she looked down at him, one eyebrow raised. "Are you looking to get a beating?" She waved for him to follow her. "You're lucky it was me who found you."

He stayed where he was and let out a sharp yip as he jerked his head in the other direction.

"What is it, dog?"

He barked again. She gave in and followed him. They rounded the corner and Deor took off running. Lorelai lifted her skirts and did the same. She couldn't remember the last time she ran and joy filled her chest as they passed servants who looked on quizzically. Every ounce of happiness crashed inside of her when she followed Deor into an abandoned corridor and found Davi.

He sat with his back against the wall and his head rocking from side to side in his hands. A groan escaped his lips.

"Dav." She crouched down in front of him, pushing Deor out of the way. "What happened?"

"It hurts," he whispered. "Everything is so muddled." His voice dipped, but she was sure she heard a strangled, "Rissa."

Her mouth fell open in shock. Were his true memories returning and overcoming the false ones? Part of her hoped they were. Then she could stop lying to him. No, she couldn't let him become an enemy of her uncle's. Even though Davi was the king's son, that wouldn't save him if he remembered the life he'd led and the people he'd left behind.

"Davi," she whispered.

He raised tortured eyes to hers. "I can't tell what's real."

Cupping his cheek, she brushed away a tear with her thumb. "I'm going to help you. I promise. First, I need you to stand."

She helped him to his feet, but he stumbled against the wall when he tried to take a step. "My head. I can't... Too dizzy."

She didn't have to think before slinging one of his arms across her shoulders and wrapping her arm around his waist to keep him steady. "Come on, big guy."

He tried to say something, but it came out too garbled to understand. He leaned all his weight on her, but she had a bit of magic stored up to bolster her strength.

Luckily, the man she needed to see wasn't far. Ramsey Kane was being kept under guard in a locked room. The guard eyed them suspiciously, but unlocked the door and let them enter.

Davi fell through the door, almost dragging her with him. She was forced to let go, and he slumped to the ground.

Ramsey jumped up from where he was seated at a small desk. The Tri-Gard member didn't hesitate in running forward. "Shut the door," he ordered Lorelai.

He easily lifted Davi off the ground and put him on the bed. It was easy to forget that the Tri-Gard members didn't need to draw power from the earth. It was a part of them, just as her sight was part of her. But without his crystal, his power was no more than anyone else's.

Calis had taken his crystal many years before. The Tri-Gard's crystals came from deep in the earth. They'd appeared the moment the magic from Dreach-Sciene was taken. Some said the Tri-Gard held that kingdom's magic within those stones, but the ancient triad held their secrets tightly.

"What happened?" Ramsey asked, raising dull gray eyes to hers. She stopped, locked in his gaze for a moment. She remembered a time when everything about him had been bright and cheerful. Just like his daughter.

But then he'd been kept prisoner for twenty years.

"Lorelai." His harsh tone snapped her back to the present.

"I think his true memories are returning."

His eyes darkened at the news, but she couldn't help noticing the slight quirking of his lips. Ramsey Kane might have taken and reshaped Davi's memories but he didn't do it of his own free will.

"What did he say to you?" Ramsey cocked his head.

"He called out for Rissa."

"Is that so?" He tried and failed to hide his smile. "She's her mother's daughter, that one. Changing his memories of Rissa was the hardest magic I've ever attempted. Much more difficult than just erasing his memories in the first place. It was like everything inside him fought against any ill feelings toward her."

Davi mumbled something, his eyes still closed.

Ramsey's smile dropped, and he blew out a long breath, looking as if he wanted to say more. But he didn't trust Lorelai.

The next words out of Lorelai's mouth felt like poison to her soul. "If he's fighting the changed memories, maybe you need to remove her altogether. Like when he first came here. Make him forget."

Ramsey rubbed a hand across his face. "I can't do that without my crystal and your uncle…"

"Will question his loyalty if he knows," she finished for him.

Davi groaned, his eyes shifting beneath closed lids. "Just make it stop, Ri." His voice was strangled and tears leaked from the corners of his eyes. "Please."

His hands shot up to tear at the sides of his head as he shook it back and forth. Lorelai met Ramsey's alarmed gaze.

"We may not have a choice, Ramsey. Look at him. We can't let this continue."

It was the first time she'd seen such indecision in the Tri-Gard member. Even after decades of torture at the hands of her uncle, he'd remained strong. He never spoke of it before, but she remembered. He'd forced his counterparts to carry out Calis' wishes and strip magic from the land. It was unnatural and cruel, but they'd done it anyway because they trusted Ramsey and he'd convinced them it was the only way to prevent both kingdoms from destroying each other.

But she'd seen the armies Calis was building once again. The war hadn't ended all those years ago, only postponed. This time, Dreach-Sciene wouldn't stand a chance.

Ramsey moved to the bed and sat near Davi's head, whispering soothing words. He couldn't use much magic in the palace without his crystal, but he was still an ancient being. A steward of the earth. And that meant something.

But the cracks in Ramsey's armor had begun to show. He was just as helpless in this palace as Lorelai. Magical being or not.

Three years after the war ended, they received news that the queen of Dreach-Sciene had died. Calis found Lorelai crying over Marissa's fate and thought a lesson was in order. Her new task had been to inform Ramsey that his daughter was dead.

She'd never seen a man break before.

After that, he'd stopped fighting. The strength was still in him, in his refusal to give Calis any aid, but it was as if he no longer cared.

Until them. Until Calis showed him his grandchildren. The girl with Marissa's flaming hair and the boy with her fierce determination. Calis could send people to kill or capture them easily and Ramsey knew it.

Davi was just collateral damage in his quest to protect them, in his obedience to Calis. But each time Ramsey was forced to touch more of Davi's memories, he wandered further down a dark path.

One day, he'd be too far gone to come back.

"Ramsey." Lorelai gripped his arm, to shake him out of his quiet trance. "You don't have a choice."

"Choice?" Ramsey lowered his eyes to Davi's shaking body. "Have any of us ever had a choice?" At the sound of his own words, he snapped his eyes up, his mouth dropping in fear. "Forget I said that."

She gave him a reassuring smile. "I won't tell my uncle. But we have to go to him now."

She was preparing to call the guards to help lift Davi when the door to the room burst open and Calis marched in.

"Uncle," she breathed, half in relief and half in fear. "We were just coming to find you."

A scowl darkened his face. "I thought my guards must have been mistaken when they told me you and Davi were here."

Of course, he had eyes everywhere.

He continued. "You do not have access to Ramsey Kane without my permission. I expect better from you, Lorelai."

Her cheeks reddened, and she shifted her eyes away. "Davi needed my help."

He shook his head. "You two are becoming too close. He does not need your influence."

She opened her mouth to protest. She was a grown woman, for earth's sake. Not a child. But Ramsey jumped in.

"Do you have the crystal, sire? Davi just needs one of our sessions to get his mind in order."

"What's wrong with him?" As if noticing his son's state for the first time, Calis gazed down as Davi.

"His mind has gone through a lot of changes. It's perfectly understandable that it would rebel a bit."

"Rebel?" Calis' eyes narrowed in suspicion.

Lorelai sent Ramsey a pleading look.

Ramsey scratched his nose. "What's real will always be more powerful than what's false and Davion is a strong young man."

"If he were strong, he wouldn't be having this problem." Calis pulled the necklace from around his neck, the clear crystal attached to it. Light from the candles flickered in the stone and as Ramsey took it, a peace settled over his face. The Tri-Gard members were not supposed to be separated from their magic.

He shifted, turning toward Davi and placed a hand on each side of his head. Closing his eyes, he let the magic flow out of him. It encompassed the room in a tranquil quiet. None of them spoke.

Davi's body stopped shaking and his breath evened into a slow and steady rhythm. A few more moments passed and his eyes opened slowly, a dreamy look clouding his face.

Ramsey eased off the bed and Davi stared at the ceiling while they all held their breath.

He lifted his head first and then slowly scooted his body up into a sitting position.

"Where am I?" he asked.

Lorelai wanted to run to him in relief but she restrained herself in the king's presence.

"Welcome to my lair," Ramsey said jovially.

"What happened?"

"Nothing, son." Calis stepped forward and put a hand on his shoulder as he held his out to Ramsey who dropped the crystal into it. "From here on out, I'm going to take over your magic training. You and Lorelai are not to spend time together. The kinds of things she's done are not the sort I want corrupting you."

He spoke as if she wasn't there and she reeled back. He may as well have slapped her.

"What?" Davi dropped his legs over the side of the bed. "I can't…" His eyes glassed over and he fell back.

"Son, you will do as I say."

"My head feels weird," Davi said, seemingly unable to argue any longer.

"That's to be expected." Ramsey helped him to his feet as Calis pulled open the door and strode into the hall, expecting him to do the same.

"Ramsey was just recovering more of your memories from Dreach-Sciene." Lorelai hated herself for the lie.

"Oh… good."

Her eyes met Ramsey's. "There's a lot in there about Trystan Renauld."

Davi grunted in disgust and Lorelai pushed on.

"And also his sister, Rissa."

Davi lifted his eyes to hers. "Is this a test? He doesn't have a sister. Dreach-Sciene has no princess and I've never heard of this Rissa."

CHAPTER 9

The stew bubbled, entrancing Alixa as she stared into the murky sea of mutton and carrots. Her mind blanked, giving her one blissful moment outside her own head—aware from the pain that'd become like a second skin.

The pop of the fire jerked her back to the task at hand and she stirred the dinner, thankful for the mindlessness of the motion.

Her heavy eyelids drooped but never closed. If she let them close, she'd see it all over again. Her father. Ella.

There'd been a time when she loved her father. When she wanted to make him proud. Children fail to see the greatest faults of their parents until the damage is already done, and it's too late.

Edric sat nearby with his shoulders hunched forward. He'd barely looked at her since they left the high walls of Cullenspire behind two days prior. She didn't fault him for blaming her. His sister was dead because she'd helped Alixa. Because Alixa dared to care about someone, anyone.

No, her father wouldn't have that. People who cared were dangerous. They acted on emotion. He'd worked hard to drive the emotion from his children.

All he'd done was turn any love she had into pure, unadulterated rage. It didn't matter who he was. Not anymore.

"I'm going to kill him."

It wasn't until she noticed the group around the fire go completely still she realized she'd said the words out loud.

She waited for them to speak. Trystan and Rissa at least never held back their many opinions. It was like some family trait—thinking people wanted to hear everything that was in their heads.

But neither said a word.

"I mean it," she said. "He's a dead man."

Trystan grunted.

"Good," Rissa finally said, pulling her cloak tighter around her shoulders. "Just… good."

Were these the same people she'd set out on this journey with? The ones with oh-so-noble sticks up their royal asses?

"Did you hear me?" she asked. "I said I'm going to murder my own father."

"What do you want us to say, Alixa?" Trystan's steely gaze met hers.

"You're supposed to tell me I can't spill the blood of my own family or some honorable bull like that."

His jaw clenched. "I'm going to have to kill my own uncle."

"Oh." She leaned forward to stir the pot again, bathing her face in the warmth of the flames. It'd grown warmer since leaving Cullenspire, but a chill continued to linger in the air. "Stew's ready."

She filled the wooden bowls Lady Yaro had provided, and they dug into their food silently. Alixa had never enjoyed mutton, but she'd found she could eat anything after a long day of travel.

Nearby, a horse neighed from where they'd been tied for the night. It had taken a lot of effort to find some place dry to stop. The melting snow pooled along the ground, making for a miserably wet trip.

Once the stew was finished, Alixa put away the supplies and retired to her bedroll, a blanket pulled to her neck.

Stars winked between the overhanging trees, beckoning her with their brilliance. For the first time since their fight at Cullenspire, she found herself drifting off.

Ella appeared in her dreams, too good to be pulled into her father's schemes. The night of the fight replayed in her mind. She'd thought Ella was dead already and hadn't recovered from losing her the first time. As the knife slid across Ella's throat, a scream ripped through the dream and Alixa was torn from the scene by two strong hands shaking her.

She thrashed against his pull and bit off another scream.

"Alixa." The voice was familiar. "Wake up. It's me. It's Trystan."

She opened her eyes in a daze, her breath coming in gasps. His face swam before her. Light hair. Strong jaw. Warm eyes. Trystan. It was Trystan. Her breath evened out. "Someone was screaming."

"That was you."

She looked down at his hands continuing to hold on to her and then back to his face. "You uh… you can let go of me now."

It was as if a spell was broken and he was shocked to realize he was still touching her. He snapped his hands back to his sides and sat back on his heels. "Sorry." He scratched the back of his neck and looked away.

In the dim light of the fire, she could barely see the color flood his face.

She pushed herself up, so she was sitting and pulled her knees in to rest her chin on them.

"You were dreaming?" he asked.

"About Ella." She blinked back tears.

He looked unsure for a moment before moving to her side and patting her back awkwardly. Only last week, she'd been comforting him over his own loss.

They couldn't escape it—this feeling. The world was crumbling around them, but it was the pain of their individual losses that brought them to their knees.

A question burned in the back of her mind as she went over everything her father said and did. He'd been there for a reason. "Where was Royce?" she asked suddenly.

"What?"

"Royce. My brother. He's always at my father's side ready to do his dirtiest work, but he didn't come to Cullenspire. Why?"

"I don't pretend to know any of your father's reasons." Trystan held his hands closer to the fire for warmth.

"No, you don't understand. There is always a plan, always a purpose." She thought for a moment. "He'd only show up without my brother if Royce had a more important task." Her eyes widened as realization struck her. "He never meant to win that fight in Cullenspire. The retreat was planned as well. He hadn't come for the fight, nor to take you and Briggs to Dreach-Dhoun. What was the single most important thing he did?"

Trystan's brow furrowed. "He brought us news of my uncle's actions."

"Yes." She nodded quickly. "He told you your throne had been taken."

"You think he was lying?"

"No. I think he wanted us to go back to the palace. Calis doesn't want us crossing into Dreach-Dhoun where we'd have access to the magic in the land."

"So he made a deal with my uncle." Trystan was catching on.

"Royce will be there. I'm sure of it. Just as I'm sure your uncle is going to try to kill you."

Without thinking, she took his hand in hers and laced their fingers together. "I don't want you to die."

"Because if I die, we may never unite the Tri-Gard."

"No, you idiot." She sighed and leaned against his side. He stiffened for a moment before relaxing. "Because my heart's been broken too many times. Once more and I'm not sure I'll be able to piece it back together again."

A sad smile flitted across his lips. "If I were Davi, I'd make a joke about you actually caring about me."

"If you were Davi, you'd get away with it." She rested her cheek against his shoulder.

"I miss him." His breath whooshed out and his eyes flicked to Rissa. "I can't say that to Ri."

"I miss Ella." A tear slid down her cheek.

"And my father."

She smiled at that. "My father used to tell me stories of yours—none of them flattering. He spoke of your father as if he was a coward who let the magic be taken, conveniently leaving out the part about him siding with Calis when they captured the Tri-Gard."

Trystan stiffened beside her, so she was quick to speak again. "I didn't believe him. Marcus Renauld was a good king."

"He was." Trystan's voice thickened.

"You'll be a good king too."

He forced out a laugh. "You wouldn't have said that back when we first met."

"Yes, I would have. I was just difficult and… unhappy. I'm sorry."

"Please don't apologize. You brought me out of my sheltered life among the palace elite. Don't ever be sorry for that." He was quiet for a moment. "I may not even win my throne back, let alone sit in it with honor."

"You will."

"You really believe in me?"

"People will follow you, Trystan. Let's face it, I could probably best you with a sword. I have more knowledge of your own kingdom than you do. But someone like me could never rule. You know why?"

He shook his head.

"Because nobody likes me. I'm brash and stubborn and yes, sometimes cruel. But not you. People will follow you. They will put their lives on the line for you. I don't care if you're the noble man that stupid prophecy spoke of. Even if you're not, you're the one who is going to save us. I know it."

As soon as the last word left her mouth, Trystan turned. Alixa felt his eyes on her and she sucked in a breath.

"What?" Her voice came out soft. "Why are you looking at me?"

He reached forward to trail his fingertips down her cheek and she leaned into his touch.

"You have so much faith in me," he whispered.

Her lips curved up, and she finally looked at him. "Well, yeah. I'm not an idiot. Even I can see you were born for-."

He cut her words off by pressing his lips to hers. Shock froze her, and she didn't respond. An overwhelming urge to run washed over her. The rightful king of Dreach-Sciene was kissing her, the daughter of a traitor duke. But it was Trystan, she reminded herself. Just Trystan.

And one day he'd have to marry someone from a family who wasn't only spoken of in hushed voices.

It was too much when her heart was still broken. His was too and so she made a decision that was best for the both of them. She pushed away from him and blew a dark curl out of her face.

"I'm sorry," he said quickly, running a hand over the top of his head. "I shouldn't have done that."

"It's okay," she said, her voice shaking.

"No, it's not. I just… since Davi… I haven't had anyone to talk to. Rissa is in no place to think about anything other than her own grief. My best friend…" He wiped at his tired eyes. "I took advantage of your friendship and it was a horrid thing for a king to do."

"Hey." She touched his arm gently. "It's okay. Really."

He let out a strangled laugh. "I think I liked it better when you were mean to me."

She surprised him by slapping him upside the head. "You're an asshole. Seriously, the biggest idiot king I've ever read about in all the histories of Dreach-Sciene. You're going to get us all killed, Trystan Renauld." She shot him a grin. "Better?"

"Much." He pointed to her bedroll. "Now, try to get some sleep. You were practically falling off your horse yesterday."

She rolled her eyes but settled back under her blanket. This time when she closed her eyes, there was nothing but peaceful emptiness.

The morning light brought with it the realizations of a new day. They were once again traveling to Whitecap to gather anyone loyal to the rightful king.

Ella was still dead.

With a fresh mind came clarity. There would be a time for grief when all the battles had been won. But now was a time to fight. A time to get vengeance for the ones who were no longer with them.

Alixa sidled up beside Edric as he packed the saddlebags on his horse.

"You're really going to kill him?" Edric asked.

"If it's the last thing I do," she responded.

He nodded and flipped the bag closed before turning to her. Fire burned in his gaze. "Make it hurt."

"I'll make him regret the day he ever laid eyes on Ella."

He grunted. "Royce is mine."

She nodded once in agreement.

For you, Ella, she thought. *And for everyone else they've hurt.*

CHAPTER 10

The dreams had stopped, and Davi finally settled into a comfort at the palace. It was as if his mind was free of some force that had held it hostage for so long. As if it no longer had to fight.

Gone was the sense that there was something he was forgetting. It was replaced by a singular purpose. Get revenge for his years in captivity.

He liked the palace at night. It no longer seemed cold to him. Instead, he felt protected. It was a formidable fortress built to show the strength of Dreach-Dhoun, his father, his kingdom.

He'd grown accustomed to the constant ringing of blades. To the blacksmith shop that always had the fires going for new armor and weapons. His father was building a force the likes of which hadn't been seen since the days of Trystan the Bold.

It was a tale told to children in Dreach-Dhoun as a warning about what too much magic can do to you. Trystan died. Just the name of the man from legend set him aflame because it was shared by his enemy.

He took the steps two at a time, enjoying the burn as he climbed to the top of the tower. A fierce pride bloomed in his chest as he scanned the horizons. One day, it would all be his. He'd be king.

After a while, he climbed back down and greeted the guards

stationed around the palace. They only acknowledged him formally, but it didn't stop his friendly grin. He wanted someone to talk to him as more than the prince. To stop being so scared of his father. But none of them did. When they sparred with him, they let him win. The last time, he'd thrown his sword across the practice yard and stormed away. The guards behind him muttered about just how like his father he was.

He longed to talk to his cousin. Lorelai didn't treat him like a broken prince who'd known more years as a prisoner than free. But his father was keeping them apart. He didn't fully trust Lorelai, but Davi couldn't figure out why.

Screw it. Before long, he found himself walking towards her rooms. If she was sleeping, he wouldn't bother her, but his father couldn't control the one friendship he had, possibly the only one he'd ever had. Did prisoners make friends? He rubbed his jaw, the stubble scratching his fingers.

He needed a shave.

But he kind of liked it. He'd never worn a beard before. As least he didn't think so. He still didn't trust all his memories.

Lorelai's hall was dark except for a single torch along the wall, but the orange flow from the fire seeped out beneath her door. Would she have put it out before going to sleep?

He stopped outside her door and raised his hand to knock, freezing when a loud grunt sounded through the wood.

It was followed by a rhythmic slapping and a grin formed on Davi's face. Arching a brow, he turned to go, proud of his cousin for taking what she wanted.

Then he heard it. The tiniest whimper of pain. Figuring he imagined it, he waited. A muffled "no" filled the air before Lorelai cried out.

Davi didn't think twice before twisting the door handle to open it. Locked. "Dammit," he snapped. He could really have used his magic right then, but it'd been a while since he was outside and he was drained.

Scanned the door quickly, he realized there was only one thing he could do. He stepped back and took a running start to slam his shoulder into it. Wood cracked, but it didn't budge. So he did it again. And again.

An angry "Shove off" came from the room, and pain seared through Davi's shoulder.

He growled. It was no use.

But he didn't stop. He started to run at it again but the door was yanked open and Davi's momentum carried him right into the chest of the naked man yelling at him to go away.

"Davi," Lorelai shrieked, lunging for a robe to cover herself.

The man righted himself again, turning cold eyes on the intruder. Davi didn't meet his gaze as his eyes darted wildly around the room, his heart slamming against his ribs. A broken chair sat to the side of the rumpled bed and clothes were strewn everywhere, but his eyes landed on his cousin, and the tears streaking down her face. She didn't bother to wipe them away.

"What's going on?" he asked, directing the question to her, not the man who was sizing him up.

At least he'd found someone who didn't care that he was the prince.

"Lorelai and I have an arrangement that's no business of yours," he drawled.

"She's my family, it is my business." Remembering their conversation in the tavern, Davi pointed to the man. "Is this the guy?"

Lorelai nodded.

Davi finally met the man head on. "My cousin is no whore. She does not trade secrets for her dignity."

His lip curled up. "Hate to break it to you, prince, but she already has." He narrowed his eyes. "What's to keep me from telling the king that his greatest enemy's blood is on my hands and not his darling niece's?"

"Thom, please." Lorelai scrambled forward.

He stepped towards her, studying her face. "Slut." It happened so fast. He raised his hand and backhanded Lorelai. Hard. She twisted to the side and fell back.

Davi lunged. The man had no clothes for Davi to grab on to, so he slammed his shoulders back against the wall before slicing his fist through the air and connecting it to the other man's jaw. Davi didn't stop. Anger burst free of him and he pummeled the man who could bring his cousin down.

Davi took a fist to the eye but spun away before another hit could reach him. The man advanced and Davi was ready.

What he wasn't ready for was the knife the man swiped from the table. He leaped for Davi, but the prince easily avoided the blade.

The two men stared at each other for a long moment.

"You're a traitor. Look at you all cozy in Dreach-Dhoun when only months ago, you were enjoying life as a favorite of king Marcus."

Davi growled. "You're lying." He hated Dreach-Sciene. They'd kept him prisoner. How dare this foolish man say otherwise? He didn't know a thing.

Davi knocked the knife from the man's grip and flipped it in his own hand. His blood boiled with a desire to gut the man who would dare call him a traitor. Who would take advantage of his cousin? He flicked his eyes to Lorelai for the briefest of moments. He knew what he had to do.

His mouth set in a grim line as he advanced, blocking every jab directed his way. He didn't like it, but sometimes evil things must be done.

The man pressed up against the wall, fear finally breaking through his cold glare.

He jumped forward to try to take the knife and in one swift jerk of his arm, Davi buried it up to the hilt in the man's neck. Blood sprayed free, speckling Davi's skin with the evidence of what he'd done.

Surprised etched across the man's face as he crumpled to the ground.

Lorelai ran to Davi's side to watch the final gurgles from the man's throat and then took Davi's hand and led him to the wash basin.

"Dav," she whispered. "Look at me."

When he did, he hardly saw her. All he saw was the blood on his hands. All he felt was the adrenaline coursing through him.

Tomorrow. Tomorrow he'd hate himself for what he'd done, what he was feeling.

Exhilarated.

Energized.

Powerful.

All he'd known was captivity. Now he was the captor. He had the power.

Lorelai dabbed at his face with a wet cloth. "Thank you."

He only nodded and rose to his feet.

Guards rushed in followed closely by the king.

"Lorelai," he barked. "Davion. I heard reports of a commotion." His all-seeing eyes landed on the dead man.

"Who did this?" he asked.

Lorelai sent Davi a panicked look, but he faced his father. "I did."

Calis took in Davi's dour expression, and the blood sprayed across him with calculating slowness. He nodded, a proud smile forming on his lips. "I take it you had a good reason?"

"I did…"

His father held up his hand. "I don't need to hear the reason. I'm proud of you for taking care of matters."

Nothing about the man made sense. Davi had killed one of his father's men, and all he got was a pat on the back.

But when his father spoke again, Davi began to understand.

"You may have more steel in you than I thought, son."

To Calis Bearne, slitting a man's throat was a sign of strength. Davi tilted his lips up tentatively. He so desperately wanted to make his father proud. A new rush replaced the one from his actions before as he met his father's eyes. His father. In each memory that Ramsey brought back to him, there was a longing for home, for family. He'd been alone for so much of his life in a land full of enemies. Taunted and beaten and kept in a cell.

Now he had everything he'd dreamed of, and he was going to do everything he could to keep it.

Because when his father's pride was directed at him, he was more powerful than any magic could ever make him. He could do anything.

And he would.

CHAPTER 11

Whitecap had changed from the last time they'd been there. Gone were the colorful sails of the trading vessels and the happy banter of the fishermen toiling along the pier. The docks were empty of life, the ships barren of their colors and bobbing in the icy breeze coming off the water. Not even the seagulls could be heard screeching in indignation as they fought over stolen morsels. A pall hung over the usually boisterous town. A veil of shadow, like it had endured way too much recent sorrow.

Trystan glanced around in unease as they rode through the deserted, waterfront street, trying to pinpoint where his gut feeling of *wrongness* was coming from. Even the tavern where they had rested on their first trip here seemed to be closed for business though it was well into the afternoon. The door was barred tightly shut, and not a glimmer of light shone through the cracks in the shuttered windows. It appeared abandoned; as empty as the rest of the town.

"Where is everyone?" Alixa asked at his back, speaking out loud the question in his mind.

"Not here, obviously," Briggs answered, as Rissa snorted in derision.

"Good to see you didn't lose your keen sense of observation while you were pretending illness."

Briggs turned in his saddle and glared Rissa's way.

"There was no pretending, girl. You and your brother dragging me all over the mountains and almost freezing me to death caused me to become severely ill."

"Maybe at first. But those last few days were just you refusing to get your cowardly butt out of bed. Don't bother to lie because you know it's true."

Briggs huffed in indignation and pointed a dirty nailed finger her way. "You know, you could be a little more respectful. I am a member of the all-powerful Tri-Gard. I could bring a horde of locusts down on your head if I so wished. And trust me, I'm getting close to doing just that."

Rissa narrowed her eyes in retaliation. "Your threats don't scare me, old man. You and your precious Tri-Gard have already done the worst thing possible. You stole Dreach-Sciene's magic. The possibility of you bringing it back is the only thing keeping you alive right now. You'd be wise to remember that."

Briggs whipped his head over his shoulder, his glazed eyes focusing on something none of his companions could see. "Yes, I know her sharp tongue is just like her mother's. Yes, I know she's the princess.… But her insolence is becoming old and… Fine. I'll let it drop."

And just like that, Briggs hunched over his horse's neck, refusing to speak another word. A tiny smile tugged at Trystan's lips when Rissa grumbled, "Crazy old hermit." He raised his eyes, meeting Alixa's, and they shared a moment of amusement before her smile disappeared and she dropped her gaze. His smile vanished too, for he knew what she was remembering. That kiss.

Dammit. Why had he done something so stupid? He and Alixa were finally getting along. She was finally treating him as a friend instead of a silly, pampered prince. And then he had to ruin that. Alixa did the right thing by stopping it, but that didn't stop the sting of humiliation.

"No matter," he called over his shoulder, shrugging off his embarrassment. "Maybe it's a good thing no one is around. The fewer that know of our presence here, the better."

"Sire," Avery interrupted and lifted her chin as Trystan looked her way. He followed her gaze. Hmmm, the town was not as empty as they first believed. A boy of about ten peered out at them from a vacant husk of a building, his look of curiosity mounting to fear at knowing he'd been seen. He turned to run but Trystan yelled at his back, "Hey, boy. Come here. There's a gold coin in it for you if you answer my questions."

The boy stumbled in his tracks and swerved back as quick as he'd run. He came closer but still kept a wary distance between him and the party on horseback.

"You lyin'?" the boy asked as he turned skeptical eyes on Trystan. "Cause you don't look like no wealthy man. No sir-ee. You all look like a bunch of poor travelers." He eyed them all up and down before standing straighter as he decided on his course of action. "Give me the gold coin first and I'll tell ya everythin' you want to know."

"Fat chance of that happening, you little runt," Briggs snorted his way. "You'd take it and run first chance you got. Do we look that stupid?"

"*You* do," the boy replied in all seriousness, and it took all of Trystan's will not to crack up at Briggs' look of offense.

Trystan pulled the gold coin from his pocket and rolled it smoothly across the back of his fingers, pretending to toss it to the boy. The boy grabbed at the empty air and scowled as he realized Trystan was toying with him.

"Answers first," Trystan said as he palmed the coin.

"Fine," the boy huffed. "What do ya wanna know?"

"Has there been any army activity in town? Have you seen Isenore soldiers or even unknown soldiers coming and going? Have they taken everyone away?"

"No, there ain't been no soldiers 'round. None other than Lord Coille's men that I've seen."

Not the answer Trystan was expecting.

"Then where is everyone?" he asked in puzzlement.

"At the ceremony. Where you should all be instead of here askin' me silly questions." The boy cocked his head to the side and stared at Trystan like he should already know this.

"What ceremony?"

The boy rolled his eyes. "The ceremony they's havin' for the dead royal family. Don't you people know nothin'? You just crawl out from under a rock? They's all dead. The king, the prince and the princess. All of 'em gone. Lord Coille is havin' a memorial for 'em all today outside his estate. The whole town is supposed to be there outta respect."

Trystan stared at Rissa in shock, her eyes just as wide as him. Everyone thought they were dead?

"Why are you here in town then," Rissa averted her gaze to the boy. "Why aren't you at the ceremony? You up to no good?"

"What?" The boy turned to Rissa, guilt written all over his face. "No... I ain't up to nothin'. And don't turn this 'round on me. I answered yer questions, now give me my coin."

Trystan threw the coin, and the boy snatched it out of the air, turned tail and ran as fast as his scrawny legs could carry him.

"They think you're both dead," Alixa reiterated the boy's words as soon as he vanished amongst the alleyways. "Why would they think that unless they've been told some story?"

Trystan nodded in agreement and spoke softly, keeping the unease in his gut hidden from everyone. "Dear old uncle Drake was no doubt planning on making the story come true."

Briggs took no effort in hiding his fear. "You thought we would have all died if we went back to the castle? When were you going to tell us that?"

Another snort escaped Rissa's lips. It seemed to be her favorite form of communication nowadays.

"What did you expect, old man? That he was going to steal Trystan's title and then welcome us home with open arms? Yes, he would have killed us all, except you of course. I'm sure he would have made a good trade with Calis for you."

Briggs visibly paled at her words. "That doesn't make me feel any better, girl," he whispered, and she stared back with her cold, empty eyes.

"It wasn't meant to."

"Enough," Trystan interrupted before the exchange could snowball. "Whatever the reason behind the lie, we are still thankfully very much alive, and I'd like to make it to Coille's estate in one piece. No more talk. Like our governess used to say, Rissa, the walls have ears. Move out. And I advise you all to pray on the way that we still have allies willing to help us take back the throne."

Lady luck decided to be on their side for a change. Although they encountered numerous villagers making their way back to town, no one paid them any attention. The townsfolk appeared too engulfed in their grief and conversation to even notice the pack of dirty travelers. But then their luck ended. The moment they approached the stone gates they were swarmed by soldiers and ordered to dismount at sword point. Alixa knew Rissa was about to lose her temper from the way she slid from her horse, threw her hood back and glared at the soldiers, but Alixa grabbed the princess's arm and shook her head in warning. And then a small miracle happened. Rissa actually clamped her lips shut in a tight grimace. Alixa blinked in surprise as the princess pulled back, allowing Trystan to do the talking.

"Let us through," Trystan commanded as he stepped directly in front of the guard that had ordered them to dismount. "We must speak with Lord Coille."

A couple of the guards straightened in surprise at his authoritative tone, but the one in front of Trystan sneered in suspicion.

"Oh really? Then you're out of luck. Lord Coille isn't seeing anyone right now. You had your chance to speak at the memorial."

"He will see us," Trystan added as he crossed his arms and stared the guard down.

"Oh aye? You think so now, do you? Move along. My orders are not to let anyone through. There's been some less than savory characters spotted around here lately. Dreach-Dhoun spies some are saying. No one is allowed inside without an invitation from Lord Coille."

Trystan's stance never changed. He never even reached for his weapon, but his gaze pinned the guard with threatening steel. "Go get Lord Coille, now."

No threat was uttered but Alixa could feel the quiet menace radiating off Trystan and the fine hairs on the back of her neck stood on end. She stared at him through new eyes. Where had this Trystan come from? Where was the pretty boy, slightly soft prince she'd met at the Toha ball? That was not the same man who stood before her now. This Trystan was determined. Driven. Gone were the clean shaven, slightly rounded cheeks of the man she'd first met. Weeks of adversity and loss showed in his hard eyes and chiseled, set jaw. The bristly stubble and unkempt hair giving him more of a mountain man look than a royal prince. He seemed forceful and in command. He seemed like a king. The guard must have felt it too since he backed away a couple of steps and called over his shoulder to a comrade still inside the wall.

"Go get Rion. Tell him to come to the gate."

At the name Trystan jerked his head and met Alixa's eyes. Rion? The young soldier who'd been traveling with Trystan and Avery when she first met them in the forest of Alderwood? The one Trystan tried to get her to return to the castle with?

They waited in silence, the guards eyeing them up and down in suspicion until the soldier returned with another body in tow. The newcomer's slight frame was dressed in new Alderwood colors, but Alixa recognized the boyish face beneath the shaved head.

"Rion?" Trystan called out in part doubt, part relief. The young man brought up short and his look of puzzlement quickly escalated to wide-eyed amazement as if he'd just seen a ghost. Much to his credit, however, he didn't utter a single name. Instead he turned his attention to the guard barring them entrance.

"Let them through," he demanded, and the guards obeyed without hesitation. The gate groaned in protest as it was pulled open, allowing the weary travelers access. Rion approached them as they made their way inside. He came to a stop in front of Trystan, his head bowed.

"Your Maj…" he began, but Trystan cut him short.

"No, not here." The young man looked up in confusion at the quiet words. "Seems everyone believes us dead? Let's keep it that way for now."

A slight smile crossed his weary face. "It's good to see you. All of you."

"You as well, Rion," Trystan replied as he grasped the boy's shoulder. "Can you confirm the rumor we've heard that Lord Drake has taken the throne back in Dreach-Sciene?"

The young man nodded. "It is so. Drake has pronounced the royal family as dead and taken the title for himself." There was no denying the disgust in the boy's words and Alixa could see Trystan's lips tilt in a tiny smile.

"Drake? Not King Drake?"

"Even believing you all to be dead, he was never my king. There are many still loyal to King Marcus and they won't accept Drake as king even when they think the rest of the royal family is dead. Most of them are here, including Lord Coille."

"Good. Then let us go inside. There is much to discuss."

WITH RION LEADING the way they received no more resistance from any guard. The boy had risen quickly in the ranks from the young soldier Alixa had first met. Her eyes fell on Trystan. Then again, a lot of changes had occurred in the past few months.

"Is the council meeting already underway?" Rion marched straight to a soldier standing at the bottom of a stairwell situated in the middle of the large room they now found themselves in. The room had been grand and elegant at one time, no doubt. Back when there was magic. Alixa saw the wear and tear of the sparse times in which they now lived reflected in the threadbare rug beneath their feet and the splintered, warped stairs that badly needed replacing. Lord Coille didn't seem to be as tenacious in keeping up appearances, unlike her father.

The older man nodded as he squinted at her and the rest through red-rimmed eyes.

"Yes. The nobles in attendance stayed behind after the ceremony. It's being held in the chapel." The soldier huffed as he placed his sword across the stairwell, stopping Rion's progress as the boy tried to continue on. "But, you know the rules. When council's meeting, there are to be no interruptions, even if that meeting is not taking place in the council chambers."

Rion stepped back. "I know the rules. But Lord Coille will want to see these people as soon as possible."

The red eyes stared closer. "Hmph. Lord Coille don't have no need for this bunch of dirty, smelly heathens."

Dirty, smelly heathens? Was there really any need for that? Alixa looked down at her stained, tattered britches and cloak. Well maybe he wasn't far off the mark.

Rion squared his shoulders. "That is for Lord Coille to decide, not you. Now out of the way, Sharpe."

Sharpe's response was drowned out as a squeal of disbelief pierced the air, causing Alixa to wince in pain. A tiny blonde girl appeared at the top of the stairs, her porcelain pale skin enhanced by the wide blue eyes staring down at them. She blinked in rapid succession as her hand flew to her mouth, to stop any more ear rupturing screams Alixa hoped. The girl's perfectly curled hair and clean gown only made Alixa feel that much more the dirty heathen Sharpe spoke of. The girl appeared familiar, but Alixa couldn't place her at first.

"It cannot be. My eyes must be deceiving me." She descended

halfway down the stairs before stopping to stare. "Trystan? Rissa? Is it really you?"

Alixa's eyebrows shot up in surprise as the first genuine smile Rissa had given in weeks, spread across her face.

"Willow!" Rissa yelled as the girl nearly bowled Sharpe over and ran down the stairs into Rissa's open arms. The two girls embraced like long-lost sisters, and recognition finally set in. Willow. Of course. Lord Coille's daughter. The memory of meeting the girl at the Toha ball was faint, but there.

Willow finally stepped back and held Rissa at arm's length as tears streamed freely down her face.

"I knew you weren't dead. Even as I sat through the funeral ceremonies, I just knew it."

She glanced over at Trystan and her tears flowed harder as he opened his arms and she fell into them like it was where she belonged.

Alixa resisted the urge to roll her eyes in irritation at the girl's loud sniveling as she hung off Trystan's neck like a wet rag. Instead, the recollection of the Toha ball came back with a vengeance, and Alixa drew a sharp breath. She remembered now. The girl had stared after Trystan all night with those enamored, beautiful eyes. Following his every move, her emotions on her face for all to see. She was in love with the prince. Any fool could see it. What had Davion called her? Trystan's possible future queen. It made sense. Merging the two fine houses of the Renaulds and the Coilles was a smart move. The only move. So why did it leave such a bitter taste in her mouth?

Trystan gently removed the girl's arms from around his neck. "It is good to see you, Willow. But we must speak with your father immediately."

"Of course." The girl wiped the tears from her eyes with a tiny laugh and a fleeting moment of hatred filled Alixa's heart at the girl's still impeccable features. She even cried pretty.

"He's still in the chapel. I'm sorry. It's just... I'm so happy to see you. All of you. But... where is Davi?"

Alixa heard Avery's sharp intake of breath as her gaze switched to

Rissa. The smile that had softened the princess' face faded at the mention of Davi's name. It was like watching summer turn to winter. The green eyes crystallized with ice and her face fixed into a hard mask, her mouth a grim line. The silence following the question seemed to last forever, before Rissa finally growled, "Davion is dead. Do not mention his name to me again."

"No! But how? What happened?"

"Willow, your father," Trystan stopped the words flowing from the girl's mouth and Alixa knew it was just in time too. Rissa's features grew frostier by the moment.

"Yes, of course." Willow was visibly shaken, but she pulled herself together and straightened her slim shoulders. She clamped her lips shut and stopped her silly flow of words. An admirable trait of a future queen, Alixa noted with annoyance. Something she herself hadn't learned to do yet.

"You're right, Trystan. We will have time to talk later. You need to join the council. Follow me."

Willow led them down the hallway. The lone guard standing outside raised a brow as she commanded him to move aside, but he didn't budge an inch.

Willow tried again. "I said move aside. Allow us entrance."

"Sorry, my lady. You know better than that. Your father said they were not to be interrupted for any reason."

Alixa had had enough. This silly pomp and display of importance was carrying on much too long. They needed to see Lord Coille and if Willow's whispery words weren't enough, then she would make it so. Enough of being denied. Much to the guard's surprise, Alixa pushed Willow aside none-too gently and threw open the heavy doors before he could stop her. Numerous pairs of eyes stared in surprise as she practically pushed Trystan into the room and presented their dead prince, alive, if not quite whole.

CHAPTER 12

An audible gasp came from somewhere in the room, the only sound in the tense moment. Trystan stood in the doorway; his hand gripped the wooden beam.

Most of the faces in the room were unknown to him, but the familiar gazes of two stole the words from his mouth. Lady Destan, the young Duchess of Sona, covered her mouth with her hand. Beside her, Lord Coille's wide eyes shone.

No one spoke.

They didn't move.

Trystan opened his mouth, but a breath was the only thing to escape.

Willow entered the room behind him and put a hand on his arm. She'd recovered from her shock quickly.

"Lords and Ladies of Dreach-Sciene." Her voice was high and clear. "May I present Prince Trystan Renauld."

"The prince is dead," someone said.

Rissa pushed him aside and came into view for the first time. A sob escaped Lady Destan.

"Like hell he is," Rissa snapped, making for the front of the room where an altar sat bathed in candlelight. She stopped at the raised platform. "Does he look dead to you?" She turned her glare to all in attendance. "Your rightful king has just entered the room. Rise," she demanded.

"Rissa," Trystan chastised with a shake of his head. He'd risen from the dead. His people would need time.

Lord Coille rose first. His voice shook as he spoke. "Welcome home, your… Majesty."

Trystan's gaze drifted over the people between him and the duke. His nobles. The ones who'd had their king die and thought his children dead along with him.

Did they know the mission he'd been sent on? Or how empty handed he was in returning? That he'd failed to do anything but get Davi killed?

He strode into the room slowly before stopping beside his sister. "With all due respect, my lord, Whitecap is not my home. My home has been stolen from me."

Lady Destan got to her feet and stepped around Lord Coille. "Not for long." Her voice thickened as her eyes scanned the other faces. "Our king has returned."

One by one, they stood. Lady Destan faced Rissa. A smile touched her lips, and a tear broke free of her eye. "Thank the earth you two have returned." She pulled Rissa into a tight hug as Lord Coille gripped Trystan roughly.

"We've failed you, Trystan." His voice was rough. "Your uncle sits on your throne."

Once again, Trystan took in the nobles who'd stayed after the ceremony to prepare to fight for Dreach-Sciene.

Trystan gripped the Duke's shoulder. "No, my lord. You've lost the throne, but not Dreach-Sciene. My kingdom is a people, not a palace."

Lord Coille closed his eyes and released a breath as if he'd been holding it since the day his king died. "That's something your father would have said."

"My father was a great king."

"He was. And an even better friend. I'm so sorry, Trystan."

Trystan shook his head. Every time he thought he was past his father's death, it hit him with the force of a battering ram. Maybe if he'd been there, his father would still be king and none of this would be happening.

But then they'd be no closer to restoring their magic.

"There will be much time for talk." Lord Coille's eyes found something near the doorway and narrowed. "Guards!"

Trystan followed his gaze to Alixa. He tried to stop him but Lord Coille sprinted to the door. "Guards. Alixa Eisner, you are under arrest for treason against Dreach-Sciene."

Alixa backed up but two guards grabbed her arms.

"Stop," Trystan yelled. No one heard him through the pandemonium.

Trystan pushed through the nobles blocking his way to find Alixa kicking and struggling. "Trystan," she screamed.

Rion ran up to Lord Coille and whispered to him furiously, pointing toward Alixa. Lord Coille's brow furrowed, but he didn't order his guards to stop.

A roar ripped through Trystan. "I order you, as King of Dreach-Sciene, to unhand the woman." He pulled his sword free. "I will cut off any part of you that is still touching her in three seconds."

When no one moved, Trystan swung, deliberately missing the guards, but close enough to cause them to lurch out of the way. Alixa stumbled and Trystan caught her. "I got you," he whispered.

Her body shook as she leaned into him, her face a mask of anger.

"Trystan," Lord Coille snapped. No 'your Majesty' or 'my King' this time. "Put that bloody sword away and come with me."

He kept an arm protectively around Alixa as he followed Lord Coille from the room, leaving the panicked people behind.

Rissa stepped up beside him. "That was brilliant." She shot him a smile. A true, honest to God smile. The kind he rarely saw from her anymore.

Lady Destan met them at the door to the council chambers and leaned in. "I quite enjoyed that." She laughed fondly.

Rissa yawned.

"Are you okay, princess?"

"It's been a long time since I've had much of a rest."

"It's going to be a long night for Trystan, but the rest of you should eat and sleep." She waved Willow over. "Would you show Rissa and Alixa and the rest of their company to adequate rooms?"

Trystan glanced over his shoulder. They had yet to introduce the others. Avery, Edric, and Briggs hadn't entered the council room with Trystan and Rissa, but they followed at a close distance now. It was probably best that Briggs' presence only be known by a few.

To his surprise, Rissa went willingly and even Alixa failed to put up a fight, leaving Trystan alone with Lord Coille and Lady Destan.

The door shut with a definitive slam and Lord Coille spun. "I'm assuming you have a reason for protecting Alixa Eisner."

Trystan ran a hand over his tired eyes. "Did Rion tell you how she came to join us?"

"He told a tale of her escaping her father, but I thought you'd inherited your father's brains, boy. The Eisners are not to be trusted. Royce Eisner is right this very moment—"

"Advising Drake?" Trystan cut in. "I came to that conclusion myself."

Lady Destan pulled out a chair and dropped into it gracefully. She folded her hands in her lap. "You forget yourself, Adrian. Remember to whom you speak."

The Duke sighed. "You're right. I am sorry, your Majesty." A wry smile appeared on his lips. "Sometimes it is hard to see those you watched as children as anything else. To me, you're still the boy who'd run through the palace with little Davion pretending to be knights while tracking mud along the halls."

Trystan fell into a chair and put his head in his hands, exhaustion and sadness winning out over decorum.

"I can't imagine what you've been through since leaving the palace, Trystan, so I don't want to tell you to be careful. You already know that."

"Davi," he whispered. "That's what we've been through. Davi is dead."

Lady Destan closed her eyes. "That boy…"

"I'm sorry." Lord Coille clutched his shoulder.

Trystan lifted his head. "You aren't aware of everything that's happened and I'll tell you some of it. But you need to trust me when I tell you Alixa Eisner is on our side."

They both nodded. Lord Coille gave him a final pat before taking a seat. "When Drake announced your death and Rissa's, the soul was ripped right from Dreach-Sciene. I think I stopped breathing when you walked through that door."

Trystan met his stare. "The Renaulds aren't this kingdom's soul. Magic is. Or it was."

Lord Coille raised a brow. "Soon after you left, your father told me you weren't sure you believed in magic."

"I didn't. But I trusted my father."

"What changed?" Lady Destan asked. "Why do you believe now?"

He paused for a moment, considering the impact of his next words. "We found Briggs Villard."

A smile crept across her face.

"The old man is here?" Lord Coille asked.

Trystan nodded. "And Lonara Stone won't be far behind us."

Lord Coille released a laugh and looked to the ceiling in relief. "It seems we aren't as hopeless as we thought."

"That's where you're wrong." Lady Destan smiled. "We were never hopeless. Not while Trystan was out there fighting for us."

"We thought he was dead."

"Correction, you thought he was dead. Some of us had more faith than to trust the word of a spineless man like Drake."

"That's why you're here." Trystan ended their bickering as he glanced between them. "You're not in Sona. There has to be a reason. What are you planning?"

Lord Coille grunted and Lady Destan let out a laugh. "As perceptive as Marcus always was." She bit her lip, considering him. "There will come a time when the Tri-Gard is the most important tool for our survival, but before we look to our enemies across the border, we must first deal with those who are tearing our kingdom apart."

Lord Coille's face lit up. "Briggs. He can end this right now. We take him to the palace and he uses his magic. Drake won't stand a chance."

"No." Trystan's harsh tone caused them both to jump. "The armies under Drake's command were some of my father's soldiers. I won't use magic against our own people."

Lord Coille deflated.

Lady Destan stood and brushed off her skirt. "Nothing will change by morning." A knock sounded on the door and Willow poked her head in. "Perfect timing. Trystan needs to be shown to a room before he collapses right here."

Trystan opened his mouth to protest. It had been a long day, but there was still so much to discuss. A wave of exhaustion crashed over him and he sighed. "Okay."

Lady Destan led him to the door. "It's still hard to believe you're here, Trystan, but now that you are, we have work to do."

"My uncle won't be allowed to rule." He gripped the doorway, his knuckles turning white. "We always knew Calis Bearne would come, but I never imagined fighting my own people." He hung his head and followed Willow. His eyes drifted to her slight frame, her perfect skin. So familiar, yet it seemed like another lifetime growing up with her.

When she spoke, her voice was soft. "I'm glad you've come back to us, Trystan."

He smiled at her honesty, but his eyes caught on her hands rubbing together nervously.

"Are you okay, Willow?"

She stopped in the middle of the hall. "I don't want to marry you," she blurted.

"What?"

She turned and paced the length of the hall before returning. A servant passed but gave them a wide berth. "I thought I wanted it, but I didn't understand."

"Understand what?"

Her shoulders tensed. "I don't want to hurt you. We've known each other for so long and you wanted this."

He held in a laugh. As far as he knew, she was the one who'd pushed for a betrothal.

"You chose me and I'm flattered," she continued. "But, Trystan, I don't love you." She exhaled heavily. "There may have been a crush once upon a time, but…"

"My death got you out of the betrothal." This time he didn't hold back his laugh.

She huffed and red crept up her pale neck. "I didn't want you to be dead and my heart soared when I saw you in that hall, but I don't love you as anything more than my friend and my king."

Trystan hid his smile behind a cough. He'd never seen Willow flustered, and it worked for her much better than her usual shy mousiness.

When he didn't say anything, she continued, "After Lord Drake announced your death, father promised I could choose my husband, but now…"

"Willow." He put a hand on each shoulder to stop her fidgeting and met her eyes. "Our betrothal was never made formal. Even if your father insists, I'll deny you."

"No," she gasped. "Can you imagine my reputation?"

A laugh burst free of him. "What do you want from me? You don't want to marry me, and despite what you think, I don't want to marry you either. Yet, I can't refuse you?" He released her. "Trust me, your father has bigger things to worry about." He narrowed his eyes. "Who is it?"

"What?" she stumbled back.

"If you're this adamant, you obviously have a husband in mind."

Her cheeks flushed. "His name is Rion. He's a guard."

"Rion?" Trystan grinned. "You love him?"

"More than anything."

"He's a good man. If your father pushes, don't take no for an answer."

Her jaw dropped open. "You want me to disobey him?"

"Willow, I'm going to tell you something I wish someone had told both me and my sister. The only person who has to live your life is you. No matter who you are—whether it's the nobleman's daughter, the prince, or even the penniless guard, you deserve good things."

The edges of her mouth curled up, and she stretched up on her toes to press a kiss to his cheek. When she spoke, her breath was warm on his skin. "And that is why we will follow you into the very wastelands of Dreach-Dhoun." She stepped back and dropped into a curtsy. "Your Majesty."

"Goodnight, Willow."

She hurried back down the hall and he turned toward his room, seeing the open door next to his for the first time. Alixa's golden eyes peered out at him, her lip wedged between her teeth.

"Did you just hear all of that?" he asked.

She opened her door wider and stepped out with a tiny nod. She'd been given a silk gown to sleep in, pale against her dark skin. Her chocolate hair fell about her shoulders in waves.

She stepped closer, one bare foot peeking out from the bottom of the nightgown.

"What you said to her." She reached for the front of his jacket and pulled him against her.

He gripped her hips and lost himself in her gaze.

"I refused to see it when I first met you," she whispered.

"Didn't see what?"

"You're a good man, Trystan." She reached up and brushed her lips across his gently.

She leaned away, and he missed her kiss instantly. He brushed a fingertip down her soft cheek. "What was that for?"

"Thank you."

"For what?"

She shivered as he traced the outline of her ear. "You stood up for me today. And at Cullenspire. I've never had anyone who…"

He placed a finger across her lips to cut her off. "I don't know how many times we have to tell you this, but you're one of us now, Alixa. I don't care what anyone says, you aren't simply a traitor's daughter. You're brave and kind—"

She snorted.

"You are. You know what you aren't?"

"What?" she whispered.

"Alone. Not anymore. You have a family who will fight for you, protect you."

"I don't need protection."

He smiled. "Everyone needs protection sometimes, but you're right. You can stand on your own. You've done it many times. Just know you don't have to."

She wrapped her arms around his back and pressed her face to his chest. "Thank you."

He rested his chin on her head. "You've done far more for me than I ever have for you. All of you have. You. Ri. Avery. Da—" He clamped his lips shut and squeezed her tighter.

"I think you're crushing me." Her words snapped the tension, and he released her. "Sleep well, Trystan. Tomorrow will be a long day."

He entered his room and closed the door. Food sat on a tray next to a pitcher, but he had no desire to eat.

Instead, he cleaned up and changed before collapsing into bed. Dreach-Sciene would soon know their king had returned. Their true king.

CHAPTER 13

By the time morning came, Trystan's mind whirled with everything that must be done. Somehow, he'd have to get to the palace and face his uncle. Could he challenge him to a duel? Would Drake accept?

No. That would be too honorable, risking himself rather than his people.

But war? Trystan rubbed his throbbing temples. War was unacceptable. At least among his own people. They could fight, but for what? A throne that would sit empty as soon as Trystan needed to leave again? He had to face the truth. The mission to find Ramsey Kane couldn't be postponed.

How was he supposed to lead his people from enemy territory?

But Drake must not be allowed to hold the throne either. If what Alixa said was true and her brother was with the pretend king, Lord Drake had chosen his side.

Grabbing an apple from the bowl on his bedside table, he bit into it while sliding one arm into his tunic. The day started unbearably warm, a far cry from the freezing temperatures they'd experienced in the weeks before.

Three short raps sounded on his door and he opened it expecting to find Alixa or Rissa. Instead, a stranger peered in at him. He appeared slightly older than Trystan and a grin stretched across his face.

"Uh," Trystan squirmed under the man's curious gaze. "Can I help you?"

He laughed, and the sound was lighter than anything Trystan had heard in a long time. He crossed his arms over his chest and waited.

"I'm sorry, your Majesty." He shook his head. "I seem to be at a bit of a loss in meeting you."

Trystan nodded slowly. "Why don't you start with your name?"

"Oh, I'm sorry. Wren." He stuck out his hand and Trystan looked at it in amusement before taking it in his.

Wren didn't bow or keep his distance. Instead, he laughed again.

"Wow." His breath rushed out. "Your grip is strong."

Trystan released him, but Wren didn't step back.

"Is there a reason you're at my door this morning, Wren?"

"Of course. Old Man Coille assigned me to you. I'm to show you around and make sure no one sticks a knife in your belly."

"Old Man Coille." Trystan laughed. "If I called him that, he'd be the first person in line to stick a knife in me."

Wren waved the words away. "He scowls every time, but I've known the man since I was a kid on the battlefield with him."

"Battlefield?"

"THE battlefield. I was just a boy when Coille and Marcus led the army against Dreach-Dhoun. It was epic until…"

Trystan could imagine what he was going to say. Dreach-Sciene had been winning the war until their magic was stolen. He peered at Wren again, realizing he must be slightly older than he looked. Twenty-five? Thirty?

"Marcus? You knew my father?"

Trystan's father let very few people call him by his first name and this man had done it with the ease of familiarity.

Wren's grin widened. "When I was ten-years-old, your father became my hero and kept that title until the day he died." He glanced back over his shoulder. "Come on. You have a lot to see."

Trystan stepped into the hall and shut his door. "Just a moment." He walked to the room a few doors down and pounded on the door. "Open up, old man!"

Briggs scowled when he appeared. "What?"

"When you're not in your room, you will be by my side at all times. Come." To his surprise, Briggs didn't protest.

"Who's that?" he asked, jerking his head toward Wren.

"Bless the earth," Wren gasped. "You're Briggs Villard. I saw you once during the war." His eyes widened as he glanced from Briggs to Trystan. "You're reuniting the Tri-Gard."

"No," Trystan said, but there was no conviction behind the word. He marched down the hall.

Wren ran after him. "You are." He sucked in a breath through his teeth. "I should have guessed it. You are Marissa's son, after all."

What was that supposed to mean? Trystan rubbed the back of his neck. "This knowledge cannot get out. What we have to do… if we don't succeed."

Wren nodded furiously. "I won't say a word." He whistled and studied Briggs once more. "Wow. The Tri-Gard. It's all really happening again, isn't it?"

Briggs narrowed his eyes. "Who are you, boy?"

Wren held out his hand as he'd done to Trystan but Briggs looked at it with distaste. Wren's smiled didn't falter. "Wren Yaro, at your service."

The name rang through Trystan's mind. "Yaro?"

Briggs finally relaxed. "You're Lady Yaro's boy?"

"From Cullenspire?" Trystan asked.

"That's me. After my da and brother…" His smile fell for the first time. "Well, Ma thought it was time we joined the fight, so she sent me here to an old friend."

"We've just come from Cullenspire. Your mother and sister aided us greatly."

Wren's eyes widened. "They're okay? They can't get word to me from inside Isenore. It isn't safe for them anymore, but they won't leave. It's home."

Trystan gripped Wren's shoulder. "They're doing as well as they can. They probably saved our entire mission when they nursed Briggs back to health."

Wren exhaled heavily, his smile returning. "Good. Good. Come on. There's something you need to see."

The halls were mostly empty as Wren led them out into a courtyard where the sun beat down mercilessly. Trystan shielded his eyes.

The estate at Whitecap sat on the cliffs overlooking the ocean with the fishing village down below. Behind it were large, grassy, normally empty plains.

As soon as they passed the gatehouse and rounded the edge of the walls, he saw it. A sea of tents as colorful as the sails of the ships down in the harbor.

Trystan's steps faltered. "What…"

"Yesterday, they mourned their king as well as their prince and princess," Wren said quietly, gesturing to the people among the tents. Some stoked morning fires, others sharpened crude weapons. A few practiced sword-play.

"Today," Wren pushed on. "They're a little lost." He scratched his head. "We thought you were dead. I was in the room last night when you appeared and think my own heart stopped. When it started again, it was as if the ice thawed from inside and the darkness receded a little."

"You a poet, boy?" Briggs asked.

Wren's cheeks reddened. "In another life, I'd have liked to be a minstrel."

Briggs grunted. "I hate poetry. Never trust a man who can't speak plainly. Just say you were happy Trystan hadn't been sliced open in the godforsaken mountains of Isenore."

Trystan closed his eyes and sighed. He was used to Briggs' insults, but others weren't.

Shock flashed across Wren's face before a laugh burst from his lips.

And then another. "You're worth all the gold in Dreach-Sciene, my friend."

"What gold? Dreach-Sciene is a poor kingdom."

"Watch it," Trystan said.

Wren shot Briggs a wink. "Aren't we only poor because you and your Tri-Gard friends decided to steal our magic?"

"That's what I've been telling him," Rissa said as she joined them. Her eyes scanned the tents. "Amazing, isn't it, brother?"

"Uh… Pr-Princess." Wren stuck out that hand again.

Rissa glanced at it and then at his face. "I'm not shaking that. I don't even know you. You might have the plague… just no."

"Ri, this is Wren Yaro. Wren, meet my sister. I promise, this attitude is a new development."

"I like attitude." He winked.

"Ugh. Okay, brother, I'm going to go. I need to get away from all these people and find somewhere I can just listen to the earth."

Wren's eyes widened. "You have the Tenelach?"

"I do." She turned to leave, but he called after her.

"Wait!" His eyes searched the crowd. "I have someone you need to meet."

"Why?"

"She has the Tenelach too."

Rissa stopped, her entire body freezing. Her hand went to the necklace at her throat, the one that belonged to their mother.

"You look like her." Wren's words were awed.

"Like your friend?"

"No. Like Marissa." He smiled, but it held sadness this time. "That's her family sigil, isn't it?" He pointed to the necklace and his eyes flicked to Briggs. Briggs nodded shortly in silent communication.

Wren dropped his hand before walking toward one of the tents. A woman with chestnut-brown hair and warm amber eyes greeted them. Her eyes held questions she didn't voice.

"Mira," Wren whispered. "This is Rissa. She has the Tenelach too."

Mira's eyes widened and bounced between Trystan and Rissa.

Wren went on. "I didn't get a chance to explain this morning."

"But… but we attended their funeral yesterday."

Wren shrugged as if that explained it all.

Once the shock wore off, Mira dropped into a clumsy curtsy. She didn't move with the grace of someone who'd been trained in the ways of court as Wren did.

"Where have you come from, Mira?" Trystan asked.

"A village on the northern edge of Aldorwood, s-sire."

Rissa's pained eyes met his. They'd seen one of those villages. The starvations. The distrust. The anger.

Mira pushed back her messy hair. Wren, now unbothered by the king's presence, pulled her in for a quick kiss.

When he pulled back, his lips curved. Was this man always smiling?

"Many of the people here are from the villages. Some have come for food, but most because they don't accept Lord Drake as their king."

Rissa squeezed her eyes shut. "You mean our people have come to fight? They shouldn't need to do that. Not yet."

Trystan placed a hand on her shoulder and she covered it with her own. "We'll find a way to prevent it."

She shrugged him off. "How, Trystan? Drake is sitting on our father's—on your throne. Do you expect him to just abdicate?"

A quake ripped through the earth and the surrounding people screamed. "What was that?" Wren asked.

Rissa and Mira locked eyes and spoke at the same time. "Magic."

Trystan turned to Briggs, but he'd already taken off running. Trystan's longer strides caught up quickly, and he grabbed the older man's arm, jerking him to a stop.

"Unhand me," Briggs yelled, fear shining in his eyes. He looked to the sky. "Yes, I know she's in danger," he said to the imaginary being that always seemed to be with him. "If this idiot king would let me go…"

"Who, Briggs?" Trystan yelled. "What's going on?"

"Lonara. Her magic grows weaker. She's almost used it all up."

Trystan opened his mouth to call for horses, but Rissa was already on it. They'd taken four of them from people nearby. Unhealthy looking beasts.

Wren offered Rissa help mounting, but she pushed him aside and climbed on before taking off. Trystan, Wren, and Briggs galloped close behind.

They flew away from the tents across the plain until Lonara came into view. Horseless, she stood her ground, throwing out weak bits of magic easily dodged by her circle of attackers. It was all she could do just to stand when she pulled her sword free.

The first attacker rode for her, preparing to trample her. Rissa jumped her horse into the path and brandished her sword. It met steel with a loud crash.

Trystan counted six soldiers in Isenore green.

"Rissa," Briggs yelled. "Out of the way!"

Wren rode for her and intercepted the next thrust of the man's sword before expertly dispatching him.

Rissa rode hard toward Lonara.

Briggs mumbled something under his breath before light blasted from his palms, striking each Isenore soldier in the chest. They flew from their horses and landed motionless.

The thunder of a galloping horse reached Trystan's ears, and he turned to find a final Isenore man riding hard toward the horizon of tents. Briggs sent jolts of magic, but the man dodged and weaved until he was out of reach.

Digging his heels into his horse, Trystan chased after him. He couldn't be allowed to see the people residing on the Coille estate. If that information got back to Lord Drake…

He caught up to the man as he reached the first row of tents and lunged from his saddle, knocking the man to the ground. He hit hard, landing on his shoulder, but he pushed the pain away as he rolled to his feet and wrapped his fingers around the hilt of his sword.

The Isenore man attacked first, lurched forward with a thrust. Trystan blocked it effortlessly. He twisted his sword in an arc above his head as the clang of steel on steel rang in the air. People ran from their tents to see what the commotion was.

Sweat broke out across Trystan's brow as he played the game, performed the dance. A man from Isenore would not beat him. No one would. Not until he'd succeeded in bringing his people what was rightfully theirs.

The man was skilled. Trystan was better. The man was quick. Trystan was quicker.

His body worked separately from his mind, doing what it needed to do.

When his blade finally met flesh, there was an audible exhale from the crowd. His sword slid through skin like butter before sliding back out again. The man's eyes widened in surprise before he fell back, his body landing in a cloud of dust.

Silence descended, but it was short lived. He didn't know where the cheer began, but people rushed forward.

They didn't recognize him as anything other than a warrior. To them, Trystan Renauld was dead.

Wren, Briggs, and Rissa returned with Lonara and lowered her carefully.

"Is she okay?" he asked once he'd caught his breath.

"Just exhausted," Briggs explained low enough for only them to hear. "Using a large amount of magic drains a person."

Lonara mumbled something.

"What, Lona?" Trystan asked.

She raised her voice. "Your Majesty." She reached out to touch his face, but he stilled as a murmur worked through the crowd.

"The king. The king is alive."

He straightened his spine and turned to meet the people at his back.

Lord Coille and Lady Destan pushed to the front.

"What has happened?" Lord Coille asked. "Are we under attack?"

Rissa coughed. "No, but if you don't give these people answers, we might be." She jerked her head to the crowd.

Lord Coille's gaze found Lonara. "Lona. Is she okay?"

"I'm fine." Lona sighed. "The woods of Aldorwood are crawling with Isenore men."

"It's been a long time, Lona." Coille rubbed the back of his neck.

"This is great and all," Ri interjected. "But priorities."

"Right." Lord Coille pursed his lips.

Lady Destan put a hand on his arm. "Let me. Telling of our king's survival is..." She released a breath.

Lord Coille gestured towards the crowd.

She smiled. "Men and women of Dreach-Sciene. Children. Lords. Ladies. Even the very birds should hear this news. A miracle appeared to us yesterday. Trystan and Rissa Renauld were thought to have perished. Our information was false, a lie fed to us by a man who wanted the throne for himself. Your king and your princess live." She gestured to Trystan and Rissa.

Murmuring rippled over the crowd as Trystan and Rissa found themselves under intense scrutiny. Most of the crowd stared dumbfounded while others openly wept at the realization.

Lady Destan turned to Trystan. "It's your show now, my king."

Trystan scanned the faces before him. "Many months ago, my sister and I were sent on a mission." He breathed in deeply. There was no way to keep the secret with Lonara's presence or her use of magic. "My father charged me with the task of reuniting the Tri-Gard. It is a task I will not fail."

He ignored the gasps of shock and continued. "Briggs Villard and Lonara Stone are here to help us find Ramsey Kane. I have not abandoned you. My sister has not abandoned you. We have lost much in this pursuit, but without it, we stand to lose everything. My father knew this. He was a great man."

The rumble of agreement made him smile.

"He was cut down by a coward and his throne was stolen by a man worse than that. I'm not going to lie to you. Both Briggs and Lonara used magic on this day. Anyone with the sight now knows of their presence. It is no longer safe here. Are you ready to take back your kingdom?"

A cheer wound through the open fields.

Lady Destan wiped a tear away and gave him a nod.

Wren stepped up to Trystan. When he spoke, it was loud enough for everyone to hear.

"I would have followed your father into certain death." He pulled his sword free. Rissa jumped forward, but Trystan waved her back.

Wren stuck the blade tip down into the ground and lowered himself onto one knee. "And I will follow his son. Trystan Renauld, though no crown sits on your head yet, you are my king. I pledge you my sword, my heart, my life. We will take back your throne and protect it until the day you return to us."

He bowed his head. Trystan laid a hand on his hair. "Rise, Lord Yaro. Wren. My sword. My subject. My friend."

They were his father's words. Trystan witnessed many oath swearings. Marcus Renauld always finished with *my friend*.

"Trystan," Lord Coille boomed. "Your father was my best friend. I watched you grow and learn and become a man. I want more than anything for you to now be my king. When you appeared yesterday, I thought it was a ghost, but it wasn't. Your father led me into war once and we failed. I'm ready to rewrite our wrongs."

He knelt and repeated Wren's words.

Others he didn't know stepped forward and Trystan accepted each oath as they were freely given.

"Help me kneel before my king," Lonara whispered.

Rissa helped her kneel.

"My allegiance will forever be to Marissa and her children."

It wasn't the same oath but Trystan took it all the same.

He held back the emotion threatening to pull him under as his people put their faith in him.

Avery and Edric knelt among them.

When Alixa approached, a nervous buzz surrounded her. Her

family name had been passed around and the distrust was evident in their eyes.

She didn't bring a sword but knelt in front of him.

"If I'm going to follow you into the darkness of Dreach-Dhoun, I sure as hell am not going to miss any other battle." The teasing glint left her eyes. "Trystan Renauld, you arrogant, stubborn man. Every part of me is yours. My king. My friend."

The crowd held their breath, wondering if he'd accept the oath of Eisner's daughter.

"Rise, Alixa."

When she stood, her eyes latched onto his. "I will take your oath." He dropped his voice. "I'll take everything."

She smiled and stepped back.

Rissa was the final person to approach.

He shook his head. "You're my sister, Ri. A princess of Dreach-Sciene. I don't want your oath. I don't want that between us."

"Would you let Davi kneel?" she asked, her voice thickening but no tears falling.

He didn't respond, so she answered for him. "He gave you his oath once when you chose him as your second in command. He'd have insisted on this, needed it." Her voice shook. "Truwa, brathair."

A tear tracked down his face. "Trust, sister."

"Let me do this. For him. Please, Trystan. You may not think you need my oath, so can I give you his?"

He brushed another tear from his eye and nodded.

Rissa lowered herself to her knees. Someone sniffled, probably Lady Destan, but all he saw was his sister and next to her, he imagined Davi smiling up at him, watching him take his rightful place. He'd have been proud.

Rissa shook bright red hair out of her face and flicked her eyes sideways as if seeing Davi as well.

When she raised her face to Trystan, there was no smile, only grim acceptance. He wasn't coming back. He didn't get to be a part of this. To see his best friend claim his birthright. To fight alongside them.

"I pledge you my sword," Rissa began.

Trystan held back the tears threatening to spill over.

"My heart." She held a hand over her heart.

Her lip shook as she tried to push out the last phrase. The part of the oath Davi had already fulfilled. He didn't know how she kept the tears from falling.

Sucking in a breath, she pushed it out. "My life."

He waited a moment to calm his breathing before responding to her. "Rise, Rissa. My sword. My sister." He paused. "My friend."

Rissa stood, and he imagined Davi rising along with her.

He pushed those thoughts from his mind and turned to his people. "Prepare, for soon we must leave."

Lord Coille stepped up beside him.

"They'll know I'm here with Briggs and Lonara," Trystan whispered.

Coille nodded. "I guess it's time we face your uncle."

"We must avoid a fight."

"I wish you'd re-consider the use of magic."

Trystan shook his head. Magic could do more damage in a moment than a battle could in a day. He couldn't risk it. Not against his own people. "Out of the question."

"We may not have a choice."

Trystan turned to trudge back toward the estate. "We'll find another way."

CHAPTER 14

His people. Trystan had always been the kingdom's prince. The day he'd been named Toha had changed his world. His father's words came back to him now, and he closed his eyes.

You are to be the kingdom's shield against the darkness. Their hope.

He'd barely had time to perform the function of Toha and now he was king.

So, yes, they were his people before, but now it was... more. He held their oaths in the palm of his hand. Their lives sat on the edge of his blade.

And he was ready.

Not in the sense that he knew what he was doing, because he didn't. But he would learn. He'd grow. He wanted to lead them. Needed to create their path.

He ran a shaky hand through his hair as he stood on the long balcony surrounded by redbrick pillars. What would his father say of him now? Would he be proud? Would Davion?

His eyes drifted out over the land beyond the estate walls where the people of Dreach-Sciene prepared to take back the throne. Pride bloomed in his gut. They'd come from the towns and the villages. There were nobles who'd abandoned their estates to join in with the common folk.

Even before they'd known Trystan still lived, they'd recognized Drake as the enemy he was. There was more bravery, more strength in his kingdom than he'd ever imagined and it gave him hope. When the time came, Dreach-Sciene would rise against Calis Bearne. They'd fight for their homes and their king. Maybe they'd even win.

If he managed to re-unite the Tri-Gard and reclaim their magic.

He turned from the railing. Taking his throne back from his uncle was necessary, but every day they remained here was another day their mission went unfulfilled. The truth of the matter was Ramsey Kane's recovery seemed as impossible a task as ever.

"Your Majesty," Lord Coille said as he joined him.

"My Lord." Trystan nodded.

A large hand landed on his shoulder. "Your father was my greatest friend, let's dispense with formalities, shall we?"

Trystan smiled. "Of course, Adrian." It should have felt strange but instead, there was comfort in the familiarity. Trystan had allies.

Adrian looked out across the sea of tents. "Your father would have loved to see this." He shook his head. "The people rose for us the last time we went to war and we were nearly destroyed. He once told me he wasn't sure if they'd come for us again."

Trystan thought for a moment. "He always underestimated how much they loved him."

"No truer words have ever been said." Sadness crept over Adrian's face. "He was a good man."

"The best." Trystan breathed out slowly and then turned to face the lord. "What happened? Why is he gone? How did someone…"

Adrian averted his eyes and rubbed his chin. "Your father was arrogant. In the best possible way. He thought that because he could wield a sword better than any other, he didn't need constant protection. Before magic was taken, there was no man in Dreach-Sciene with more power than Marcus Renauld. But in the end, it wasn't his skill that failed him or his vigilance."

"Then what?" Trystan pressed.

"It was his heart."

"I don't understand."

Adrian Coille sighed. "Your mother has been gone a long time, and that was Marcus's one weakness. He'd never loved anyone like he loved Marissa, but that didn't mean he couldn't feel anything. So, when the seer…"

"Lorelai?" Trystan's eyes snapped to the lord's, horror burning in his gaze. "She killed my father?"

Adrian's slow nod was all the answer he needed. The woman who continued to haunt his dreams. The girl with the cold voice and stinging words.

Someone you love will die by your hand.

Someone you love will sacrifice their life for yours.

Someone you love will forsake your name.

He backed away from the duke.

"She was an agent of Dreach-Dhoun," Adrian explained.

Trystan's head jerked from side to side in disbelief. And then he froze. It all made too much sense.

She'd played his father with prophecies and promises.

Was the curse false?

The sacrifice had already come true, but was it real?

"She wants us to bring them to her," he said suddenly.

Adrian looked to him in question.

"The Tri-Gard. She wants us to take Briggs and Lonara into Dreach-Dhoun. Lorelai set us on the path to finding Briggs. She convinced my father of the necessity with her prophecy." His mind flashed through everything he knew of the seer. Finding her in the woods. Davion. He covered his mouth. "Davi."

Adrian's wide eyes didn't leave Trystan as he too sifted through every bit of information they had. "What about Davi?"

"Lorelai knew him. She was the person who convinced my father to take him in as a boy."

"What does that mean?"

"I don't know." Trystan turned back to the balcony railing and gripped it until his knuckles turned white. "Maybe nothing now that Davi is…"

"Do you really believe it had no purpose?"

"No." Trystan pushed out a breath.

Anger spiked through him and he spun as he let out a growl. "Everything we've done, every action, every decision has been orchestrated. And all we have to show for it is loss. I'm tired of losing people."

He pointed toward the people below. Alixa and the rest of his friends were among them. "Every person that helps me could be walking into their own deaths."

Adrian put a hand on his arm and pushed it down. "A fact they were all aware of before pledging themselves to you. Trystan, my king, I miss your father and Davi didn't deserve to die, but you can't stop now."

Trystan's shoulders fell. "I know." He sighed with a shake of his head. "I know." He met the duke's understanding stare. "We let her into the palace. I carried her through the front gates myself. We healed her. We trusted her. And she killed him. Do you know how it happened? Where it happened?"

"Trystan-"

"I need to know."

"I was told it was in his rooms in the late hours of the night."

Trystan closed his eyes. "He didn't deserve that."

"No."

"My father deserved to go out on a battlefield where he belonged, fighting for his people."

"Trystan." Adrian's gaze reminded him so much of his father's. "No one deserves the battlefield. Your father was a warrior, but in the end, a fair life would have seen his end come after he'd grown too old for it. And he would have had your mother at his side."

"I wish I remembered them together."

Adrian chuckled softly. "Trust me when I say this, my boy, if you ever want to know what your mother was like, all you have to do is watch that sister of yours."

Trystan smiled as thought of the Rissa that existed before this mission. Sarcastic, but quick to smile at the same time.

Adrian patted him on the back once more and bowed quickly. "Your Majesty." He left Trystan to his thoughts.

Lorelai.

This changed things. He couldn't just walk into Dreach-Dhoun with Briggs and Lonara. Not now that he knew Calis wanted just that.

He hated to think what that meant.

It seemed never ending. Their fight. He re-entered the estate to go over tomorrow's preparations. Lorelai's actions had set off the events that led them here. She'd set them on this path to civil war.

But he refused to fight his own people inside the palace walls. Not when there was another way.

Trystan's mind worked swiftly over the new information and his eyes did not see her before he almost ran over her. Rissa hid near the balcony door.

She set her jaw and turned hard eyes on him. "It was her?"

"You heard us speaking?"

"What do you think?" She took a step away from him. "All this time."

Was she putting Lorelai together with Davi in her mind? Making the connection? That knowledge had thrown everything he knew into question. Even Davi's loyalty, and he hated himself for that.

He refused to cloud Rissa's feelings with doubt. They might never know why Lorelai wanted the orphan boy in their household.

No, if she didn't think of it, he'd let her anger rest solely with the seer.

She shook her head, her pleading eyes finding his. "Please." She rubbed her hand over the hilt sticking up from her belt. "Tell me I get to fight something tomorrow. I need..."

"Ri." He stepped towards her but she backed away.

Her jaw clenched. "We need to take it back, Trystan. They stole Father from us. They cannot have our home."

Lord Coille might be right. No one deserved the battlefield. But some yearned for it. For the first time, he saw that desire in his sister.

There were no words he could say to make her see any different, and he wasn't sure if he should even want to. He'd need Rissa fired up when they reached the palace. But that didn't mean he had to like it.

Taking a deep breath, he met her gaze. "Yes. Tomorrow, we will push them from our home."

He wished he could say something to clear the fog of anger from her mind.

He was angry too, but he was also king. And a king didn't have the luxury of giving in to his anger.

Once they regained his throne, he'd tell her what he'd pieced together from Lorelai's treachery. He'd tell them all. Because there was one thing he was now sure of.

They couldn't risk taking any of the Tri-Gard members to Calis. Briggs and Lonara would have to stay behind.

They'd be forced to enter Dreach-Dhoun without their new allies' magic to protect them. But not yet. Tomorrow, he had an uncle to defeat.

CHAPTER 15

"I never thought I'd be this terrified to come home."

Rissa's whisper was meant for Trystan's ears alone rather than the small army of two hundred strong behind them. There had been no shortage of volunteers once word got out that Trystan was marching on the castle. He had selected a few to accompany him. The others were left behind to protect Whitecap. With Briggs and Lonara's use of magic, the Dreach-Dhoun soldiers would soon be crawling over the town and someone had to be there to protect the people.

The chosen followed his orders without question. He'd never truly realized how deep Dreach-Sciene's loyalty lay with his father until he'd seen the gathering at Coille's estate. Drake would soon find out stealing a title did not a king make.

The trip to the palace was uneventful to say the least. No one seemed to be traveling far in these dark times. No doubt, Drake's claiming the throne and Calis' stronghold on their lands had a common link. Even with the deserted roads, they had taken no chances. They'd forgone the open road the closer they'd gotten to the castle, choosing instead to push their way through the dead forests of Aldorwood. Not that Trystan was foolish enough to believe they could enter the castle without being seen. Two hundred could not sneak in without someone noticing. But he wanted to give them as little notice of their arrival as possible for the plan to work. They should have no time to prepare. Drake was expecting Trystan's small party of six, not two hundred.

Lonara suggested the evening arrival and Trystan had agreed. Arriving after dark meant fewer servants and innocent villagers cluttering up the courtyard. Any attack meant casualties, and the fewer innocent victims, the better. Only the guards were expected to be patrolling the grounds and most were not traitors to Marcus and his children. The majority, Rion had told them, were told of the deaths of Trystan and Rissa and had no choice but to put their faith in the remaining king. But, Drake did not accomplish this feat of taking the throne alone. There were a few in Drake's inner circles that were not so innocent. Royce Eisner was one. There would be a battle. Trystan was just hoping to keep the death toll of his people to a minimum.

He turned slightly in his saddle to look at Rissa, her pale skin shone bright in the watery moonlight. "Terror is only one of the things I feel right now, sister." Glancing back over his shoulder, he raised his voice. He infused it with steel, admitting to none of the fear he felt inside. "The plan stands. We all know what we must do. Wait for the signal and pray we achieve this with minimal loss of life."

"Trystan." Lonara's voice floated softly out of the dark. "Are you sure you don't want to take the castle with magic? Drake will be waiting for you, and he will not be as concerned to the wellbeing of the innocents as you are."

"We can't use magic when we don't know where we stand. Magic cannot differentiate between loyalists or traitors. Let us decide that. You just make sure you and Coille get everyone inside at the signal." Nudging his horse, and with a slight wave of his hand, Trystan started down the small incline to the castle below. Only five others followed his lead; Rissa, Avery, Edric, Alixa, and Rion. The rest remained hidden in the shadows as commanded.

The towers of the castle, visible above the gates, were awash in welcoming light and back-lit with a thousand stars. The sight of it was inviting and welcoming and would have warmed his heart if he had any heart left to care. Knowing his father no longer waited inside, but instead his treacherous uncle, filled him with a deep-seated need for revenge.

The horse's hooves echoed in the arid night air. The weather had changed again. Cold escalated into a simmering heat, relieved only by the coming of dusk. The heat of the day still lingered on his skin and he wiped the beads of sweat from his upper lip.

"Ri, as soon as I give the order, raise the signal. We cannot have the guards locking our people out. Avery, you take the left guards, Rion, the right. Do not take any unnecessary lives. We do not wish to cause harm to any still loyal to us—"

"We know what we have to do, Trystan." Rissa's curt words interrupted his. "Drake and Royce are the only lives we take tonight."

"For once we agree, princess." Alixa's voice floated over Trystan's shoulder, adding to the unease caused by his sister's callous words, but he ignored it. He had much bigger things to worry about at the moment.

Torches burned at the castle wall entrance, firelight glimmering off the thick iron gates. Shadows lurked beyond and disembodied voices floated out to them as they brought their horses to a standstill just out of the range of light.

"Who goes there?" a voice asked. "Identify yourselves."

"Is that you, Fields?"

Silence followed Avery's question. Then, "Who's askin'?"

"It's me, Avery. Open the gate. I've brought the prince and princess back home."

A longer silence.

"You lie. The royals are dead. King Drake said so."

"King Drake? How can Drake be king when Trystan Renauld is still very much alive?"

Murmuring and shuffling from inside met Trystan's ears. The guards argued amongst themselves. Sliding from his horse, he walked slowly into the firelight. "Avery does not lie, soldier. I have returned and I am your rightful king. Open the gate and let us in."

The guard's broad, flat nose squished as he peered through the iron bars in disbelief. "Impossible. You all died in the Isenore mountains. The king said so. He also said we ain't supposed to open the gate for no one without the captain's permission." He squinted into the torchlight. "Although you do kinda look like the young prince under all that hair."

Trystan spread his hands wide, trying to assure the guard of his identity. "My uncle was… mistaken, as you can clearly see. And I understand you not wanting to disobey orders. Call for Captain Brown, then. Tell him of our return. He will know what to do."

The guard grew silent and shifted his eyes away as if struggling with his words. "Brown ain't the captain no more. King Drake had him arrested and imprisoned for treason weeks ago. Patterson is our captain now."

"Treason?" Trystan snorted in derision. "And you believe that? Brown was as loyal to my father as I was. There was no way the captain was involved in any sort of treason. You lot should be ashamed of yourselves for going along with that sham."

"Who said we went along with it? And it ain't King Marcus he's accused of treason against. It's King Drake. Can you prove you're the young prince?"

Trystan narrowed his eyes. "Can you prove I'm not? And if I am, will you take the chance of disobeying me, Lieutenant Fields?"

Fields hesitated for a moment before flashing a mouthful of broken teeth. "Well played, young sir, and I believe you. But I still can't disobey captain's orders without risking my neck." He turned and cupped a hand to his mouth. "Go fetch Captain Patterson. Tell him he's needed at the gate."

"The Captain's already retired for the night. He's not going to like being interrupted," a voice answered back.

"Yeah, well you ain't gonna like my boot up your arse, boy. Now go fetch him and tell him we have someone at the gate claiming to be Prince Trystan."

"Prince Trystan?" Trystan heard the questioning voices as more faces crowded the gate and stared out at him.

"It can't be him, can it?"

"It looks like the young prince, but it's too dark to see proper."

"Yeah, I think it is."

"It's an imposter. Has to be. The royals are all dead. King Drake said so."

Trystan ignored the blabbering as his companions dismounted from their horses and joined him at the gate. This was it. He glanced over at Rissa as his hand settled on the hilt of his sword.

"Ready, sister?"

"As ready as I'll ever be."

Another commotion followed in the courtyard and the staring guards scattered as a bevy of soldiers emerged from the shadows. Even in the low firelight, Trystan observed the shining new armor and honed blades. As they approached, he identified the colors of Isenore. These were not his father's men.

"Open the gate." A taller shadow moved into the flickering light and Trystan recognized the hawkish features of Patterson, a man he remembered as an average soldier, but yet was now somehow the captain of the guard instead of the fiercely loyal Brown. Patterson had clearly chosen a side, and it wasn't Trystan's.

Trystan's heart pounded in time with the clanging of the metal gears as the heavy gate began its ascent. Walking abreast with his companions, Trystan slowly made his way into the courtyard of what was once his home. The rising gate made one final jump and settled against the stone wall with a resounding clank that faded into a pregnant silence.

Fields broke the stillness. "Captain, the young prince has returned home. King Drake was mistaken—"

"Imposters!" Patterson bellowed. "Trystan and Rissa Renauld are dead. Arrest these frauds."

"Drake is the only fraud in Dreach-Sciene." Rissa's steel tone cut like blades through the courtyard, halting the soldiers headed their way. "He is not your king and those who follow him willingly are traitors. Your king stands right here. Trystan Renauld and I, Rissa Renauld, are alive and well and are back to claim what is rightfully ours."

Rissa threw her hood back at the same time Trystan drew his sword and held it high above his head. The unmistakable Renauld emblem sparkled in the firelight.

"My sister speaks the truth. I've come to take my kingdom back from the false king you've been following, and with the sword my father bestowed upon me, I will do just that. Who will follow me in the name of my father? In the name of King Marcus Renauld?"

Gasps and shouts filled the courtyard.

"It's really them."

"It's the Toha's sword, all right."

"They're alive."

"Nonsense!" Patterson screamed again. "The Renauld children are dead. Arrest these people immediately. King Drake has ordered them to be brought to the throne room."

The finely dressed guards at his back moved in unison to do his bidding, showing clearly where their loyalties lay.

"Now, Ri!" Trystan yelled as the rest drew their weapons and prepared to fight.

In one swift movement, Rissa drew the oiled arrow from her quiver and stuck it into the nearest torch. As it burst into flame, she aimed it high into the ink colored sky. The fire arrow was met with the thunderous sound of pounding hooves and battle screams as their reinforcements answered the call.

Trystan could see the moment realization set in on Patterson's face.

"Close the gate!" Patterson screamed.

"Avery," Trystan swallowed the acrid taste of fear that coated his tongue and bellowed at the sword master. She was closest to the gate and the only hope to stop the soldier about to slice the heavy rope keeping the gate open. She moved at Trystan's yell, but before she could intercept, Fields leapt at the Isenore soldier, tackling him to ground. Yanking the soldier's sword out of his grip, the squat-nosed guard smacked the hilt into the soldier's face, blood and teeth splattering the pristine tunic. The man stilled as Fields turned wild eyes on Trystan and teeth flashed in his wide grin.

"Welcome home, your Majesty." Field's gaze switched to the shocked gate guards. "Men, protect our prince and princess at all costs!"

The order was all they needed to mobilize them into action. Field's men surrounded Trystan on both sides just in time to collide with the oncoming horde of Drake's new soldiers.

"Protect Alixa and Ri," Trystan yelled at Edric, but his command was lost in the clanging of steel against steel. Trystan ducked just in time as a broadsword came straight for his head. Pivoting low, he shot out with his own blade and struck the soldier in the back of the knee. The soldier screamed and fell as his leg nearly severed at the joint.

Leaping nimbly to his feet, Trystan yanked his sword up to his chest as another blade crashed against his. Both men stared into each other's eyes, swords locked, as Patterson lowered his head so his nose almost touched Trystan's.

"You shouldn't have come back, you stupid boy," he hissed, spraying Trystan's face with spittle as he spoke.

"You shouldn't have chosen the losing side. So who's the stupid one, really?"

Trystan stepped back far enough to break the stalemate and slashed low at Patterson's stomach, but the man blocked his attack effortlessly.

A smile of complete arrogance crossed the older man's face as he stepped around Trystan. "You forget, boy. I've watched you train with Avery and the rest of us since you were a lad. I know your every move. There's nothing you can do that will surprise me so—"

His words cut off abruptly as an arrow sliced clean through his eye and protruded through the back of his head. Trystan caught a movement in his peripheral and whirled, sword up, as Rissa hurtled into view.

"You were taking far too long, brother, and we still have to find Drake. Our soldiers can handle this."

She pointed with her chin at the people now storming through the gate, Coille leading the way. Their screams and battle cries were meant to intimidate but were totally unnecessary. It took only mere moments for the Isenore soldiers to throw down their arms once they realized they were severely outnumbered.

"Trystan," Alixa gasped in relief as she ran to his side, her eyes devouring him for any sign of injury.

"I'm fine," he assured her. "But we need to do what we came for. Patterson said Drake was waiting for us in the throne room."

"Aye, with a hundred more guards, no doubt." Edric said as he joined them. "And Royce Eisner."

"Doesn't matter if he's guarded by a thousand loyal to him," Rissa growled as her grip on her bow tightened. "This ends tonight."

Trystan gave a quick nod of agreement. "Lonara, Fields," he called, and the Tri-Gard member and guard strode across the courtyard at his command.

"Fields, how many more of those new soldiers does Drake have at his command?"

"Probably another twenty or so inside, your Majesty. They are Isenore soldiers. I always thought something wasn't right about 'em being here. And about Brown being imprisoned for treason. None of us thought that was right, but the few who spoke out about it got thrown in the dungeons too, so we learned to keep our mouths shut about it."

"So the rest of your soldiers are still loyal to us?"

"Until the day we die, sire."

Trystan was moved by the truthful conviction in the guard's voice and he placed a hand on his shoulder. "Thank you. Now grab some men and come with us. We have a usurper to dispose of."

COMPARED to the battle sounds of the courtyard, the castle was like a tomb. The only noise was the echoing of their footsteps as they made their way across the marble floor of the great hall to the arched doors of the throne room where King Marcus once held court with his people. Trystan had many fond memories of that room and they all threatened to overwhelm him right now. The realization that he would not find his father sitting on the raised dais but his uncle instead, hit him like a punch to the gut. Taking a couple of deep breaths, he ignored Rissa's questioning glance and straightened his shoulders. Two very nervous looking guards on either side of the familiar, carved doors watched them approach with apprehension.

"Stop, in the name of King Drake." One had enough gumption to hold out his spear in protest at their approach even though the sheen of sweat covering his ashen face belied his order.

"Out of the way, fool. Do you not recognize your own prince and rightful heir to the throne?" The guard's eyes opened wide at Fields' words.

"Prince... Prince Trystan?" The guard stumbled over his words. "But it can't be. We were told you—"

"—were dead. Yada, yada, yada." Rissa twirled her finger at the guard. "Do we look dead? Now out of the way and let us through to Drake."

Both men bowed their heads in respect as they stepped away from the doors and Rissa barreled past them, slamming against the huge doors. They didn't budge.

"What? They're locked." Rissa slammed her palm against the carved oak. "Drake, we know you're in there. Open this door and face us, you miserable little coward."

"Move aside, Princess," Lonara called softly and Rissa did just that. The older woman wrapped a hand around the crystal hanging from her neck and gave a slight wave toward the door.

Even though being around the Tri-Gard made magic much less of a shock now, Trystan still watched in amazement as the two massive doors fissured and cracked, then fell inward, creating a floating cloud of dust. Stepping through the dust, they entered the throne room, only to be greeted by a wall of Isenore guards. Their shrill cries of attack resonated off the high ceiling and Trystan raised his sword ready to defend his people, but there was no need. With another toss of her hand, Lonara sent the soldiers flying in the opposite direction and they crashed none too gently into the stone walls and slid to the floor.

Silence surrounded them once again. Tearing his gaze from the incapacitated soldiers, Trystan centered his attention on his father's throne. There Drake sat, a newly crafted jeweled crown atop his dark head, much more elaborate than the one his brother had worn. More guards flanked him. Trystan wasn't prepared for the wave of hatred that originated in his gut and rippled through his body, sucking his very breath away.

"Not fair, Trystan. You've brought a Tri-Gard member to fight your battle."

"Just as fair as you betraying your own brother and stealing his throne."

Drake spread his palms wide. "I had nothing to do with Marcus' death. My hands have no blood on them."

"Yet you've made a deal with the very people who orchestrated his murder. I doubt your hands are clean, Uncle."

Drake's sigh bounced around the room as he stood up. "Trystan, you silly, silly boy. Why couldn't you have died in the mountains like you were supposed to? You're as much a fool as your father was."

"Shut your filthy mouth," Rissa spat as she stepped toward the dais, but Trystan grabbed her arm and held her back. She shook off his hand but stayed where she was, glaring daggers at Drake. "My father was no fool. Say one more ill word about him and I swear I'll rip out your poison tongue and feed it to the hounds."

Drake raised his bushy brows in surprise. "Be that as it may, girl, Marcus was a fool. All the nobles are. You think you can beat Calis with his army and magic? The only way Dreach-Sciene can survive is to ally with Calis. Your father was too pigheaded and proud to see that. He put his own pride before his people. That was his downfall as it will be yours."

"So is that what you did, Uncle? You chose Calis over your own brother? And what was the deal for us? Were you to hand us over as well? Or were we to die by your decree?"

Drake shrugged with indifference, but Trystan saw through the facade. His uncle was afraid. "I guess now it doesn't matter. I cannot go up against a Tri-Gard member. You surprised me, Trystan. I never dreamed you would succeed in your mission. But yet, here you are, with Lonara Stone in tow. I'm impressed. But what does that mean for me? What's next?"

Trystan sheathed his sword and studied his uncle through weary eyes. "What's next? You will be arrested. Put in the dungeons to await your execution for treason against the crown as will any of your known allies. Guards, arrest them all."

As Fields and his men advanced on Drake and his soldiers, all hell broke loose.

"Let me go!" Alixa's scream startled Trystan, and he whirled in time to watch her be yanked back into the shadows. His heart leapt into his throat as the torchlight bounced off the blade at her neck. Royce Eisner stared at him from over his sister's head, desperation burning bright in his eyes.

Trystan stepped toward them, pulling his sword, but Eisner only tightened his grip.

"Stay back, Renauld, or I will slit her throat."

"Let her go, Eisner," Trystan growled.

"Not happening. I am not dying in this miserable hellhole. You are going to let me walk out of here and my dear sister is going to help me do that, or else she dies. Understood?" To emphasize his point, he dug the knife tip in and a bead of blood formed and dripped down Alixa's neck.

"Trystan," Rissa yelled from over his shoulder. "Drake is getting away!"

A quick glance showed Drake indeed making a run for the halls at the back of the throne room. Indecision and fear immobilized Trystan. What to do? Go after Drake or help Alixa?

"Stop him, Ri," he finally ordered as he leapt Eisner's way. He heard Rissa's bow sing at the same moment a knife whizzed past his head and planted hilt-deep into Royce Eisner's forehead. The look of surprise etched on his face didn't waver as Royce fell to his knees. Alixa scrambled away as her brother crumpled to the floor. She fell into Trystan's arms and he pulled her tight.

"It's just a flesh wound," she murmured, answering his unspoken question as he ran a gentle finger over her neck. Suddenly stiffening under his touch, she pulled away and cried, "Edric."

Trystan turned to face Alixa's rescuer. Edric's face was a sickly shade of gray and he swallowed a couple of times, like he was fighting hard against nausea. Winning the battle, he wiped a shaky hand across his mouth and nodded Alixa's way as he whispered, "For Ella."

He wobbled a little and Alixa caught him, wrapping her arm around his back for support. She glanced up at Trystan.

"I got this. Go help Rissa."

"Ri," Trystan whispered, finally realizing he couldn't see her. Or Drake. Pushing through the flood of battling guards, he ran towards the back halls, fear filling his chest. Where was she?

He found her standing armed and ready over an injured Drake. Their uncle hadn't even made it out of the throne room before she'd taken him down. The tip of an arrow protruded from his shoulder and he clutched at his bloody wound as he stared up at Rissa with tear-filled eyes.

"Have mercy, niece," he cried as she lifted her bow once more.

"Ri," Trystan called out, but it fell on deaf ears.

"Rach a dh'ifrinn," she cussed at Drake as the arrow found its mark, right between his eyes.

CHAPTER 16

The silence fell over them like a fog, thick and choking. It only lasted a few seconds, but it felt like an eternity as Trystan stared at his sister.

"Rach a dh'ifrinn," he whispered her words with a shake of his head. "Go to hell." How many times had he imagined saying the very same thing to his snake of an uncle? Drake deserved the arrow sticking out of him. He deserved to have the life seep from his veins.

But Rissa? What did she deserve? It wasn't the blood that now soaked into the sleeves of her shirt from battle. Or the lack of remorse on her face.

She just killed her uncle, shot him as he lay helpless, and her eyes were blank.

She didn't deserve to be broken.

The fog lifted and the clang of swords against stone snapped him back to the reality of their situation. The guards who'd chosen his side formed up around him, their eyes watching Drake's men drop their weapons.

Trystan's chest heaved, his breath thundering through his lungs.

Lieutenant Fields barked out orders. "Kneel before your king." He circled the room, stopping in front of each soldier who'd been loyal to Drake and brandished his sword. "Get on your knees, traitors."

Chaos spilled in from the hall as the loyal Dreach-Sciene soldiers continued to disarm the others.

Soldiers who'd been ready to fight him only moments before, lowered themselves, waiting for their judgment.

Trystan slid his sword into the scabbard at his side and wiped a hand across his brow. Royce's body lay at an odd angle, his legs bent under him. His eyes were still open but they no longer saw the mess he'd created.

It should have filled him with pleasure to see Eisner's son dead at his feet, but all he saw was another body to go into the soil of Dreach-Sciene. Another man who wouldn't return home. There'd be many more of them before this was finished. He crouched down and slid Royce's eyes closed.

He raised his face and found Edric sitting on the ground near the platform. His knees were pulled up to his chest. Alixa stood in front of them.

"You did it," she said. "Edric, that was for Ella."

He buried his face in his hands. "I thought it would help, but it won't bring her back, Alixa." His back shook and Alixa bent to wrap her arms around him.

Trystan tore his eyes away and rose. Avery joined him. "The palace is secure, your Majesty."

"That was fast." He pushed out a breath.

"Once the palace guard heard of your arrival, they turned on Drake's men. Most of the traitors were Isenore soldiers and they're being rounded up as we speak."

Trystan nodded and scanned the faces of the men and women who still knelt near the back wall. They put as much distance between themselves and the guards as possible.

A man ran into the room and Trystan recognized him instantly, even under all the dirt and grime of his captivity. Captain Brown's eyes scanned his surroundings until landing on Trystan. A grin spread across his face and he hurried over. "Your Majesty." He bowed. "I didn't want to believe you were dead but there's been no word of you."

Tears danced in the big man's eyes, but they didn't fall. "Welcome home, sire. Welcome home."

Trystan put a hand on the captain's shoulder and squeezed. "I should be the one thanking you."

"For what, sire? I've been in those dungeons for a while."

"Exactly. Your loyalty won't be forgotten. We have tough times ahead, but tonight, I want to enjoy being home."

Brown bowed again and walked off. Avery went with him, their heads close together as they talked.

Lord Coille spoke with a few others near the door and then gestured to the Isenore soldiers. Two guards drew their swords and herded the traitors from the throne room.

Trystan walked toward Lord Coille.

"How does it feel to be back?" the lord asked.

Trystan surveyed the room, a chill settling over him. "Empty," he said honestly. "This place feels empty."

"I know what you mean."

Trystan didn't doubt he did. His father had filled the palace with his presence. Davi had filled it with laughter.

His eyes caught on Rissa's red hair as she bent forward to pull her arrow free from Drake's head. "I don't want to waste an arrow," she explained to Fields, her voice matter-of-fact.

Fields watched her in shock as she yanked it and didn't flinch at the blood and skin that flew out with it. She wiped the tip of the arrow clean on her shirt.

"Princess," Fields choked. "You shouldn't—"

She held up the arrow. "See? Clean."

Fields turned abruptly, the look of disgust on his face unmistakable.

Trystan walked forward and grabbed his sister's elbow to pull her away. He leaned in and spoke lowly, "There are eyes on you right now. Stop this behavior."

She clenched her jaw stubbornly, but he didn't miss her quivering hands. Like most things with his sister lately, this too was an act. He should have seen it sooner. Her shoulders dropped, and he pulled her into a hug, the arrow that killed their uncle wedged between them.

"I'm sorry," he whispered, pushing her hair back. "You shouldn't have had to do that."

She buried her face in his chest and his shirt muffled her words. "But I did, brother." She looked up at him. "I know you. You wouldn't have been able to do it. You'd have kept him alive. We can't afford mercy because we will be shown none. He wanted to kill us."

He breathed out slowly and pressed his lips to her forehead. "I'm not going to stop being sorry."

"I took the oath too. And I meant it. I will be loyal to you until I die."

He flinched at those words, but she continued.

"And my loyalty means I will even save you from yourself. He took your throne, Trystan. Father's throne."

"I know he needed to die. I just wish I could protect you for a little longer."

She released him and stepped back. "You can't. I am in this. I have been from the moment we set out. I am no less capable than you and I have just as much right to risk myself—whether it be physically or morally—as you do."

She was right as hard as that was to admit. Being king meant trusting others to get the job done. He wouldn't always be there. Rissa wasn't a child. He couldn't keep the world from hurting her. A smile tilted his lips. "Okay."

"Okay?"

"Just… I love you."

She grinned, and the sight was so rare and so foreign on the heels of a fight, he shook his head.

"I love you too, big brother, but I'm not the only one." She pointed behind them to where the guardsmen now stood at attention, waiting for their king's orders.

Once again, his sister was right. His people deserved his attention now. He turned to Avery and Brown. "Wake the palace. Gather everyone in the palace who hasn't been arrested. Guards, servants, ordinary soldiers. I'll meet them in the courtyard."

He walked from the throne room with Fields and another guard trailing him. When they'd rushed in to confront Drake, he hadn't had a chance to really look at the halls of his childhood. They hadn't changed. Stone archways stretched before him, interspersed with wooden doors that had been carved to depict scenes from Dreach-Sciene's history. It finally hit him. After everything, he was back at the palace. His palace.

He trailed his fingertips along the wall, wanting to hold on to every memory he had of the place. Racing through the halls with Rissa. Stealing food from the kitchens with Davi. Standing at his father's side and feeling like the most important boy in the world.

He could have waited for the sun to rise in a few hours before greeting his people, but they needed to know of his return. Once the guards had roused the sleeping members of the court from their beds, he entered the courtyard to find a crowd cheering. Many wept. Most faces were familiar. Those who'd cared for his family for years.

His breath shuddered as he held up a hand. The roar continued.

"Let the king speak," someone yelled. Alixa. He shot her a smile. The people here didn't react the same to her presence as they had in Whitecap. His family's servants and guards trusted that if she was with him, there must be a good reason.

"Quiet!" Brown's voice boomed.

The cheers died down and Trystan swallowed, suddenly nervous.

"I'm sorry to wake you all from your dreams. As you can see," he began. "My sister and I are not dead."

Laughter echoed off the stones.

Rissa stepped up beside him and gripped his hand. He squeezed hers in thanks.

"We've returned home to find an imposter on the throne. Drake Renauld is dead. Royce Eisner is dead." He paused to let the words sink in. "But you all are not. You have remained loyal, joining me as soon as I arrived. For that, I have no words."

He paused, breathing deeply.

"Drake and Royce are not the only ones who are gone." He closed his eyes briefly. When he opened them, he saw his own sadness reflected back from the people before him. "Let us take a moment to remember my father, the greatest king Dreach-Sciene has ever known."

Rissa's hand was heavy in his as the next words left his mouth. "And Davion. You all knew him. You helped raise him into the man he became. The man who gave his life to save mine."

Alixa wiped at her eyes and she wasn't alone. Rissa stood very still.

"I wish I could tell you this was the end, but that would be a lie. The road ahead is very difficult. It will test us and bend us, but we will not break."

A few people cheered at that.

"You all deserve to know where my sister and I have been these long months and why I cannot stay. Not yet."

A few disgruntled words reached him, but he didn't stop. "Dreach-Sciene is dying." He let that sink in. "You can all see it, I'm sure. My father set Rissa and I out on a task with a few others. We've been seeking the Tri-Gard. We're reuniting them. Magic will once again run through Dreach-Sciene."

Disbelief rang out in the form of gasps and mumbled curses.

"The Tri-Gard is gone," someone yelled.

"They betrayed us once," another called. "They won't help us."

As more and more people yelled their arguments, Lonara and Briggs pushed through the crowd to stand at Trystan's side. Lonara held her crystal in one fist. A flash of light struck overhead and before he knew what was happening, Trystan rose in the air.

He kicked his feet wildly as fear surged through him. "Lonara," he yelled. "Put me down."

She flashed a wicked smile. "As you wish, your Majesty."

Trystan's feet crashed into the ground and he stumbled forward. Rissa caught his arm and helped him stay upright.

"They needed proof," Lonara explained.

"It's Lonara Stone." The chant wound through the group.

Briggs yelled to be louder than them. "And Briggs Villard. I've returned too." But they didn't hear him as they surged toward Lonara.

"Stop," Trystan called, waving his arms over his head. They obeyed. He'd never get used to being king.

When they quieted again, he spoke. "We have two members of the Tri-Gard but a third is being held in Dreach-Dhoun. We can't waste any time. I must leave in two days once we're re-provisioned. Lord Coille, the Duke of Aldorwood, is to be left in charge of Dreach-Sciene. His command is my command." He met the duke's eyes. "I trust him with your safety."

Lord Coille nodded and Trystan stepped back. Finished with his speech, he turned to walk back inside, but Coille called him back.

"Your Majesty." He gestured to someone behind him. "There is something we must do before you leave again. Everyone is already gathered."

A servant Trystan recognized as his father's steward stepped forward and extended a crown to Lord Coille. A crown? Trystan shook his head. His father's crown. No. He wasn't ready.

"Breathe, Trystan," Alixa whispered. He hadn't realized she was behind him and he immediately relaxed. She pulled him back around to face the crowd. They looked on with excitement.

Coran, the steward, placed a velvet pillow on the ground and gestured to it. "Kneel, your Majesty."

Trystan's knees bent of their own accord and his heart thundered in his ears. Lord Coille wore a proud smile. "I was at your father's side when the crown became his in the middle of a battlefield and I am honored to be here to see it fall to you. Under Dreach-Sciene law, the coronation is but a formality. You've been king since your father's final breath. But it is so much more than that. As I place this crown on your head, we get to bear witness to the turning over of history. Your mother used to say that war has a memory. That the earth remembers every soldier who falls, and every one who remains victorious. It creates scars. Well, I like to think the earth remembers these moments as well. Moments that see us embrace the hope that has been so long forgotten. And in these memories, the earth heals."

Rissa gripped Trystan's shoulder, lending him her strength. Lord Coille stepped forward and set the ruby encrusted crown atop his head. The weight of it was unlike anything he'd felt.

"No longer Toha," Coille said. "Now, you're more. You are no longer only the one who fights for us, you're the one we fight for. Rise, your Majesty."

Trystan stood and faced the crowd as a cheer wound from one end of the courtyard to the other.

Coran turned to him. "Please, your Majesty, return to us."

"I will and I'll bring our magic with me."

Well-wishers mobbed him. He hugged people he'd known all his life. Guards he'd grown up with and trained alongside. Servants who'd been like a part of his family.

It reminded him what the sacrifices were for. For them. For Dreach-Sciene. His home. He would fight for them until he no longer could.

A FAMILIAR CALM settled over the palace the night after the king reclaimed his home. Trystan remembered it well. He'd loved to wander the halls that were busy during the day as they lay still, their inhabitants sleeping in their rooms.

It had been a long day sorting through everything that had happened in Dreach-Sciene since he left. He hated the thought of abandoning them again.

His jacket lay across his shoulders but the buttons sat unclasped. His sword still hung at his waist. He couldn't bear the thought of not having it on him. Not yet. Not so soon after he'd had to fight in these very halls.

He shook his head to rid himself of the dark thoughts. Would this place be forever tainted?

He sighed and continued walking. As soon as he reached his destination, he had his answer. No. He wouldn't let his uncle ruin this place.

The bodies had been removed from the throne room. Drake would be given a royal burial in the forest where all those of royal birth were laid to rest and returned to the earth. He may not deserve it, but he was a Renauld.

Royce Eisner would be sent to Isenore.

The throne room looked as though the events of the day before hadn't happened. As if blood hadn't been spilled on the very stones leading up to his father's seat. He guessed it was his seat now.

His father's presence was stronger in this room than any other.

Stand up taller, Trystan.

Look like a prince.

He heard the words so clearly.

You can't let Davion continue leading you into trouble. That particular warning had been repeated many times over the years and always with affection. Marcus Renauld loved Davion as he did his own children. Trystan thought he'd even been secretly amused by Davi's antics.

The last one rang loudest through his mind.

I'm proud of you, son.

His father's voice was not something he could ever forget. It had been stern, but never lacking for warmth.

Trystan faced the throne. "I'm ready, Father." He took the steps slowly and lowered himself onto the seat. He didn't know if he'd been expecting some momentous awakening, the birth of a king, or what, but nothing happened.

He didn't feel any different.

He drew his sword and examined the symbol on the hilt. He let the tip of the sword touch the ground and spun the hilt so the blade rotated quickly.

"I thought I might find you here," Alixa's voice drifted toward him.

He jerked his head up and stilled the blade.

She sauntered forward. "I've got to say, you don't look any different." She pursed her lips. "No, the crown hasn't improved your face. Still an oafish bore, I see."

He raised an eyebrow and rubbed the side of his face. "Still the impertinent lady I met at the ball."

She flashed him a grin. "Only with you."

A laugh burst past his lips.

Her steps brought her close until she was standing in front of the throne looking up at him. She gestured to his sword. "Planning on fighting someone tonight?"

He'd forgotten he still gripped the sword tightly. His fingers loosened. "I just—"

"I know," she cut in. "This place doesn't seem as safe as it once did. I feel it too."

"I grew up thinking it was the best place to be in all of Dreach-Sciene. Nothing could touch us behind these walls. At the ball when you told me I knew nothing of my people's suffering, you were right. Because their suffering didn't extend to within this palace. We were happy. I was…" He lowered his head, resting his forehead on the hilt of his sword.

"And now that's been stolen, just like everything else," she said. "I get it. I wish I grew up as you did. With family who protected me and guards who were more interested in training me than groping me. But Trystan, this palace has never been safe. Nowhere is. The change you feel, it isn't real."

He raised his gaze to hers. "I thought I'd have a moment when I sat on this throne and knew how I would rule. How stupid is that? As if a chair could tell me how to be my father."

She ascended the steps and put two fingers underneath his chin to tilt his face up. He sucked in a breath as her lips touched his. Her hand wound around his neck and she deepened the kiss. Every time he doubted himself, she'd been there. His moment came. Clarity.

"What was that for?" he asked against her lips.

She straightened. "Do you have to ask that every time I kiss you?" Her hands flew to her hips. "It kind of ruins the moment when you're always questioning my motives. Can't I just want to kiss my king?"

He laughed. "No. That's not exactly how people show their loyalty."

"You're infuriating, Trystan Renauld. What are you looking for here? Do you want me to tell you I haven't been able to stop thinking about kissing you since Whitecap?"

He relaxed back into the chair with a ridiculous grin on his face.

"You've been wanting to kiss me again?"

"Argh." She spun once before facing him again. "I hate you."

"But you like my lips."

"As long as nothing is coming out of them."

He laughed and jumped from the chair to grab her around the waist. She yelped but didn't stop him from pulling her against him and kissing her. His hands sank into her hair. She gripped his biceps as if she'd fall.

He missed his father and Davi, but they weren't there anymore. Alixa was. Rissa was. Sadness fell away from the room.

Alixa pulled away first, her breath erratic and her cheeks flushed. She cupped his jaw. "You're going to be a good king, Trystan Renauld."

"How do you know that?"

"Haven't I told you before?" She tapped her thumb against his lips. "I know everything."

He laughed and buried his face in her neck. "Thank you."

"For what?"

"For making sure I smiled again."

"That was all you. You're not the stoic asshole you'd have people believe."

"I never wanted them to think I was an asshole."

She ducked out of his arms. "Could have fooled me." Her laughter filled the room, and he thought of the last time they'd both been there. Alixa wasn't who she'd wanted people to believe either.

He pressed his hand against the arm of the throne. "I'm coming back," he promised it, feeling like Briggs for talking to an inanimate object. "I promise, Father. Dreach-Dhoun will not be the end of me."

Alixa paused at the door and turned back. "Who are you talking to?"

Trystan's gaze circled the room. "No one. He isn't here anymore."

She seemed to understand. "Of course they're not in this musty old room." She reached for him as he neared and put her hand against his chest. "Because they're in here."

As they walked back toward their rooms, Edric rushed to follow. He bowed. "Your Majesty."

Trystan smiled and motioned for him to rise. "Can this wait until the morning? I'm exhausted and we leave soon."

"I'm sorry, sire, but it cannot."

"Go on."

"I won't be coming to Dreach-Dhoun."

"What?" Alixa asked harshly. "Edric—"

Trystan cut her off. "Explain."

Edric looked from Alixa to Trystan. "I've had my revenge for Ella's death and it didn't matter. It didn't mean anything."

Alixa opened her mouth to protest but Trystan squeezed her arm.

Edric went on. "I want to help in this fight. You're going into Dreach-Dhoun, but you don't need me. It'll be better for you to have a smaller traveling party. Lord Coille has offered me a position in his guard. I can make a real difference here. He wants me to help train the flood of new soldiers we'll be getting." He lowered his head. "I'm sorry if you think me a coward."

Trystan put a hand on his shoulder. "You aren't a coward, Edric. Your task here will be just as valuable as ours. Stay. Train the soldiers to become warriors as great as you."

"Thank you, sire."

Trystan patted Edric's back as he walked by him. Alixa hung back to talk with her friend. It was one less person he'd be leading into Calis Bearne's hands.

He wished he didn't have to take any of them, but as his sister had told him so many times, that was not his choice to make. With one more glance back at Alixa, he vowed to do whatever he had to do to ensure they all made it out of this intact.

CHAPTER 17

Lorelai scrubbed the feel of Thom from her skin as she sank lower in the water and leaned her head back against the metal rim of her soaking tub. It'd been days since Thom's body lay in front of her fire and she could still feel his touch.

She could still see the look in her cousin's eyes when he plunged the knife into Thom's neck. He hadn't looked scared, barely even shocked. The fire had lit his excited face in an eerie glow.

She closed her eyes. He'd looked like his father.

A shiver raced down her spine despite the warmth of the water. Breathing out slowly, she dipped down to rinse her hair.

He hadn't hesitated. Not like when she had Marcus on his knees.

The king of Dreach-Sciene's forgiving eyes would haunt her for as long as she lived.

And her allegiance to her uncle, her obedience, would be the noose around her throat for just as long.

She was stuck. Trapped.

There was one person who was trapped with her. Someone she'd been neglecting of late.

Rising to her feet, she let the water run from her body and squeezed her hair as the chill of the room hit her. Stepping from the tub, she reached for her underclothes and pulled them on her still damp body before shrugging on a simple shift dress.

Her hair hung limp on her shoulders, soaking the material of the dress, but she paid it no mind as she hurried into the hall and around the corner to her mother's rooms. The king liked to keep his sister as far from his wing as possible.

Being a seer meant seeing a lot of things others didn't want to know about. Lorelai rarely discussed her own visions. She'd learned a long time ago that it was better that way. Her mother didn't have the mental capability to hold back.

And her visions were always honest and mostly dark.

She didn't twist them to give Calis what he wanted to hear like Lorelai sometimes had to do.

After issuing three heavy knocks on her mother's door, Lorelai waited, listening intently. No sound came from inside the room so she tried again.

Nothing. She tried the door, and it opened easily.

"Mother," she called, stepping into the space.

Emptiness greeted her.

Her mother was always there. She didn't leave her rooms unless Lorelai accompanied her. Where would she have gone?

A young man appeared, his eyes widening when he saw her.

"Kor." Lorelai approached him because he hadn't moved. Her mother's servant pressed his lips together as if willing himself not to speak as his eyes scanned her sopping hair and simple dress.

She didn't look like herself, but she didn't care.

"Where is my mother, Kor?" She fixed him with a cold stare.

He bit his lip, his eyes darting around the room frantically. "She… she told me not to tell you."

A scowl settled on Lorelai's face. "Boy, if you don't tell me where she is, I'll take you to my uncle."

He swallowed noisily. "Mistress Bearne went into the village."

"Dammit." Lorelai reeled back and turned on her heel, not bothering to ask why. She had to get to her mother before something happened to her. She ran back toward her room and threw her cloak over her shoulders as she twisted her hair under a cap and set out again, this time for the stables.

A messenger slid down from his horse outside and before the stable lad could take the reins, Lorelai snatched them. "I need to borrow your horse."

Recognizing her immediately, he didn't argue. Instead, the messenger gave her a boost into the saddle. As soon as she was situated, she dug her heels into the horse's flanks and thundered through the palace gates.

Her surroundings blended together as she nudged the horse onto the path to the village, avoiding the ruts made by traveling carts and wagons.

Her mind worked in overdrive, imagining every possible scenario, every misfortune that could fall upon a woman who was more than a few pieces short of a bale of hay.

A woman who no longer knew how to use earth magic. Whose visions haunted her day and night.

A woman who wasn't strong enough to handle the life of a seer.

Lorelai's one goal in life was always to avoid her mother's fate. Too many seers found their minds scrambled until they didn't know what was real anymore.

She lifted her rear in the air and hunched forward, snapping her reins. The village came into view and she didn't know what she'd find there.

The path turned to cobblestone as she entered the village streets and passed storefront after storefront. Places she'd loved exploring as a kid. Now, it only instilled fear. Her mother could be anywhere.

She turned the corner and pulled up on the reins as a large crowd moved toward the center of town. Foreboding filled her chest.

A voice rang out, echoing off buildings, and she recognized it immediately. Someone was using magic to amplify her mother's voice. The crowd parted to make space for her horse and whispering hissed in the air around her as she was recognized. But she focused on the woman who stood with two men on a makeshift stage.

"I have seen it," she said. "The future."

Her mother had discarded her plain dress for an extravagant silk robe. It had been a present from Lorelai, but she'd never seen the woman wear it.

Her hair curled neatly down her back as if she'd taken great care with it. It was a far cry from the usual nest that sat atop her head.

Lorelai had never seen her mother look so beautiful. And it scared her. She had to figure out what was going on.

As she neared, she recognized one of the men with her mother as her friend from the tavern but the other was a mystery.

"We are heading down a dark path, my friends," her mother said. "My vision was of our kingdom burning. Of death. Of ruin."

Her mother's eyes found her and Lorelai dismounted to stand at the edge of the stage.

"Dreach-Dhoun is going to lose this war," she said. "And it's because we deserve to. We have done unspeakable things. Our king will lead us to destruction."

As her words sunk in, shouting erupted through the alleyways.

"It's the prince!" someone shouted as they ran in every direction. "The army is here."

"Run," someone else screamed. "No one is safe."

Lorelai jumped onto the stage and gripped her mother's arm to pull her down. She had to get her out of there unseen by her uncle.

"Mother, what were you thinking?"

Her mother ripped her arm free. "I won't go back there."

"You know what he'll do to you."

She raised her chin. "Yes."

Lorelai looked for the men who'd stood with her mother, but they were nowhere to be found. There was no one to help her.

Even if there had been, it was too late.

Davi buckled his sword belt and slid a knife into the sheath around his leg. He was prepared.

It was his first mission for his father. A messenger had arrived that same hour to tell them of unrest in the village. Rebel activity.

It was his chance to prove himself.

He would bring them to justice.

His horse was waiting for him, as anxious to be out of the palace as he was. He didn't have any magic stored up in his body, but he had the feeling he wouldn't be needing magic for this one.

Using magic against the king's men was a capital offense. No villager would dare attempt it.

He mounted up and joined the soldiers who would accompany him. He told his father it was overkill. They didn't need to send the entire guard to deal with one instance of unrest in a single village, but his father hadn't listened.

Davi turned to face them. "Once inside the village, you will hold back. I will take a few select men with me to investigate. We don't want to overrun the place if we don't have to. If you're needed, I'll send a runner to you." He shifted in his saddle. "Move out."

They sounded like an army racing across the plains, pounding the earth into submission, and maybe they were. Did two hundred men constitute an army? Were they invading their own villages now?

Pushing all indecision from his mind, he let out a yell. "For the king!"

The sentiment was echoed behind him.

They slowed as they crested the hill overlooking the village. Davi nodded to the four men he'd selected and together, they continued into the village.

The streets were deserted. Davi met the eyes of the man on his right, confirming the air of apprehension surrounding them.

"Where is everyone?" he asked.

No one answered him.

There was a noise up ahead and at first he thought he was imagining it, but the closer he moved, the louder it became. It sounded like… a crowd.

Before rounding the corner, he held up a hand to the other men and craned his neck to peer around the buildings into the town square.

His breath stuck in his throat. Every person who lived in the village must be there. And up on stage was a woman he hadn't seen since first coming to the palace, but he knew her all the same.

Lorelai's mother.

His aunt.

And there was her daughter moving through the crowd on horseback.

They'd missed the first part of her speech but the ending chilled him.

"Dreach-Dhoun is going to lose this war, and it's because we deserve to. We have done unspeakable things. Our king will lead us to destruction."

Davi rubbed a hand across his face and stared at each of his men in turn. They were missing one. "Where's Jeffers?"

"He went back to bring the troops. There's no way we can take on this many rebels at once."

Davi cursed. "That's the entire village. We can't arrest them all."

He had to think fast. Soon, they'd be overrun with Dreach-Dhoun's deadliest soldiers. He heard them before they arrive and then a villager spotted him and screamed. He couldn't make out their words, but the crowd started running in every direction.

He looked toward the platform again but he'd lost Lorelai and her mother.

He cursed again and kicked at a man who tried to drag him from his saddle.

Pulling his sword free, he motioned for his men to follow him. They had to find Lorelai. A few brave villagers tried to get in their way but they were quickly cut down. Davi didn't see any faces. He didn't notice the accusing eyes or fear that sat heavy in the air as his force bore down on the unsuspecting village, spreading out like a swarm of bees destroying everything in their path.

Battle instinct took over, and all Davi knew was his objective. Get his cousin out of there, no matter how many people were hurt in the process. He'd lost any control he had over the army the minute they entered the village.

Maybe he'd never really had control.

He sliced his way through the crowd, looking for that white-blond hair before realizing she'd been wearing a cap.

Villagers threw themselves through doorways to avoid being trampled or cut to ribbons. They cowered under tables, mothers cradling their children and fathers keeping them hidden.

Remorse bloomed in Davi's gut, but he shut it down.

They were rebels. All of them. They'd listened to his aunt's traitorous talk.

How was he supposed to wrap his head around that? His aunt was a traitor. He wouldn't be able to save her. But Lorelai. She could be saved.

"Your Highness," someone barked behind him.

When Davi turned his horse, something cracked inside of him. Two guards held Lorelai and her mother.

"We got the traitors," the man said.

Davi jumped down onto the street that now ran with blood. He leaned in close to Lorelai. "Why were you here, cousin?"

There was pain in his voice that he did his best to hide. If Lorelai was a traitor too, it'd be like a knife to the heart.

"I had to save my mother." Lorelai looked down at her hands. Hands that were stained with blood, Davi noticed.

"She killed two king's men, my prince." The explanation came from a woman behind him.

Davi closed his eyes.

He'd been wrong. He couldn't save any of them.

He turned his back on his cousin to speak with the woman who was cleaning her blade on her pant leg. "We're done here. This village needs to be put back in order. Select ten of the army's most powerful magic wielders. Take them into the glen to draw power from the earth and then return to wipe away what has happened here."

The woman nodded and took off to obey her orders.

Davi faced his cousin once again. The look she sent his way nearly broke him.

"You can't erase this, Davi. No amount of magic can bring back the people your men have killed here today."

He shook his head. "Before today, they were your men too."

"They're supposed to be Dreach-Dhoun's men. The ones who protect us. Not the ones who make us bleed."

THE KING CROUCHED DOWN to look into the wild eyes of the woman who knelt on the very platform she'd spoken from only hours before.

Hushed murmurs wound through the crowd. The army had gone into each house, each storefront, to force the cowering villagers back into the town square. All talk of rebellion was gone, leaving only a heavy despair in the air. Too many were dead.

Davi steeled his eyes as he scanned the horizon.

"Sister," his father cooed. He lifted her face to meet his, but any lucidity she might have previously displayed seemed to have fled her mind. She didn't know what was happening.

"You should know better than to betray me, sister."

Her bottom lip quivered and Davi averted his eyes, finding Lorelai instead. Two guards held her by the side of the platform. She refused to meet Davi's eyes.

A sick feeling washed over him. She'd never forgive him for leading the army against the village. For reporting everything to his father.

He was the prince. He shouldn't have to apologize to anyone.

Two others knelt on the platform. Rebel leaders. He'd met the first one before in the tavern. But the second was an older man who looked as though he'd seen his fair share of hard years.

Davi didn't know what to focus on. His father who was still speaking lowly to his aunt? The rebels, traitors to the crown? Should he watch Lorelai as every bit of love left her eyes? Or maybe the crowd and their scared, accusing stares.

The king stood and Davi made his decision. His father should have his focus, his loyalty. He'd do anything to be the son Calis Bearne wanted. The son he'd lost and found again.

His father's voice boomed out, cracking the stillness like a battering ram. "These are your kingdom's betrayers." He pointed to his sister. "This woman speaks nothing but lies. She lost the sight many years ago."

He was lying. She hadn't lost the sight, only the sanity to decipher it.

"These men," he pointed to the other rebels. "Have led you astray long enough."

He raised a hand into the air and twisted his wrist in one quick movement. The two men fell forward, their bodies thudding into the wooden platform beneath them.

The crowd gasped. Someone cried out. But no one moved. Fear was power and in that moment, the king held every ounce of their fear in the palm of his hand.

None of their magic could touch him. Combined it wouldn't even be enough.

Not for the first time, Davi was glad to be on that man's side in the battles to come.

No air moved through the courtyard. No birds flew overhead. The sun beat down upon them mercilessly as they waited. And waited.

Would he do it? Would he execute his own blood?

Not even Davi knew the answer to that.

Lorelai's sobs were the only sound to reach Davi's ear. "Please," she cried. "Mother."

Her mother lifted her eyes as if seeing her daughter for the first time and a smile softened her face. Sanity returned to her eyes. "I saw this day."

Davi swallowed roughly as Lorelai gasped. "You knew this would happen?"

The older woman nodded and closed her eyes as she spread her hands out before her. "I am ready."

Davi studied his father as if willing him to realize he didn't have to do this. He'd say it was a lesson to his people. No one was safe from his wrath. But it didn't have to be that way. He didn't have to be... evil. Calis Bearne could be a good man.

For the first time since returning home, Davi saw remorse in his father's eyes. Hesitation in his movements.

Davi closed his eyes, unable to watch. When the thump of a body hitting wood sounded in his ears, he opened them. His aunt's eyes were wide as if still in this world. But she wasn't. She was gone.

"No!" Lorelai screamed, fighting against her guards. "Bring her back. Bring her back to me."

With the last words, she slumped against one of her guards, every ounce of energy leaving her as she sobbed.

The guards dragged her away. Davi should have gone after her. He watched them retreat before turning back to his father. Why didn't he go after her?

The crowd was allowed to disperse, and the bodies were taken away for burial. Traitors weren't buried on the palace grounds even if they were members of the royal family.

The king stood motionless until he brought a hand up to rub his tired eyes. His breath shook as he pushed it past his lips. "I had no choice, son."

Davi didn't believe that, but his father needed him to be on his side. "I know." He gripped his father's shoulder and squeezed.

His father put his hand over Davi's. "This doesn't end here."

"I know that too."

"I have enemies, even in my own kingdom."

"You have friends too." As he spoke, a horseman appeared in the square and his father's face relaxed.

The king stepped away from his son as if their moment never

happened and jumped down from the platform to greet the new arrival.

"Duke!"

The portly man dismounted and bowed. "My king."

"I am glad you've returned. You must meet my son."

Davi didn't like the way the man scanned him from head to toe with narrowed eyes. "It's a pleasure to see you again, your Highness." He inclined his head.

Davi tried to recall meeting the man and an image of a young woman with the same dark tones to her skin appeared in his memory. Had she been a friend or foe in his captivity?

Then a man appeared in his mind and a shock of hate went through him.

"It's okay, if you don't remember me, my prince," the duke said. "It seemed like another lifetime."

His father clapped the man on the back, his smile at odds with the events of moments before. "Lord Eisner here is an old friend and ally. Come. Let's return to the palace."

"I would have brought my son with me, but he had important matters to attend to in Dreach-Sciene."

"Too bad. Davi spends too much time in the company of his cousin. A woman is not such great company. Unfortunate business today though. My niece is actually residing in the dungeons now."

"That is a shame," Eisner said with a lecherous grin. "I enjoyed her company the last time you sent her to me. I should have liked to see her again."

Calis shook his head with a grin. "One woman is just like any other. They don't really change much. I have many others for you to choose from."

As they rode to the palace, Davi's mind was still back in the village. With his aunt. With his people. Leading the army against unarmed villagers was the kind of thing he'd remember for the rest of his life.

A giant of a man was waiting in his father's office as they strode in. He turned from the window and bowed immediately.

"Your Majesty."

Calis nodded in approval. "I see they continue to make them big in the mountains."

The duke smiled at that. "Yes, we ran into one of your border patrols. Mountain men make the best warriors."

"Hmmm. Now, have a seat. I believe you have a report for me and honestly, I need a drink. It's been a trying day."

"Anything I can help you with?"

"No. Just get on with the reason you're here."

A servant poured them each a small glass of brandy. The king downed his in one go and held his cup out for more. Davi sipped his, enjoying the burn in his throat as he watched the two men. Eisner. His mind put it together now. He remembered him as the Duke of Isenore. He was from Dreach-Sciene. Why should they trust him?

Eisner leaned forward, his elbows resting on the arms of his chair. "Trystan Renauld is in Whitecap. I received a message from your man close to him to pass along. They will soon be on their way to Dreach-Dhoun just as you said they would."

Calis lip curled. "Has my man been able to decipher if any of the Tri-Gard members will be with him?"

"They don't know for certain, but it's possible."

"Stupid boy."

The duke reported on many other things, but Davi was lost in his own mind. The prince of Dreach-Sciene was coming to Dreach-Dhoun.

He'd have his chance for revenge.

CHAPTER 18

Trystan had never been to the border separating the two kingdoms, but he had heard many stories depicting the beauty of a land with magic. But this? What they were looking at on the other side of the valley below them? Words could not do it justice.

A river ran swift and clear between Dreach-Sciene and Dreach-Dhoun, like a veil between life and death. The brown, brittle weeds that crunched under their feet as they dismounted from their horses disappeared on the other side of the waterway; replaced by green grass so vivid it didn't seem real. Beyond the bank, trees covered in mossy bark grew thick and tall saturated with leaves of red and gold. After days of traveling with nothing but the dull, dreary mountains of Isenore as background, seeing this much beauty and color was almost hard to look at.

The fear and unease that had been his constant companion ever since leaving the castle was pushed aside for the moment as wonder replaced it. So lost in the beauty of the landscape, he wasn't even aware that Alixa had joined his side until her whisper startled him.

"So this is what magic looks like."

He nodded. "This is what Dreach-Sciene once looked like too and hopefully will again. If we succeed."

"*If* we succeed. Doesn't exactly instill confidence, my king."

My king. The words seemed foreign. Wrong. He didn't feel like a king. Even after the ceremony and the show of fidelity from his people, it still didn't seem real. To him the king was, and always would be, his father. He hoped deep down inside he would do his father proud.

"I wish I could give more assurances, but ours is not the best plan of attack. Actually, allowing ourselves to be captured by the one man we should avoid at all costs? Not the smartest move."

"Not the smartest," Alixa agreed with a tiny nod, "but the only option. We need Ramsey for this whole plan to work. The only way we can get to Ramsey is to be inside the castle. Briggs assures us that all we need to do is reunite the Tri-Gard member with his crystal and then they will get us back out. Easy, right?"

Trystan's sharp bark of laughter caught the attention of the others and Rissa threw a disapproving glare their way.

"Right. Easy. Find Calis' prisoner while we ourselves are prisoners. Steal the crystal back from the all-powerful Calis and somehow let Briggs and Lonara know we have Ramsey and the crystal both so they can break us out. All the while keeping Briggs and Lonara out of Calis' grip. All in a day's work."

Alixa's deep sigh echoed his gloom. "When you put it like that—"

"Do not give up hope before we've even begun." Lonara's tiny frame squeezed between the two of them, her strange gold eyes berating their dismay. "Calis needs to believe he's captured you against your will. He will never believe you came to him willingly. He will think an attack on his castle more likely, but any attack could lead to Ramsey's death. We cannot take that chance."

"Why *is* Ramsey still alive?" Alixa questioned. "We need him to return Dreach-Sciene's magic, but Calis already has taken his crystal. He's powerful enough with it, he doesn't need Ramsey alive. It doesn't make sense why he would keep him prisoner all these years instead of getting rid of our only chance to heal our lands."

Lonara's lips tilted up in a sad smile. "Calis Bearne does not do much that makes sense to us. He enjoys playing God with people's lives. He enjoys bringing them suffering and pain. There are many reasons he's kept Ramsey alive. Reasons we do not have time to get into right now, but the main reason? He takes pleasure from making Ramsey suffer horribly in any way he can. Even with that, if he ever fears we will free Ramsey, he will most likely kill him at the first opportunity. That's why we can't attack with magic. He desires our crystals to make his power complete, but he is well aware that reuniting the three of us could lead to his downfall. He will kill Ramsey before he allows that to happen. You need to get to Ramsey and the crystal first before we attempt any rescue."

"Lonara, if this was meant as a pep talk I have to tell you, you've failed miserably." Alixa crossed her arms across her body and hugged herself tight. "I can't believe we're willingly walking into his hands. What's to stop him from just killing us all on sight?"

"He won't. He's much smarter than that. He wants something we have, and he knows killing you will make his goal that much more unattainable. He'll use you all as a bargaining tool."

Alixa shook her mop of dark curls. "Not making me feel any better."

Lonara's smile was genuine this time. "Do not fear, girl. We're not sending you into the lion's den with no protection. Our plan will work. Especially with this." From her pocket, she pulled a strap of worn leather with a yellowed crystal dangling from the end. Whereas her Tri-Gard crystal was rounded and Briggs' diamond shape, this one was more oval. Trystan blinked in surprise.

"You have another crystal?"

"A fake. A replica of Ramsey's. The third crystal. Once you are inside, you will need to switch this for the real crystal. I've infused it with a slight magic, enough so Calis won't realize it's a fake, not until it's too late. As soon as you reunite the real crystal with Ramsey, I will know. Briggs will then lure Calis away from the castle with a show of magic that he won't be able to resist; opening a way for you to escape. Trust in Ramsey Kane. He will get you through this."

Trystan watched Rissa as she approached, grimacing to herself as she overheard Lonara's remarks. "Not much of a plan, Lona. I hope to earth we know what we're doing."

ONCE THEY CROSSED INTO DREACH-DHOUN, they parted company with Lonara and Briggs and the rest of the soldiers. They had their own agenda to follow, as they all did.

Rissa had listened to Lonara's plan in silence, hiding her doubts. Maybe it would work, maybe it wouldn't. Maybe putting all their trust into Ramsey Kane was foolhardy and reckless. She couldn't say for sure, but she was certain that if the opportunity arose to end Calis once and for all during their captivity, she wouldn't hesitate. Not for a moment.

They made their way through the thick copse of woods in silence toward the heart of Dreach-Sciene. The small group of sacrificial lambs. Their lack of talk wasn't from the sheer beauty of the scenery, or the fragrant smells of jasmine and sage inundating the air, but rather from the dizzying presence of magic. It had assaulted them as soon as they'd crossed over. It was everywhere. It oozed from the trees, the grass, the very air itself. Lonara told them it would be overwhelming, especially for Ri, considering her connection to magic. Rissa had tasted these tinges of power before but that had been nothing compared to this. This was intoxicating and frightening all at the same time. Her head was spinning from the abundance of it, like she had drunk too much wine over the past few hours.

"Ri."

It took her a moment to realize Trystan was calling her name. She turned to look at him and swayed a little in the process. "Yes?"

"Are you all right? You were stumbling."

"Yes. No. Can you all not feel that? Can you not hear it?" The humming had started out barely detectable, but now it filled her head like a thousand honeybees circling around her. Warmth slowly filled her body and flowed through her veins, bringing both pleasure and pain at the same time. She tried ignoring it, but her nerve endings were on fire and she wanted to cry out. Her mother had Tenelach as well. Did that mean she felt this way every day? If her mother could handle this, then so could she, right? Some of her fear and doubt must have shown on her face, however, since Alixa's eyes flashed bright with worry and she suddenly grabbed her arm.

"Here, why don't we sit down for a moment?"

Rissa allowed herself to be led to a fallen tree. She sat gingerly and stared around at the three worried faces in confusion. "Okay, you're all looking at me weird. Please tell me you all feel this strangeness as well?"

Trystan glanced around at their companions. "I feel... something. Like a vibration in the air. A tiny disturbance. It's faint, but it's there."

"Faint?" Rissa echoed in disbelief. "It's deafening. The humming is everywhere. It's so beautiful. Like the trees and flowers, the very earth itself is singing to me. Alixa, Avery, please tell me you feel it too?"

She knew from their puzzled expressions they didn't.

"Lonara said the Tenelach would make me more susceptible to the magic," she glanced up at Trystan. "But I wasn't prepared for this."

Trystan's worried eyes met hers. "Is it painful, Ri? Are you going to be able to keep going?"

She stood up, suddenly feeling embarrassed at her weakness and waving away the hand he offered to help her. "Of course, I can go on. We have to keep going. I just need to accustom myself to—" her words halted abruptly as a tiny yelp fell from her lips. The humming escalated into a drumming, throbbing in her head. Without warning her knees buckled, and she put out her hands to catch herself as she fell. The moment her hands touched the ground, an energy like nothing she had ever felt before surged through her palms and up her arms. She stifled the scream of surprise on her lips and tried to pull away, but it was like her hands had a mind of their own, they simply dug deeper into the dirt. Even though her instincts told her to fight it, Rissa simply opened herself up to it and the pain suddenly ebbed away, like the magic knew it was being accepted. The energy in her arms surged through the rest of her body, filling her with warmth and happiness, like something that had been long lost but was now home. A new sound filled her head and if Ri didn't know any better, she would have thought it the sweetest of music. Maybe that's what it really was. The music of life. Of the trees, the insects, the very earth itself as it made itself known to her. Tears filled her eyes as the beauty of it all moved her very soul.

"Rissa!"

She heard the others calling her name. The worry in their voices. But she didn't want to answer them. She didn't want to break the perfection of the moment as these new feelings surround her in a cocoon of peace and calm. The magic spoke to her, touching her on a level she never even knew existed.

"I'm fine," she whispered finally as she removed her hands from the dirt. "Actually, I'm better than fine. I wish you all could feel this. It's so beautiful."

She reached out and accepted Trystan's hand as he pulled her to her feet. She studied the worried faces in front of her. Suddenly Alixa made a fist and punched her in the shoulder. Hard.

"Ow! What the hell was that for?"

"For scaring the life out of me." Alixa glared at her. "I thought you were hurt or something."

"Well if I wasn't before, I am now. That's gonna leave a bruise." Rissa rubbed her shoulder and glared back at the dark-haired girl.

Trystan pinched the bridge of his nose, like he was trying to ease away a headache. "Alixa's right. You scared the hell out of us. How do you feel, really?"

Rissa stopped glaring at Alixa and fell quiet, thinking about his question. Finally, lifting her eyes to her brother, she grinned. The smile felt awkward, like her lips didn't quite know how to form a true smile anymore. "Complete. Powerful. Like this was meant to be. Like I can do anything."

"Tenelach," Avery whispered in wonder. "Magic. It came for you."

Rissa nodded. "We've missed out on so much for so long. The magic misses us too. It waits impatiently. It desperately wants back into our lands. It wants to heal and provide, like it was meant to. We need to do this, brother. We need to bring magic back to Dreach-Sciene."

"That's highly unlikely." The voice came from the trees behind them and all four whirled in surprise. They were no longer alone.

These were no ordinary soldiers surrounding them. These men and women were covered in furs and pelts, rugged and dirty. Not the least bit like the soldiers they were used to seeing. One stepped forward, tall and wide shouldered, and pointed his sword their way. "You are trespassing here, Trystan Renauld. You should not have crossed the border."

"You know who we are?" Trystan asked in surprise.

The tall man nodded. "Of course we know who you are. King Calis knows of your approach, and he has sent us to fetch you. Do not resist. It will be much easier on us all if you do not resist."

Trystan, Alixa, and Avery pulled their blades, as Rissa lifted her bow. Part of the plan or not, they weren't giving up that easily. The guards could not suspect a thing.

There was no fight, however. No blades clanged or arrows loosed. One moment they were all standing their ground, the next they were blown through the air by some invisible force. Rissa landed hard on her backside as pain shot up her back and into her neck. She watched from the ground as Trystan wasn't so lucky and he hit a thick tree, slamming hard into its solid trunk, landing on the ground in a groaning heap.

Weaponless and breathless, they were quickly surrounded and bound. Rissa should have been angry. Fearful. But the doubt and unease she had begun the morning with was no longer. Something had changed. Something within her, and for the first time since losing Davi, she felt something akin to hope.

CHAPTER 19

"My son is dead!" The Lord's voice rang through the abandoned halls. The servants and guards made themselves scarce to avoid the two men arguing in the throne room.

"Do you forget who you're speaking to?" There was no mistaking the danger in Calis' voice.

Davi peered through the door. Both men had their backs to him.

Lord Eisner stepped back. "Sire, I-"

"Oh, shut up, you ass. We have bigger issues than that fool you called a son."

Eisner's shoulders dropped. "My boy." He shook his head. "I'm sorry, my king. I still can't quite believe Royce is gone."

"Davion." Calis didn't turn.

At the harsh sound of his name, Davi snapped his head up.

"Get in here," his father ordered. "If you're going to lurk, you may as well learn something."

Davi walked toward the men slowly. He'd met Lord Eisner before, and something was off about him. He'd never been able to decipher what it was exactly. He'd betrayed his own king in favor of Davi's father. Maybe that was it. If his loyalty could shift so easily, how would they ever be able to trust him.

Calis pointed one finger at Eisner, his eyes locking with Davi's. "You see what they do to people, son? This man lost his son to Trystan Renauld." He shook his head. "And he didn't even do it himself. He had…" He looked to Eisner. "Who did you say it was?"

"A young man I raised in my own household." Eisner's jaw clenched. "Edric and his sister, Ella, were like my own children."

"I'm sorry, my lord." Davi bowed his head. He didn't like the man, but no one deserved to have their child ripped from them.

His father put a heavy hand on his shoulder and Davi jumped. They hadn't been in the same room since the events in the village. It wasn't for lack of trying. Davion searched for him day after day to plead for Lorelai's release, but he'd been a ghost.

"We received a messenger this morning," his father explained. "There's been a battle in Dreach-Sciene. It seems the young king has more backbone than we'd imagined. He stormed the palace and killed his own uncle. I don't know what kind of person kills their family."

Davi shifted his gaze to the door, unable to meet his father's gaze for a moment longer. Had he forgotten so easily? Davi could still picture it. Lorelai's mother kneeling on the platform. Tears streaming down Lorelai's face.

Was he supposed to act like it never happened? Like his father hadn't had his own sister executed?

Lord Eisner's gruff voice broke through Davi's dangerous thoughts. "After they—" He took a deep breath. "After my son sacrificed himself for our cause, Trystan left Dreach-Sciene in the hands of that dunce, Coille. The messenger said they left with supplies enough for a long journey."

"Why would he leave his palace?" Davi mused. "Everything he needs is behind those walls."

Calis paced across the room, turned, and walked back. "Not everything." One side of his mouth tilted up. "Eisner, did they have any wagons with them?"

"No, sire."

Calis rubbed his chin absently. "Then we don't have long." He turned and marched toward the door. "Take your men and make for the border. Do not intercept them. Do you hear me, Eisner? You are not to engage. Go back to Isenore. Shore up our support across the border. Buy it if you have to. Threaten if you can."

Eisner opened his mouth to protest, but Calis's footsteps echoed down the halls.

Davi ran after his father. "I need to speak with you."

"About Lorelai?" He looked sideways. "Already taken care of. We have bigger things to focus on, Davion. Guests to prepare for."

"Guests?"

Calis flashed him a wicked smile and stopped outside Ramsey's room.

Wait, what did it mean Lorelai was taken care of? His gut churned. He'd seen what his father was capable of.

Before he had a chance to answer, Ramsey's door burst open.

"Your Majesty." Ramsey bowed.

Calis pushed him aside and entered the room. "I have a present for you, sorcerer."

"A present, sire?"

Calis turned to him with the same smile he'd given Davi. "How would you like to meet your grandchildren?"

Ramsey's face paled, and he stumbled back to sit on the edge of his bed. He gripped the bedpost until his knuckles turned white.

"They're coming here?"

Davi's brow furrowed. Here? Why would Trystan Renauld leave the safety of his own kingdom?

He didn't have to wait long for an answer because Ramsey spoke again. "They're coming for me." He closed his eyes and shook his head. Pushing out a breath, he opened them again. "This must mean they're with Lonara and Briggs."

"The Tri-Gard is almost complete." Calis clapped his hands together. "We've been waiting for this."

Steel entered Ramsey's gaze. "I won't help you hurt them."

Anger flashed across Calis' face. "I don't need your help. I didn't back then and I don't now."

Ramsey sighed in understanding. "This is about her. About Marissa."

"Don't speak that name to me!"

Davi flicked his eyes from his father to Ramsey.

"I told you it wasn't healthy not to grieve for her." Ramsey's eyes pinched in sadness.

"Why would I grieve for the woman who betrayed me?"

"Because you loved her. You've been denying it for many years, but I knew you two back then. You were in love with my daughter."

Calis yelled something unintelligible and twisted toward the door. He didn't leave, but his back heaved with heavy breaths.

Ramsey's gaze found Davi in silent communication. Had this been for Davi's benefit? What did Ramsey want him to see?

When Calis finally got his breath under control, he spoke in a low, measured tone. "Marissa Kane was nothing to me but a traitor. Her children are nothing but the enemy. When they arrive, we will welcome them."

Surely Davi hadn't heard him right.

Calis sucked in a breath. "And then we will destroy them."

He walked from the room without another word, leaving Davi behind.

When Davi moved toward the door, Ramsey's voice stopped him. "Just a minute, boy."

Davi turned and crossed his arms. He'd never been alone with the sorcerer. His father hadn't allowed it.

The relationship between his father and Ramsey confused him. Ramsey was a prisoner, but there was a familiarity between the two. And Davi had never seen a prisoner treated so well. His father relied on Ramsey more than anyone else. Even his own son.

It reminded him how little of his father he actually knew.

"Speak," Davi said.

Ramsey chuckled. "You're just like your father." Despite his laughter, a bitterness hung in his words. "You have questions. I can see them in your eyes."

"My father loved your daughter?" He couldn't picture his father loving anyone.

Ramsey sighed. "There was a time when Marissa was Calis' world. They grew up together and were the best of friends. Your father wasn't always the man he is today. As a child, he was kind. Marissa was very fond of him."

"Then what happened?"

"War. It changes people. My girl was a general, and she thrived on it. Not on battle, but on leadership, independence. The first time Calis ever killed a man, he cried."

Davi's jaw dropped open.

Ramsey chuckled. "I can still see the look on his face." He shook his head wistfully and his smiled dropped. "So his father had him beaten with magic and then made him execute some prisoners himself. Marissa fought for Dreach-Dhoun for the first few years of the war. I remember the day she left so clearly. It was both the best and worst day of my life. We'd seen Calis grow colder and more ruthless. When he became king, Marissa knew she had to leave before he could force her onto the throne beside him."

Ramsey's voice dropped off for a moment. "My granddaughter looks like her. All these years we've been using blood magic to watch through your eyes have been like having my girl returned to me."

Davi's face scrunched in concentration. "You keep mentioning a granddaughter but there was only Trystan."

Ramsey stood and patted him on the back. "You'll meet her soon."

Davi couldn't help the sadness he felt for the man. He'd lost his daughter and been held prisoner most of his life.

"I'm sorry about Marissa." Davi trained his eyes on his feet. "And what has to happen to your grandchildren." He rubbed his face, giving his head a slight shake. "I want my revenge, but it doesn't seem so important anymore. When does it end? Lord Eisner was here tonight.

He lost his son. Lorelai killed Trystan's father. We're going after Trystan. I may not remember a lot of things, but I do know each time one of us strikes, it creates this hole. It's not just about the people who die, but also the ones who lose them." He raised his eyes to Ramsey as Lorelai's mother's prophecy suddenly came back to him. She said Dreach-Dhoun was going to lose. "I fear none of us will stop until we have nothing left."

Ramsey held his gaze, and the silence stretched between them.

Finally, a breath rushed from the sorcerer. "I was wrong, Prince Davion. You're nothing like your father."

Davi didn't have all of his memories yet, but he was beginning to think the memories didn't make him who he was. Since the night in the village, he'd felt like himself. Like Davion. Not like a prince or a lost boy returned home.

Was his aunt's prophecy real? If Dreach-Dhoun had no chance in the war to come, why were they hurtling toward it with alarming speed?

The royal guard trained from dusk 'til dawn. The army was camped only a few leagues away. If Dreach-Sciene attacked first, magic would be able to play its part. But his father prepared for a long trek into Dreach-Sciene. They wouldn't survive a battle against the larger kingdom if they couldn't use magic.

An ache throbbed in his skull and he rubbed his temples as he turned the corner to head toward his rooms.

His breath caught in his throat. Leaning against his door was his cousin. He ran the length of the hall and skidded to a stop in front of her. She'd been kept in the dungeon for over a week. Her clothes were caked in grime. Dark circles ringed her puffy eyes. A sickly gray pallor tinged her skin.

"Lorelai." He gripped her arm as she tried to straighten and almost fell.

"Hey Dav." She latched onto him as she stumbled again. "I couldn't stand the thought of going to my own rooms."

Without warning, he crushed her to him, her betrayal forgotten. She'd only been protecting her mother. "I'm so glad you're okay."

"Okay is relative."

The stench wafting off her hit his nose, but he didn't let go.

"Davi, I'm not going to collapse if you let me go."

He chuckled and reached behind her to push the door open before helping her through. He led her to the sitting area, and she practically fell onto the couch.

Davi stood in front of her, his fingers clenched together. "Cousin, I-I'm sorry. My father shouldn't—"

A dark look morphed across Lorelai's features, but she cut him off with a wave of her hand. "That was hardly the first time he's punished me by putting me in a cell."

He sat heavily in a chair across from her and leaned forward with his elbows on his knees. "Your mother—"

"Don't, Davi." She shook her head, her filthy blond hair falling over one shoulder.

"It's just..." He focused on his hands. "I'm sorry, okay? It sucks. My father had your mother executed. How am I supposed to get over that? How are we supposed to move on?"

"Watch your words, Davion. They sound rather close to treason."

His eyes widened. "I didn't mean... of course, I'm loyal to my father. I mean, the guy searched for me for fifteen years and sent part of his army to save me. We're family. But that doesn't mean I can't be disappointed in him."

"That's exactly what it means." She shifted uncomfortably. "I know what you're feeling. I went through the same thing. You thought your father was better than the rest of us. Good. Now you're realizing he lives in as much darkness as anyone else. The first time he ordered me to do something I didn't agree with, I tried to run because I didn't understand. Once you give your loyalty to Calis Bearne, he owns it. If you even try to break your oaths, you will pay and so will everyone you love."

Davi leaned back. He hadn't truly been reconsidering his loyalty to his own father. But who did he have that he loved? Lorelai. He met her gaze and knew he'd do anything to protect her.

"He's my father, Lorelai." Davi looked away. "I'd never turn my back on him."

She hummed in the back of her throat, but it was cut off by a horn blaring through the stone walls.

Davi jumped to his feet. "Stay here."

"Not on your life. Help me up."

He only hesitated a moment before bending to let her wrap an arm around his neck and helped her to her feet.

"I think I can walk on my own," she said.

"Are you sure you don't want to rest and eat… maybe bathe?"

"Davion Bearne, are you telling me I stink?" She shook her head. "That horn went off twice. It means a border regiment has arrived. They're the highest order of the guard and don't often leave the border."

"They're here."

"Who?" She looked to him curiously.

"The king of Dreach-Sciene."

He hadn't thought it was possible for her to get any paler.

"T-the k-king," she stammered.

Davi nodded. "Why else would bordermen leave their post? Trystan Renauld has come."

"Trystan." The breath rushed out of her. "Oh, right. Marcus is dead. I was there." She closed her eyes. "Let's go."

The halls buzzed with activity. Everyone was curious about the horn and what it meant. Davi kept a close eye on Lorelai, but his mind was elsewhere as he walked toward the meeting he'd wanted since waking up without his memories.

Trystan Renauld kept him prisoner for fifteen years. But the burn for revenge had lessened.

Guards lined the courtyard and Davi stopped at his father's side.

"It's a great day, son." Calis grinned.

The sun beat down on them mercilessly as the bordermen rode through the gates atop their tall steeds. Cloaks of fur were wrapped around their hulking frames. Many of them were stationed in the mountain section of the border.

Sweat dripped down Davi's face. They must have been burning up all bundled like they were.

The last four horses appeared with figures tied into the saddles. Davi's eyes drifted over them. Avery. He remembered her beating him with a sword, humiliating him over the years. Alixa. She'd been the sharp-tongued brat who had betrayed her own father.

Trystan was next. Even with ties around his wrists, he sat tall, refusing to look away from his captors.

The last figure had flaming red hair that covered her face. Her slight frame was hunched over angrily. She shifted and her hair fell back.

Davi sucked in a breath. He'd seen those eyes before. He couldn't pull the memory free but he didn't take his eyes from her as she was yanked from the horse. Her feet hit the ground and her knees buckled. She fell forward.

Calis walked toward them. "Already kneeling. Seems you know your place, girl."

When she looked up at him, fire flashed in her eyes.

He reached out to push her hair back.

"Don't touch me," she spit, snapping her teeth at his hand.

Trystan tried to run to his sister, but two burly guards held his arms. "Leave her alone."

"Ah, yes. The great Trystan Renauld." Calis straightened and faced Trystan. "It's a pleasure to finally meet you."

Davi had forgotten Lorelai's presence until she slid her arm down and stepped in front of him.

"You!" Trystan yelled, trying to yank his arms free as his gaze found Lorelai. "We took you in. What did my father ever do to you?"

Trystan managed to break free and ran at Lorelai before anyone could stop him. His hands were still tied, but that didn't stop him.

Enough. Davi shoved Lorelai behind him with a sudden movement before Trystan collided with him.

Trystan bounced off Davi and stumbled back, his eyes wide. "Davi?"

Davi advanced. "Do not touch my cousin."

"Cousin?" Trystan's haunted eyes searched his face. He stepped forward and raised his tied hands to touch Davi's face. "Is it really you?"

"Davi?" another voice said numbly.

The girl with fire-kissed hair climbed to her feet. A guard held her back as another took control of Trystan. All fight drained from the pair.

"Davi?" she said again, shaking her head. "No, you're dead. I saw you die."

Davi walked toward her, craning his neck to look into her emerald eyes. Familiarity struck him, but he didn't understand why. He cocked his head.

Her eyes shone with unshed tears. She gave him a tentative smile.

"It's you," she whispered.

"Who are you?" he asked.

She reeled back, agony etched across her face. "Davi," she pleaded. "Tell me you're really standing in front of me. That I'm not dreaming."

"I don't know you." He turned on his heel and left the courtyard behind. He needed a moment to clear his mind before his father summoned him as he knew he would.

A sob echoed behind him, soon covered up by the activity of the guards.

Those eyes.

How could he have ever forgotten them?

He may not know the girl, but the despair swirling in the depths of her gaze was enough to tell him he should.

CHAPTER 20

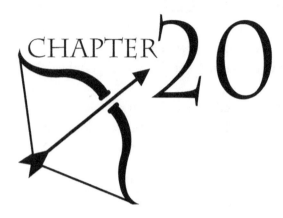

A rough hand prodded Rissa forward but she couldn't feel it. Her feet stumbled and moved of their own accord as the world around her blurred.

Noises faded to the background until the only sound in her ears was her own breath, rasping through her lungs.

"Don't touch her," someone screamed as strong fingers closed around her arms.

"Trystan," another voice called. "Don't fight them. Not yet."

Alixa. Trystan.

Rissa shook her head.

Davi.

He'd been there right in front of her. Close enough to touch. No. Impossible. Davi was dead.

Soldiers formed up around them, an imposing force. Their booted steps echoed off the cold stone and Rissa shivered.

Whoever that man had been, it couldn't be Dav. He'd looked at her without recognition in his eyes. Calis was playing some cruel joke with his magic.

A guard jerked her forward until she was right in front of the king of Dreach-Dhoun, the man who'd almost destroyed her kingdom and ordered her father's death.

Dark eyes scanned her from head to toe and widened. Hardening herself, she lifted her chin, refusing to cower. Trystan shouted something else before a guard covered his mouth, but she didn't hear him as the dark king drew her in.

He was a beautiful portrait, cold and unfeeling.

He lifted a hand and ran his fingertips down her cheek. She forced herself to remain still.

"It's remarkable," he whispered.

Rissa held her breath.

"Sire." One of the soldiers stepped forward. "We have delivered the prisoners."

"I can see that," Calis snapped. "Your men may return to the border."

The soldier barked out an order, and the bordermen marched out of the courtyard, leaving Rissa, Trystan, Alixa, and Avery in the hands of the more refined royal guard.

Calis continued to stare until his eyes caught on the golden disk at Rissa's throat.

She swallowed hard as his hand traveled the length of her neck, stopping at the chain of her mother's necklace. He lifted it off her chest and pushed out a breath.

Ghosts swam in his eyes.

Lorelai put a delicate hand on his arm and he dropped the necklace.

"Uncle," she said. "What are your orders?"

Rissa's eyes drifted to the woman who'd killed her father and wanted to laugh. The seer had seen better days. Filthy clothing and ratty hair were just the beginning. She deserved all of it.

"I see what stabbing kings in their sleep gets you," Rissa spat.

Lorelai looked away.

"Figures." Rissa jerked her head away from another touch from Calis. "Hands off, asshole."

A smile split Calis' face and he laughed. "You have her spirit as well as her looks."

"Who?"

"Marissa Kane."

Marissa? Her mother? But her last name wasn't Kane. Was it? Rissa knew nothing of her mother's life before she married her father except that she'd been in the Dreach-Dhoun army, but something Briggs once said came back to her. He'd called her Marissa Kane as well.

"Oh dear, it seems like your father had his secrets." He turned to Lorelai. "Niece, inform both Ramsey and my son that they are expected in the throne room. Then, for earth's sake, get yourself a bath."

Lorelai bobbed her head and entered the palace.

Calis looked to his guards. "Untie them. They're our guests."

Rissa rubbed her wrists as soon as the ropes were cut. Trystan ran to her as Calis turned to walk inside.

"Are you okay?" he asked.

"I can still feel his hand on me." She wiped at her cheek. "We were right. He knew we were coming and was prepared. Why didn't he just throw us in the dungeons?"

"Rissa." Trystan gripped her shoulders. "Slow down. Didn't you see what I saw? Da-"

"And what did he mean about Marissa Kane? Did he mean Mom? He must have if he thinks I look like her. Did you see the way he was looking at me? I feel dirty."

"Rissa," he hissed. "What is wrong with you?"

"For starters, I'm now a prisoner in an impregnable castle in the middle of an enemy kingdom full of magic."

"Didn't you see him?"

"Who?"

"Davi!" He took a step away from her.

"Move it," a guard ordered, pressing them through the door. Arched stone ceilings greeted them in the wide hall.

Rissa leaned close to Trystan. "Davi is dead, brother."

"Somehow, he's not. He was there. I'd recognize him anywhere."

"I thought I saw him too, but it was just a manifestation of what I wanted to see. That man didn't even know me. Calis is messing with our heads somehow."

The guards ushered them into a cavernous room. Velvet carpet spread before them in a sea of red, stopping at the edge of steps that led up to a wooden throne.

Calis waved his guards away before turning to Trystan. "You'd be wise not to consider doing anything I don't like just because my guards aren't here. Trust me, boy, I am more powerful than anyone you've ever met."

To Trystan's credit, he didn't back away from the other king's harsh stare.

Remnants of the magic Rissa had felt since crossing the border sat just underneath her skin, but it was only pieces. Inside these walls, she couldn't draw on more and she didn't know how to release the little she had.

Calis looked at something over Rissa's shoulder and smiled. "Ah, Ramsey."

Rissa turned. Trystan, Alixa, and Avery did the same.

The final Tri-Gard member stood in the doorway, his eyes rounded. He was young, much younger than Rissa had anticipated, but she knew the Tri-Gard had the ability to hide their age, the choice to remain forever young. She'd forgotten that as she traveled with Briggs who seemed ancient by comparison.

Ramsey Kane's blond hair had hints of red. His fair face grew pale.

This was the man who'd betrayed them all those years before; who'd forced the other two Tri-Gard members into draining Dreach-Sciene's magic.

Ramsey Kane.

Kane.

The name struck Rissa. "Marissa Kane," she whispered. Trystan caught her words and stared on in shock. The man standing before them—the sorcerer who'd allied with Calis Bearne—was their grandfather. How had they not realized this before?

Rissa rubbed her mother's necklace and a laugh burst out of her. Then another. She clutched her stomach, unable to stop. Their grandfather looked young enough to be their brother. They were descended from a Tri-Gard member. It made so much sense now. Lonara's love for their mother. Briggs' knowledge of her. Their father's secrets.

Trystan reached for her, but she shrugged him off. "No." She laughed again, the dam of her emotions finally breaking free.

Ramsey walked forward, concern in his fathomless eyes.

"Don't come any closer," Rissa yelled before devolving into another fit of laughter. There was no humor in any of these revelations but if she stopped, she'd tear her own hair out.

"Shut up, girl," Calis ordered.

She couldn't.

"Ri." There was a caution in Trystan's voice.

"I said shut up!"

A blast of power hit Rissa square in the chest, stealing the air from her lungs and sending her flying across the room. Her scream cut off as she passed Ramsey and slammed into someone else. They both went sprawling to the ground, Rissa collapsing across his chest.

Her limbs wouldn't work for a long moment before she finally pushed off the man whose presence saved her from crashing into a much harder surface.

Catching her breath, she hovered over him and opened her eyes.

Had she passed out? That was the only explanation for her staring directly into the eyes she knew so well.

"Davi," she breathed.

He stilled. "You're crushing me."

She'd have given anything to hear that voice again. "Say something else."

Confusion clouded his face. "Get off."

Her lips curled up, and she leaned down to press them against his. For one blissful moment, nothing else existed.

The burning started low in her chest before another blast of power struck her and her body jerked off him.

She lay still for a stunned moment, watching as he got to his feet and brushed his pants off. He walked toward Calis without another glance.

"I see you've been listening to me, son." Calis grinned.

"Keeping magic stored inside me does come in handy." He stopped at his father's side and turned to face them.

Someone extended a hand to Rissa, and she lifted her eyes to Ramsey's. Her hand was small in his as he pulled her to her feet.

"Don't let them see it affect you, my dear," he whispered. "Calis will use your emotions against you. And Davion…" He shook his head sadly. "Don't blame him for any of this."

"What's wrong with him?"

Ramsey only pointed to his head in answer before leading her back to the others.

Calis waved a hand, and the doors shut with a resounding thud. The torches along the wall flickered and the flames grew, illuminating the shadowy room.

Calis walked to a table along the wall where pitchers sat surrounded by ornate golden cups. "Wine?" he asked. He poured it into cups without waiting for an answer and passed them out. "You've never tasted wine like this in Dreach-Sciene. Without magic in the soil, they can't get the same flavor."

No one responded, so he continued to talk. "I'm disappointed in you. I expected Briggs and Lonara to join you on this ill-advised journey."

Trystan's face reddened and his fingers clenched around the wine goblet. Anger rose in him and as he saw Calis' smug face, he threw his cup against the wall. Burgundy liquid streamed down the walls. "Do you think I'm an idiot?"

Davi lurched forward, but his father held him back.

"I am sorry, young king," Calis said. "I do not mean to offend. Of course, you wouldn't bring me your greatest assets."

Trystan trained his eyes on Davi. "Do you have something to say to me, brathair?"

Davi clenched his jaw. "I am not your brother. You kept me prisoner for fifteen years."

Prisoner?

Davi had been a part of the family.

"Dav," Rissa pleaded. "Explain."

"I don't have to explain anything to you. I don't even know you."

Rissa put her hands on the top of her head and spun away to avoid their heavy stares as she broke right down the middle. What was wrong with him? She clutched at her throat, struggling for air. Her head shook. "You do." She closed her eyes. "Davi, you know me. I…" She shut her quivering jaw.

"This explains so much," Trystan said.

"Speak up, boy." Calis took a sip of his wine. "If you have a reason for spilling the wine your host so graciously gave you, I'd like to hear it."

"It's all been planned. Us. My father. Davion. It was Lorelai who convinced my father to take Davi in when we thought he was just an orphan boy."

"You mean when Marcus Renauld kidnapped me?" Davi snapped.

"Is that really what you think? Dav, that man was like a father to you."

"I have a father."

Rissa faced them once again as red crept up her cheeks. "Shut up." She ran at him. "I'll kill you, Davion." She collided with him and connected her fist to his stomach. "I'll do it. Don't think I won't. We took you in." She hit him again. "You were family, you ass. Family!" She swung once more, but he grabbed her fist.

"I am not your family." He raised his hand to strike her with magic. Before he could, Trystan pulled her back, wrapping her in his arms.

"Calm down, Ri," he said.

She pushed away from him. "Like you? Do you care about any of this? We've lost, Trystan. I don't know how we ever thought we'd be able to get Ramsey Kane out of here. We're children playing at saving the world. Well, guess what? We failed."

She held her wrists out to Calis. "Tie me up, take me to a cell. I don't care. But I'm done talking to you." Her eyes found Davi once more, expecting to see more indignation or hatred. Instead, there was only confusion.

Calis sighed. "We're finished for tonight, but tomorrow is another day." He jerked his hand, and the door opened. Two guards entered. "Show our guests to their rooms."

The stories of the Dreach-Dhoun dungeons were widespread, but those dank cells weren't where they were led.

The four of them were separated and a silent guard led Rissa to a room down a long hall. The doors opened, and she narrowed her eyes at the opulence. They were prisoners, yet the plush carpets and silk draperies spoke of honored guests. She shook her head and shrugged off her cloak. The guard left and the sound of a lock turning echoed through the room.

She shed her travel-stained clothing piece by piece on the way to the four-poster bed. After dragging her weary bones onto the soft mattress, she slipped under the covers and curled up on her side.

I don't know you.

I am not your family.

Don't blame Davion.

A tear tracked down her cheek and she wiped it away angrily. She'd dreamed of Davi's return. She'd begged and pleaded to have him back, to be able to look into his eyes once more.

But not like this.

He was the son of their enemy, but not even that would matter if he looked at her like he used to.

That Davi was gone. It seemed a stranger now walked around in Davi's body.

Her tears fell too quickly to continue wiping them away, and she sniffled. Since Davi died, none of it had felt real. She hadn't cried because that would be admitting he was truly gone.

Her body shook.

Her Davi was truly dead.

Tears dampened her pillow.

"Dav," she whispered, his name shaking on her lips. "What did they do to you?"

CHAPTER 21

It wasn't a prison cell. That was the first thought to enter Trystan's mind when he woke. They'd been in Dreach-Dhoun for three days but hadn't been taken to the dungeons. Instead, the room he'd been put in surrounded him in luxury.

It was so unexpected, he didn't know what to think.

As his mind cleared of sleep, he sat up, running a hand down his bare chest. The bruises from their capture at the border stretched down his side, sickly yellow streaks against his pale skin.

Three days and there'd been no word from Calis. He hadn't been allowed out of his room to see his sister, Alixa, or Avery.

And Davi... what was he supposed to do with the knowledge his best friend, his brother, had been in Dreach-Dhoun the entire time they'd mourned him? But he wasn't the boy he'd grown up with, was he?

A breath shuddered as it passed his lips.

This room might not look like a prison, but it was a cage all the same.

He pushed silk sheets from his legs and stood as the door opened. A servant bustled in, balancing a tray on her hands. Every day was the same. They brought him ample amounts of food and drink, filled the bronze tub with warm water for his bath, and didn't say a word.

"You," Trystan said.

The servant startled but turned her back on him and set the tray on the table.

"Why am I here?" Trystan asked. "Please, tell me something. What does Calis plan to do with us? Where is my sister? Or my other friends? I need information."

The serving girl's shoulders stilled and Trystan stepped closer, feeling as if she wanted to speak. She gave a tiny shake of her head and spun on her heel to leave. Two men entered, carrying buckets of water. They didn't look at Trystan as they filled the tub and then they too were gone. The lock groaned loudly as it shifted into place.

Trystan sighed and sank into a chair in front of the tray to pick at the food. He'd barely eaten anything they'd left over the last few days. His stomach rumbled in approval as he choked down some bread. There were two pitchers. One of wine and one of water. Opting for the water, he lifted it to pour himself a drink and his eyes caught on a scrap of paper that was stuck to the condensation on the copper bottom.

After pulling it free, he set the pitcher down. A scraping noise sounded at his door, almost as if his lock was moving again, but when he jerked his head up, no one entered.

Focusing on the paper once again, he tried to make out the words. The ink had been smudged by water and he squinted his eyes.

Turn right at the end of the hall and go through the door. I'll be waiting.

It wasn't signed. Was this a trap? Could he afford to ignore it? The answer came instantly. He had to risk it. If this person could help them... His eyes flicked to the door. But he was locked in. Wasn't he?

Slowly, he got to his feet and crossed the room. Setting his hand on the lever, he pushed, and the door opened.

Not stopping to question it, he stepped into the hall. His guard lay slumped against the wall. Trystan moved suddenly, but the guard's eyes didn't track him. They were vacant as if he slept with his eyes open.

He glanced down the darkened hallway. Were Rissa and Alixa nearby? He couldn't go banging on doors. Instead, he did as the note bade him.

The door he found led to a garden, or what used to be a garden. Flashbacks of the palace in Dreach-Sciene hit him as he stepped outside. The gardens of his childhood home had always struggled to live. But this one looked as if it had been drained of any and all life. Twisted trees stood along the high walls, their bark cracking and crumbling. Dead grass crunched under Trystan's bare feet. Flowers lay withered.

"Sad, isn't it?" A voice said.

Trystan scanned the area until his eyes landed on Ramsey Kane's small frame.

"You," he accused.

"Me." Ramsey nodded, straightening from where he crouched beside a gnarled bush.

Trystan's eyes darted around. He couldn't trust the third Tri-Gard member who'd chosen loyalty to Calis over his own daughter—Trystan's mother.

He'd had days of solitude to come to terms with his heritage and it still burned deep in his gut when he thought of Ramsey betraying Dreach-Sciene. Betraying magic.

"Calis isn't here, son. It's just me."

"I'm not your son," Trystan spat.

Ramsey looked to the sky and rubbed a hand across his face. Was he… nervous? The great Tri-Gard member couldn't look him in the eye.

"You're right," he finally said. "You are my grandson."

Trystan stepped forward. "If you think that means you have any claim over me…"

"Calm down, boy."

Trystan seethed. Ramsey might be ancient, but he looked no older than Trystan himself. He didn't get to talk down to him.

"We're done here." Trystan prepared to enter the palace once more. "I should have known better than to trust that note. You are nothing more than a sad man who forsook his sacred calling. Magic was yours to protect and instead, you drained it from Dreach-Sciene, forcing Briggs and Lonara to help you."

Ramsey froze for a moment before a booming laugh burst out of him. He held his stomach and laughed again. When he finally caught his breath, he fixed Trystan with a withering stare. "You have so much to learn, young king. Do you honestly think I could force Briggs and Lonara to do anything?"

When Trystan didn't respond, Ramsey shook his head. "Please, stay. We have much to talk about. Calis is out inspecting the army today so he won't find us."

Trystan's mind warred between curiosity of the man who shared his bloodline and hatred for the man who allied himself with Calis. His shoulders dropped, and he walked toward a bench before dropping onto it.

Ramsey's gaze swept over him. "You could have at least put on shoes… or a shirt."

Trystan glanced down at himself. He'd been in such a hurry to find some answers, he hadn't stopped to dress. He was about to have his first ever conversation with his grandfather and he was half-naked with sleep-mussed hair.

But he didn't care. Not when so many questions swirled through his mind.

"I can practically see your brain working." Ramsey chuckled. "Ask me what you want to know. I'll hold nothing back. I know what you think of me, but I'm not the evil man the stories make me out to be."

Trystan flattened his hair and focused on a patch of dead growth. "What happened here? I thought Dreach-Dhoun was supposed to be full of magic, full of life. But I don't feel it. Not like I did outside the palace. And everything is so…"

"Dead?" Ramsey finished. "Magic wielders are supposed to be conscious of the earth. Most people aren't able to draw much power at once so it's not an issue, but occasionally there are some. When too much power is taken at once, it steals all life from the ground." He gestured around them. "This was the price of saving Calis' son."

Trystan sucked in a breath. "Davi—"

"He was gone. Calis brought him back."

"That's not possible." Trystan shook his head. "Briggs told me magic can't bring someone back to life."

At the mention of Briggs, Ramsey's face darkened for a moment before the look disappeared. Trystan watched him carefully.

"Most magic cannot, that is true. But I've never seen anyone with the power of Calis. Combine that with my crystal that's in his possession and he can accomplish the impossible."

Fear shot through Trystan. How were they supposed to escape from a man like that, let alone beat him in battle? It made everything they'd gone through so far seem trivial in comparison.

"But Davi didn't come back the same, did he?"

Ramsey shifted his eyes away. "His memories have been altered."

"He's not the same man I knew."

Ramsey met Trystan's gaze sharply. "He is. I've been watching you all for many years. Calis used his son to see through his eyes. Davi may still be in there. The memories don't make the man. I have hope for him yet."

"How? Davion looked at Ri as if she was nothing. If he was still in there, he couldn't break her like that."

"He doesn't remember her." Ramsey's voice was so quiet, Trystan almost didn't hear him.

Trystan shot to his feet. "Not possible. Not for Davi."

"It's true."

"How? How did he suddenly lose all thoughts of the one person who made him whole?"

"It was me." Ramsey paced from one side of the garden to the other.

"I have been made to do a lot of things in my life that I'm not proud of."

Trystan fell back onto the bench. "You took them? You stole her from him? How could you? All these years, the people of Dreach-Sciene assumed you were a prisoner. Even after you stole the magic. We didn't want to believe a member of the Tri-Gard could be in league with Calis."

"I was protecting you and your sister."

Trystan buried his face in his hands. "That makes no sense. Protecting us from what? You? You sit here at Calis Bearne's side and call that protecting us?"

"You don't understand."

"Make me understand."

"I can't." Ramsey pushed a breath out through his teeth. "Not yet."

"That's not good enough."

"If I tell you what I know, you'll never save Dreach-Sciene."

"Sounds like a load of bull to me."

"It's not," a feminine voice said.

Trystan lifted his gaze to Lorelai as she walked toward them. His back stiffened.

"Ramsey," he said through clenched teeth. "What is going on?"

Ramsey put a hand on his shoulder. Trystan suspected it was to keep him from leaving.

Lorelai hugged her arms across her chest and shifted from foot to foot. When they'd met in Dreach-Sciene, Trystan had been entranced by the eerily beautiful seer. She'd had a confidence and calm his father had loved.

At the thought of his father, pain stabbed through him and he looked away, his lips curling in disgust.

Lorelai coughed uncomfortably. Seemed she too had changed since they'd seen each other last.

"Trystan, I believe you know Lorelai Bearne."

Trystan grunted and his hard eyes found hers. "Do you still see his face?"

She covered her mouth with her hand.

He continued. "Because I do. I imagine it. His death. He was alone in his room with only the person who betrayed him. He should have been surrounded by those he loved. My father deserved more than a knife in the middle of the night."

She bit her lip. "I see him every night." He hadn't expected her to answer.

Ramsey gripped Trystan tighter. "Lorelai isn't who you think she is. She's going to help us."

Trystan regarded his grandfather. "Since when is there an us?"

"Since you need me, boy. That's why you came, is it not? It's why you allowed yourself to be captured by the most powerful man in the world. I'm guessing old Briggs told you I could get us out of here. I'd have escaped a long time ago if I could have been assured of your safety. Calis has had you watched since you came out of the womb. But now you're here and it's time to see what freedom tastes like once again."

"Are you joking?" Trystan pointed to Lorelai. "We can't trust her."

"On the contrary, she is the only one we can trust."

This was what Trystan had been waiting for, so why did he hesitate? Something didn't seem right. If he had his way, he'd challenge Lorelai to a duel and fight for his father's honor. The honor she'd taken from him so brutally.

"Why is she helping us?" he asked Ramsey.

Ramsey shook his head. "Your arrogance makes you think your people are the only ones harmed by Calis. Lorelai has experienced her fair share of tragedies. You are not alone in that."

Lorelai studied her feet.

Did he have a choice?

He sighed. "What do we do?"

"You wait," Lorelai said. "My uncle may be away, but Davion is still here." She sighed. "I love my cousin, but he won't understand. Not about this. I was once where he is now."

Trystan couldn't help himself. "What changed?"

"Your father... he didn't deserve..." She shook her head sadly. "But then my mother..."

Ramsey gave her a sympathetic smile, but Trystan didn't know what the hell she was talking about. Lorelai had killed his father. Of course, he hadn't deserved it, but she hadn't considered that when she was picking up the blade. And her mother? Calis wasn't said to have any siblings, but if Lorelai was his niece, that must have been false. What happened to her?

Neither Ramsey nor Lorelai seemed primed to give him any answers.

"Come." Ramsey pulled him to his feet. "We must get you back to your room before anyone notices you're missing."

"Wait," Trystan pulled away from Ramsey's grasp, not quite sure if he should trust them with what he was about to reveal. Did he even have a choice? He thought back to that room he'd be returning to. The palace was a fortress. He had no hope of finding his sister or getting to the crystal in Calis' possession. What would the rest of his friends tell him to do?

Find a way out of Dreach-Dhoun at any cost.

"Lonara gave me this." He pulled the crystal from an inside pocket of his trousers. "It's a fake, of course. A replica of your crystal. She said we need to exchange the two, and to trust in you. I'm thinking either of you will have better luck getting closer to Calis with that than I will."

Trystan dropped the crystal into Ramsey's outstretched hand. Ramsey studied it with interest.

"It's a perfect imitation. Lonara has done well. We will handle this."

Trystan rubbed the back of his neck, silently questioning his decision. "I still don't understand how you think we'll get away from the palace and out of Dreach-Dhoun. Before we came, Briggs led us to believe it would be easy, but have you seen this place?"

The look from before flashed across Ramsey's face. "Don't believe everything the old man tells you." He led Trystan to the door. "As to your question. Nothing we do will be easy, but we don't really have a choice, do we?"

Ramsey ushered Trystan through the door. His words still echoed in Trystan's mind as he spotted the sleeping guard once again. With a shake of his head he pushed into his room before the guard could wake.

As soon as the door slammed shut behind him, his eyes widened. Standing near the window looking out over the palace grounds was Davion.

CHAPTER 22

Without turning, the prince of Dreach-Dhoun spoke. "It seems we have some traitors in the palace."

"Dav," Trystan croaked.

It was still surreal, seeing someone he'd thought was gone forever.

But when Davi turned, the look in his eyes was something Trystan didn't recognize.

Trystan took a step back.

"My father is going to punish that guard and the sorcerer who put him to sleep." Davi shook his head, his face darkening. "My own cousin. You've turned her. Twisted her thoughts. Ramsey doesn't surprise me, but Lorelai would never betray us again."

Us. Them. Him and Calis. He was the dark king's son.

Wait. Again? She'd betrayed Calis once before?

Davi tapped his fingers against his leg. "My father released her from the dungeons and this is how she repays him."

Lorelai was in the dungeons? Trystan wanted to ask why, but knew he wouldn't get an answer.

Davi pulled at his dark hair. "Lorelai wouldn't do this." He hung his head. "She knows what it would mean for her. How could she?"

Trystan wanted to go to him, to tell him it was going to be okay.

Instinct. That's all it was. He'd spent his life wanting to protect Davi. He clenched his fist at his side to prevent himself from doing something stupid like reaching out.

Davi's eyes hardened as he lifted his head. "You." He lurched forward. "This is all your fault." He shoved Trystan back. "Everything is because of you!"

Trystan couldn't refute that. It was true. Davi had only been taken because he'd saved Trystan.

Davi wasn't finished and his voice rose with each word. "Fifteen years. Was that not enough for you? You took me from the one place I belonged and imprisoned me."

"Dav, you belonged with us."

"Don't lie to me! I know everything. My memories were gone at first but a lot of them have returned. You and your father were cruel. I was just a boy, and you kept me locked up." He shook with rage.

"That's not true," Trystan pleaded. "You're my brother and Rissa-"

He didn't get to finish the statement before Davi's fist crashed into his face and he stumbled back.

"I don't know her!" Davi's face reddened.

Trystan touched his cheek gingerly. "I think you do." He stepped forward. "I think you know everything in that head of yours is a lie. You're one of us Davi, whether you want to be or not. You'll always be family. You can't make us stop loving you."

"No." Davi lunged and Trystan ducked out of the way.

"This feels familiar," Trystan said.

"Because you used to beat your prisoner," Davi spat.

"Because we learned to fight together." Trystan jumped forward and shoved Davi back. "Fight me. Hit me. Do whatever you need to do. I can take it."

Davi stepped back with a growl and ran a hand through his hair. It was a quirk so utterly familiar that Trystan almost laughed. How did they get here? The orphan boy who'd been raised right alongside him watched him as a predator watches its prey.

"I won't lose control," Davi said to himself, breathing in deeply. His body relaxed. "I have no choice but to tell my father about Lorelai and Ramsey's treachery. It's going to break his heart." He shook his head mumbling, "and mine."

"Dav, please, think about this. You don't have to tell him."

Davi shook his head. "You may have no loyalty, but some of us do. I love my cousin, but my father is king."

Trystan stumbled back until his legs hit the edge of the bed and he sat. There'd been a time when Davi was unquestionably loyal to Marcus Renauld. When Trystan imagined being king, the image had always included his best friend by his side. Now Davi stood beside another king.

"I'm stationing a new guard outside your door to prevent anymore wanderings." Davi's voice was cold. "At least until my father decides what to do with you."

Davi crossed the room and when the door slammed behind him, Trystan laid back on the bed, staring up at the ceiling. His face still stung, but it was nothing compared to the anger ripping him apart from the inside out.

Maybe it would have been better if Davi died like they'd thought he had. Now Calis Bearne was even destroying the memory of him. Soon, there'd be nothing left between them.

His fingers trailed over his bruised skin. At least it was proof. They were still alive.

Davi would tell Calis of Lorelai's betrayal, but maybe Ramsey had another plan.

One step at a time.

First: Save Dreach-Sciene.

Second: Save it again.

Third: Kill Calis Bearne.

CHAPTER 23

Davi fidgeted as he leaned against the wall outside the one room he shouldn't be visiting. What on earth's name was he doing there?

Two guards stood to the sides of the door.

He pressed up against the cold stone and wiped his sweaty hands on his pants. His father had summoned him that evening for the first time since he'd returned. Davi was certain it was to tell him of Lorelai's betrayal.

When he hadn't mentioned it, why did Davi keep quiet?

Because he knew what his father would do to her.

He released a long breath. Rissa was on the other side of that door. The fiery-haired princess he couldn't get out of his mind.

"You okay, your Highness?" the guard outside her door asked, looking sideways at him. "You look like you're about to keel over."

"Fine," Davi pushed out. "I'm... fine."

The guard chuckled. When they weren't in his father's presence, many of the Dreach-Dhoun soldiers dropped their stoic countenances. As soon as the king appeared, they closed themselves off, not even letting a single smile through. Davi assumed they'd seen too many of their comrades punished when his father was in one of his foul moods.

He hated that side of the man. If he hadn't seen something else in him, he'd be in a very different place. But his father loved him. He was sure of it. That was all he could ask for, right?

Except for today when the only other family member he had stood on an opposing side. On Rissa's side. Her emerald gaze was seared into his mind. She looked at him as if he held pieces of her world, but he couldn't remember.

He ran a hand through his hair, pulling it back into a tail. Why couldn't he remember? Everything else came back to him. Every moment of abuse he'd suffered at the hands of the Renaulds. All the loneliness of his imprisonment. She claimed to have been there too, but all he could see in his mind were Trystan and his father.

His father told him to be wary of the girl. She was an enchantress just as her mother had been. Lovely and deadly in the same breath. He'd seen the longing looks his father gave her as if she was Marissa Kane herself. Each time, Davi's body tensed up defensively. He couldn't explain it, but when his father had told him he had to leave again to deal with a magical disturbance at the border, he'd been almost relieved. For at least a few more days, the mysteriously familiar girl was safe.

He shook his head. Thoughts such as those were dangerous, and he had orders from his father. Orders that would finally give him everything he'd wanted since he woke with no memories.

"Your Highness?" the guard pulled him back to the current situation. Davi was a prince of Dreach-Dhoun who had no business consorting with prisoners.

That didn't stop him. He motioned the guard to unlock the door and then charged into the room.

Rissa stood near the bed in nothing but a silk nightgown they'd supplied her with. Her hair hung damp about her shoulders, but those eyes hadn't changed.

There was a challenge in them.

She raised her chin and stilled its quivering. "Yes?"

Her gaze asked the same question he continued to ask himself. Why was he there?

"What the hell do you want, Davion?"

His name held so much venom when she said it. A memory caught in his mind. A chastising voice. His lips curved up.

"Davi, you will answer me when I speak to you." She crossed her arms, her foot tapping against the ground.

"I'm the prince of Dreach-Dhoun," he said lamely. "I will speak when I deem it necessary."

Fire blazed in her gaze and she charged toward him. "I don't care who the hell you think you are." She pushed him back. "I know you aren't Davi any longer, but if you insist on walking around with his obnoxious face, you will leave this instant."

He touched his face. He was Davi. Just maybe not the Davi she thought she knew.

She pushed him again, and it was only then he noticed the tears hanging in her lashes. He grabbed her wrists when she shoved him again.

"Don't touch me." She yanked them back.

"Says the girl who is trying to push me out of the room."

"You're annoying," she growled.

"And you're angry. I understand."

"I hate you."

He shouldn't have cared but her words stung and he stepped away from her. "I only came to make sure you were still here and not escaping your room like that brother of yours."

That stopped her. "Trystan? Is he okay? What do you mean he escaped?"

He reached for her without thinking and tucked an errant strand behind her ear. She sucked in a breath and he dropped his hand.

"He's okay. For now."

"For now? What does that even mean?"

Davi turned to leave.

"Davion," she pleaded. "Don't go. What did you mean? Is my brother okay?"

He stepped through the doorway and swung it shut before she could come after him. Her voice followed his every move.

"Davi," she cried. "Please. Just... talk to me." Her voice quieted.

He suspected her next words weren't for his ears, but he couldn't walk away.

"Dav." She sobbed softly. "You can't do this to me." She was silent for a moment before she hiccupped another sob. "Earth help me." He imagined her pressing herself to the ground in prayer. "Make me stop loving him."

This was a mistake. Davi ripped himself from the door and strode away without a glance at the curious guard. If he stopped even for a moment, he wouldn't be able to fulfill his new mission. Failing his father was not something he could do.

CHAPTER 24

Trystan prowled around his room, feeling as confined as a caged animal. It had been two days since his meeting with Ramsey and the traitor, Lorelai. Two days of still not seeing Rissa, or Alixa, or Avery. Were they okay? Was Alixa okay? She shouldn't even be here with them. The rest of them, they were bound to this quest by blood. It was expected of them for who they were, but Alixa didn't deserve to be caught up in this. If anything happened to her because of him. He slammed his hand against the stone wall flanking the narrow window.

How long now since they'd been captured? Six days? And he still had no idea if Ramsey managed to switch the crystal. If truth were told, he had no idea if he could even trust Ramsey or Lorelai. What was he thinking, leading them all here with this idiotic plan? Hell, he hadn't even seen Calis Bearne since that first day. After growing up on stories of the man's ruthlessness and cruelty, being kept prisoner in this cage of luxury was not quite what he was expecting. Not once had Calis tried to question or torture him. He hadn't even called for his presence. What exactly did that mean? Maybe that was the torture in itself. Maybe him being kept here in this room while Calis tortured Ri or Alixa *was* his punishment. Or maybe he was trying to drive Trystan insane. If that was the case, then it was surely working.

Running his fingers through his hair, he stifled the groan of frustration building in his throat. Not even Davi had come back to see him after the fight. Davi. It killed him to even think the name. What Calis and Ramsey had done to him was beyond cruel. It was barbaric. Bringing him back to live this lie and not remember those who loved him the most?

"Dammit!" He took his anger out on a pile of books, sending them flying off the table in one fell swoop and crashing into the wall. He needed to do something. Ramsey and Lorelai had told him to wait, but he was tired of waiting. Enough was enough. He needed to get out of here. He needed to find Alixa. It was driving him over the edge not knowing what was happening to her. Striding across the room, he jiggled the handle of his door, finding it locked as always.

"Hey," he yelled, slamming his fist into the thick wood. "Is anyone out there? I demand you to let me out! Hey!"

He kept pounding the door, refusing to give up. Suddenly, he heard a commotion followed with yelling.

"Trystan? Trystan, is that you?"

"Alixa?"

"Yes, it's me. Step away from the door."

He stepped back in surprise just as the door flashed with a bright light and swung open, nearly knocking him from his feet. He stumbled but caught his balance as faces peered in at him from the hallway.

"What the...?"

"Trystan." Alixa crashed into his chest, her arms encircling his neck tight. "Thank the earth you're okay. I was so worried, and no one would tell me anything."

He hugged her back, the tight band of fear squeezing his heart earlier easing some now that she was in his arms. "I'm fine. You? Did they hurt you at all?"

She stepped out of his embrace, her eyes landing on his bruised face. "No, but you're hurt."

Her fingertips grazed his cheek, but he grabbed her hand and threaded his fingers through hers. "I'm fine. Had a visit from Davi is all." His eyes skimmed over her face, drinking her in. "It's so good to see you. I was so worried."

He broke off and looked over the top of her head as Avery entered the room.

"Avery, you are well?"

Avery ducked her gray head. "As well as can be, sire."

"Good." He kept watching the door expecting to see Rissa, but Avery was followed by Ramsey and the seer instead.

"How are you all here? The guards? And where is my sister? Is she not with you?" In answer to his question, Ramsey smiled slightly.

"The guards are taken care of, your Majesty. The spell I used will keep any soldiers in this wing out for a while. Your sister is being held in the rooms below us. We will get her on the way, but we must move quickly." Ramsey glanced over his shoulder in apprehension. "The guard change is not expected for another two hours, but I have no idea when the Prince might show up. He has been seen walking these hallways as of late."

It took Trystan a moment to realize the prince Ramsey was referring to was Davi, and the hope blooming in his heart shrank to pea size.

He turned to Lorelai. "Will Davi try to stop us if he finds us escaping? Is he loyal enough to his father for that?"

Lorelai's blue eyes clouded over with pain. "Yes. He will try to stop you. He has no kind memories of you, Trystan. Or Rissa. All he has is the hatred that was planted there. A hatred that has only grown and festered in his time here. Calis made sure of that. He will try to stop you and keep you here until his father returns."

Trystan rubbed a hand over the back of his neck and closed his eyes. He prayed to the gods that they would not run into Davi. He couldn't handle harming him in any way, but he knew Davi would not think twice. The rest of Lorelai's words registered then, and he opened his eyes. "Calis is gone? That must be Lonara's doing. She has lured him away." He turned to Ramsey. "Did you manage to do the switch and get what was needed before he left?"

"You mean this?" Ramsey pulled a leather cord from his tunic and held it gingerly in his palm. Hanging from it was a crystal identical to the one Lonara had given him. "How do you think I managed to take out so many guards with magic?"

"I don't believe it." Trystan's disbelief was tinged with awe and wonder as he stared at the crystal in Ramsey's hand. It was dull and lifeless right now, devoid of any power, but Trystan was well aware of the miracles this simple rock could produce. He reached out to touch it, but pulled back, afraid of what any simple contact may do. "This is the real Tri-Gard crystal?" Ramsey nodded as a tiny smile lifted the corner of his mouth.

"But how? How did you manage to get this away from Calis?" Alixa's confusion matched Avery's as they glanced between Trystan and Ramsey.

Ramsey nodded Lorelai's way. "It was all due to the seer. As much as you choose to harbor hatred against the girl, she is on our side. While I simply put Calis's guard under, she crept into his rooms and switched the crystal while he slept, much to her peril. Calis has no idea it's been switched and he will be well away from the castle before he even notices. As should we. We need to move. The crystal detects Lonara's presence drawing closer. She will be here to aid us soon. Let us not waste any more time."

The halls were eerily quiet. So quiet Trystan could hear every breath Alixa took as she crept down the stairs behind him, her hand in his. This castle was not much different from the one Trystan had grown up in. The same stone, mortar, and granite formed its foundation, but this castle felt wrong. Cursed, as if all the pain and misery it had seen over the years had permeated the walls and filled it with a deep sorrow that affected everyone in it. A shiver wracked Trystan's body at the thought of how Davi's bright light might eventually be extinguished by this shadowy place. No wonder he had not seen much of his brother in the new Davi. Light and virtue were traits that would not survive here in this palace of darkness.

Whatever magic Ramsey had performed on the floor above had not made its way to this level. The low murmurings of the guards outside of the room that undoubtedly held his sister, wafted down the hall.

All five of them ground to a halt at the sight of the still alert soldiers.

"I thought you took care of all the guards, Ramsey?" Trystan whispered in irritation and the old man shrugged.

"Apologies, sire. It has been twenty years since I've wielded this crystal. I guess I'm not as adept in my old age. My spell was not as effective as expected."

"Not exactly the reassuring words we need to hear at the moment," Alixa growled at Ramsey. "Do something already."

Before Ramsey could do as she ordered, the murmuring abruptly stopped, and a gravelly voice floated to them out of the gloom.

"Is someone there? Who's there? Who's slinking in the dark? Show yourself."

Lorelai moved into the aura of torchlight before Trystan could stop her. "Just me, Lorelai. No need to work yourself up."

"Oh, aye? And who's that with you?" The guard's voice was tinted with suspicion, and he raised his sword as he took a step their way.

"Fall into sleep." The words were spoken so quietly Trystan wasn't even sure who said it, but the brilliant flash of light from Ramsey's hand and the way the guard simply disintegrated into a puff of smoke told Trystan that the old man was not as fully in control as he wished.

"Crap!" The second guard yelled as he turned to run away, but Ramsey's power struck him dead center in the back and he crashed against the opposite wall, crumpling to the floor out cold.

"Effective enough," Trystan admitted as they hurried down the hall. Pushing the guard aside, Ramsey performed the same trick on Rissa's door as he had with Trystan's. The door swung open into an empty room. A fire roared in the hearth, filling the dark corners with light, but his sister was nowhere to be seen. A heavy dread filled Trystan's heart as he stepped into the room.

"Rissa..."

"Argh!" The scream hit his ears just before the weight landed on his back. Fingers dug into his hair and ripped, trying to pull out chunks of his skull with it.

"Rissa, stop!"

The painful ripping paused as the puzzled voice of his sister met his ears. "Trystan? What the hell?"

She fell from his back and landed nimbly on her feet as he turned to her, pain still throbbing in his scalp.

"How?" was all she said, but he shook his head at her.

"No time to explain, but we have to go. Ramsey says Lonara approaches. Our time to escape is now."

Rissa didn't ask any more questions. Grunting in agreement, she said, "Then what are we waiting for? Let's go." Glancing down at her hand, she grimaced as she noticed the chunk of sandy hair clenched in her fist. Throwing it aside, she grimaced at Trystan. "Sorry about that."

"You and me both," he whispered as he followed her out of the room, rubbing his newly formed bald spot.

Once they hit the hallway her gaze encountered Alixa and Avery, and a tiny smile lifted her lips, but the smile froze in place as soon as she saw Lorelai. Trystan groaned out loud as his sister's back stiffened in anger.

"You!" she growled as she lunged the seer's way. Lorelai stumbled back just as Trystan caught Rissa about the waist, holding her in place.

"Rissa, calm down. Despite what you may think of her, she is here to aid in our escape. She is the one who made our quest a success. You cannot harm her," he whispered in her ear, trying desperately to make her understand.

She stopped resisting him and Trystan knew his words had registered. Slowly he released her even though her back remained rigid and her eyes glared hatred at Lorelai.

"My brother tells me this is not the time, murderer, and he is correct. I will act as Dreach-Sciene's princess and not as a grieving daughter for the moment. But there will come a time when I will make you pay for what you've done."

Although Lorelai was visibly shaken, she didn't respond to Rissa's threat. Instead, she ran a shaky hand over her face and pointed down the hall. "This way. We will exit through the servant's quarters."

"Wait," Avery commanded, and Trystan paused as the sword master bent to retrieve the blade of the unconscious guard. She flipped it a couple of times in her hand, testing its weight. Finding it suitable enough, she gave Lorelai a curt nod. "Not my blade, but it will do. Now we are ready to go."

The cold, narrow passageway Lorelai led them through paled in comparison to the frigid wind that greeted them as they exited the castle. The icy air immediately tore at Trystan's lungs like sharp blades, yet he turned his face into the wind and accepted it with a deep breath. This was the first fresh air he'd breathed in a week. It felt good.

They paused in the shadows of the castle, looking out over the bobbing lanterns of the guards patrolling the grounds.

"Which way, Sorcerer?" Avery whispered and in response the old man paused, holding his crystal in the palm of his hand to shade it against any telltale sign of light. He closed his eyes and hummed to himself, oblivious to the impatient shuffling of Avery by his side. Suddenly his eyes popped open, and he grinned through the gloom.

"The west wall of the castle. Lonara awaits us there."

"West?" Alixa arched a brow. "Isn't west that way?" She pointed to the field covered in dead shrubs and trees stretching straight to the wall and crawling with guards.

Ramsey grew quiet. "I'm afraid so," he whispered.

Trystan huffed a sigh of resignation. "Of course, it is. Nothing about this can be easy."

"The magic will get us there intact," Ramsey assured them. "Just give me a moment to remember. And stay close."

"Remember?" Alixa whispered over Trystan's shoulder. "What the hell does he need to remember? If he means how to use magic, then were in deep sh---"

Ramsey bolted out of the shadows and straight into the field, startling them all. Trystan quickly regained his wits and yelled, "Go! And stick to him like a thorn to a rose." Ushering them all to follow on Ramsey's heels.

The cry went up almost instantly as they nearly collided with a guard who seemed to appear out of nowhere. His look of surprise quickly changed to alarm as he shouted, "The prisoners are escaping!"

Lights came bobbing at them from all directions, turning into more guards. Trystan's hand instinctively went to the missing scabbard normally a fixture at his hip and swore under his breath at remembering he was weaponless. Why hadn't he grabbed a weapon the same as Avery?

"Crap. You better know what you're doing," he yelled at Ramsey's back.

A mere moment after Trystan felt the air behind him tingle on the back of his neck, a bolt of light shot over his head and he ducked, disbelief escalating into fear at the realization the soldiers were attacking with magic. This was entirely new. He had no idea how to defend from magic. Pushing his fear aside, he willed his legs to keep moving as he called to Alixa and Rissa, "Keep running! Don't look back. Get to the wall."

Another bolt sailed past Trystan, splintering the dead tree towering to their left and blowing it apart. Trystan pushed Alixa out of harm's way as wooden projectiles hurtled toward them with deadly intent. Closing his eyes, he raised his arms over his head, hoping desperately to avoid serious injury. To his surprise, there was no contact. No splinters of wood tearing at his clothes or ripping away skin. There was nothing. Opening his eyes again, he blinked. The debris bounced off them like they were encased in some sort of invisible shield. That's when it hit him. Ramsey's instructions to stay close. He was protecting them with magic.

"Almost there," Avery turned, encouraging them on as the stone wall came into view. "Keep going, your Majesty."

"Almost where?" Alixa screamed as another flash bounced over their heads. "We're running toward a dead end. In case you haven't noticed, there's no gate in that wall!"

"Trust in Ramsey," Trystan yelled at her back, even though his own doubts were growing with every passing moment. Alixa was right. There was no sign of any way to escape.

"Trystan Renauld, stop running and face me you coward."

The familiar voice caused more fear than he could ever imagine churning in his gut. Davi.

"I said stop."

Trystan stumbled to a standstill just as Ramsey's shield broke. He could see it fracture and crumble like splintering ice all around them.

"No, no, no, not now," Ramsey muttered as he shook his crystal in desperation. Trystan's attention shifted to Davi. His brother stood on a slight rise behind them, a horde of soldiers at his back like hovering angels of death.

"You think I'd let you walk away that easily?" he cried out as he raised his hands and a wave of energy rolled down the slight slope, flattening everything in its wake. Trystan planted his feet, expecting to be swept away by the power, only instead, the very air in front of him appeared to solidify into a protective barrier. Davi's attack shook the barrier, but it persisted and protected them from the brunt of impact. Ramsey had gained control of his flickering power.

"Ah, Lorelai. Well done. Too bad you choose to stand with our enemies instead of your family."

Lorelai? She'd protected them and not Ramsey? Trystan glanced over at the seer, tears running down her face and her arms shaking with the effort of warding off Davi's magic.

"Fool," Rissa spat as she stared at Davi, her face a mask of frustration and her eyes wet with tears. Trystan grabbed her arm, trying to halt her words, but she shook it off. "We are not your enemy."

Davi turned to look at her then, and for a slight moment, Trystan swore *their* Davi was back. His face softened, and his eyes opened wider as if recognition set in. As if Rissa had finally gotten through. But then the *other* Davi took control, and he sneered in disgust.

"Lies. You may have corrupted my cousin with your falsehoods, but I will not fall for the same. Stop hiding behind your protectors, Renauld and face me like the king you think you are."

He pulled his sword and held it high above his head as he and his men ran down the slope.

Avery took a stance and held her blade, determined to protect her king at all costs, even as Rissa's scream of "Avery, don't!" was whipped away by the blast that shook the very ground beneath their feet. Trystan stumbled, but managed to stay upright as the dust and tiny rocks fell out of the sky, stinging his face and his eyes. Choking on the dust, he struggled to see through the plume that was settling over them all.

"This way," he heard Ramsey yell as realization finally set in. The castle wall that had been a solid barrier earlier was now just a gaping hole, Lonara Stone standing on the other side.

"Don't let Lorelai escape!" He heard Davi's order, but it only added fuel to the fire under their feet.

Magic crackled through the air and Lorelai screamed as black, gnarled roots exploded out of the soil, twisting about her legs. They dragged her down to her knees, pulling at her the more she struggled.

Trystan slowed, glancing back at her, indecision blocking his escape. Two guards grabbed hold of the magic-stricken Lorelai, keeping her from being sucked down further. She lifted her head, meeting Trystan's eyes and mouthed the word, "Go."

Guilt gnawed at him. His head swiveled, searching for Ramsey or Rissa, someone that could help the seer, but they were already on the other side of the wall. The roots began crawling with precision his way and Avery yanked him out of his stupor, making his decision to leave Lorelai behind with her scream, "Go, Sire! The other's need you. She can look after herself." So he ran, straight through perfectly formed hole, heat still wafting from the red-hot cinder blocks of stone where Lonara's magic had burnt its way through.

"Your Majesty," Lonara ran to Trystan, relief evident on her face. "I'm so glad to see you made it."

"You as well, Lonara, but I suggest we move our asses."

She nodded in agreement. "This way. My magic should block them long enough for us to escape. Help them onto the horses," she called out, and Trystan's men obeyed the command. Trystan ignored the helping hands of the soldier at his side. Instead, he leaped nimbly into his saddle, making sure everyone was accounted for before yelling, "Move out!"

As they rode into the darkness of the woods, he couldn't help but look back at the castle that had been his prison for the past week. A heavy sadness filled his heart at the thought of leaving his brother behind. Even though Davi no longer remembered that bond, it still crushed Trystan. Lorelai hadn't made it out with them either, and he didn't know what that would mean for her.

As the castle faded into the gloom of the night Trystan couldn't help but wonder if he would ever see either of them again.

"Sir, we've captured Lorelai but the rest of them got away. Should we go after them?"

The captain of the guards refused to make eye contact with Davi even though the question was meant for him to answer. He'd had too many run-ins with Calis to know failure was not an option.

Davi sheathed his sword and ran a hand through his wild hair. "No. Let them go. They won't get far."

The captain nodded in relief and rubbed at his neck, happy that it was still attached to his shoulders. If it were the king he had said those words to, he might not have been so lucky.

"Take Lorelai back to the palace."

The captain ducked his head and strode away, leaving Davi to stare at the smoldering hole left in the wall by Lonara Stone. She was powerful, he'd give her that. He could feel her power lingering still. But no matter. She would be no match for his father. None of them would be.

"It is done, father, as you requested," he whispered into the night air. "And now it begins."

CHAPTER 25

The palace of Dreach-Dhoun sat close enough to the border that it would only take a day to reach the relative safety of Dreach-Sciene.

Silence stretched between the weary group with the exception of Lonara and Ramsey who rode ahead of them.

Trystan strained his ears to catch their words.

"I have us hidden," Lonara said. "My crystal has been cloaking our movements since I found you, but I haven't sensed pursuit."

Ramsey didn't respond.

"Ramsey," Lonara said sharply. "Are you listening to me?" She sighed. "You're still thinking about that girl."

"Calis is going to ruin her."

Trystan knew instantly who he was speaking of. Lorelai.

"That's no longer our concern." Lonara smiled in sympathy. "I'm glad they were able to get you out of there."

"Because of her." His hand flew to the crystal in his pocket. "I'd never have been able to get my crystal without her and we'd still be trapped without my magic."

Trystan pulled his horse alongside the two sorcerers. "How did she get it?"

Ramsey narrowed his eyes. "I don't like what you're inferring, boy."

Trystan put his hands up in defense. "I only mean that it all seems too easy. Maybe Lorelai really was on our side or maybe something else is at work." He glanced behind him as if to look for enemy soldiers lurking in the trees.

Ramsey stopped and turned to his grandson. "Lorelai betrayed her family for me, for you, for your kingdom. And now she's probably going to pay for her crimes with her life. I will not have you question her motives. I have known that girl since she was knee high. I have watched her leave on mission after mission for her uncle. Each time she returned, there was a little less life in her eyes. She has done some bad things, but would you want your character decided by the worst you had to offer?"

Trystan's response didn't have the anger behind it anymore. "She killed my father."

"Never pretend you have the world figured out, King. Because you'll be wrong. Every time." He turned back to Lonara. "You're right. I don't sense any kind of pursuit. Calis should be hunting us down."

"I don't like it." She drew one of her long, thin swords. "We must be prepared and make haste to the border. Briggs is waiting there, but we may yet run into border guards before we reach him."

Ramsey pinned her with a look Trystan didn't understand. Understanding flashed in her eyes and she nodded. "I know."

"Know what?" Alixa asked as she, Rissa, and Avery joined them.

Ramsey grunted and resumed riding.

Lonara sighed. "Just something Ramsey and I will need to take care of once we've returned magic to the earth."

"Do you really think you can do it?" Rissa's question surprised Trystan because she'd been so quiet since getting out of the palace.

Lonara glanced at each of them in turn, taking in the doubt in their expressions. "Yes."

Darkness covered the world by the time they reached the border and left the beautiful fields of Dreach-Dhoun for the barren mountains of Dreach-Sciene.

"It stopped," Rissa whispered. "Do you feel it?"

As if they'd crossed some invisible line, the energy that'd been buzzing along Trystan's skin snapped back, fading as if it'd never been there at all. He shivered and pulled his cloak across his body to protect against the chill in the night air he hadn't noticed before.

His limbs grew heavy, finally succumbing to exhaustion after their long trek to the border. Without magic, his body barely had the strength to keep going.

"Can we stop for the night?" Alixa asked. "I don't know how much farther I can walk."

Ramsey slowed. "In Dreach-Dhoun, the magic was bolstering your energy. What you're feeling is the sudden loss of it."

Lonara's eyes were sympathetic. "We're almost there. We need to perform the ceremony before anyone from Dreach-Dhoun can catch up in case they decide to pursue us after all."

"Ceremony?" Trystan asked.

Ramsey, seemingly over his aggression from moments before, winked. "How else do you expect us to return every bit of power to the earth?" His thumb rubbed over his crystal.

Avery gestured for Trystan to pull back and ride with her so they weren't overheard. "Your Majesty, are we really sure we can trust the Tri-Gard?"

Trystan considered her question. It was warranted. He wasn't sure he liked his grandfather. Ramsey Kane had spent too much time in Dreach-Dhoun. Trystan also wasn't fond of Briggs, but the old man had stuck with them.

But Lonara? His gut told him that of them all, she was the one he could put his faith in, just as his mother once had.

"We need them," he said. "Everything up to this point has been about uniting the magic keepers. We don't really get to decide whether or not they deserve our trust."

"Do you think they'll stay true to their word and return the magic?"

He rubbed the back of his neck and glanced towards Ramsey and Lonara. "I guess we'll find out tonight."

Lonara led them on a path that wound down into the forest rather than farther up into the mountains. The last time they'd been in Isenore, the air chilled them to the bone. Not much had changed in the short time they'd been away.

"Stick close together," Lonara warned. "Don't ride off the paths. There are some areas that drop off and we don't need anyone injuring themselves in the dark."

Rissa pulled her horse up beside Trystan. Re-entering a land without magic affected her most of all.

Leaving Davi behind had as well.

Trees rose up on either side of the trail, casting shadows in the dark. They came to a small clearing with a cave at one end.

Rustling sounded up ahead and Lonara flicked her hand, creating a ball of soft light to illuminate their surroundings.

Trystan released a breath as Briggs appeared at the mouth of the cave. A grin spread slowly across his face and he looked to the sky. "See, I told you they'd make it."

"No time to waste," Ramsey snapped at the old man as he slid down from his horse.

Briggs continued to smile, but there was something behind his smile that made the hair on Trystan's arms stand on end.

"It's good to see you, old friend." Briggs's voice sounded more sane than Trystan had ever heard it. "And so... intact."

"Intact?" Ramsey growled. "Until the last few months, Calis kept me in his dungeons. Do you know what happens to people there, Villard?"

Trystan flicked his eyes between the two men. One seemed older than the earth and the other was young, but he knew appearances were deceiving. They were close in age.

Ramsey's words stuck in Trystan's mind. He'd heard stories of the Dreach-Dhoun dungeons. The living conditions. The torture.

He sucked in a breath. "That's why you're so worried about Lorelai. You truly do know what will happen to her."

Ramsey met his eyes, sadness sparking in their depths. For one moment, Trystan got a glimpse into the man his grandfather truly was. The rest of them dismounted slowly.

Lonara pushed herself between the other two Tri-Gard members and threw her sword to the ground. "Now is not the time. We must perform the ceremony. Tonight. Avery, Alixa, go stand watch. We cannot be interrupted. The prince and princess must stay close."

The two women nodded and disappeared into the shadows at Lonara's request.

She walked by Trystan and Rissa, ignoring their eyes on her as she rolled up her right sleeve to reveal the sigil etched into her skin. "Briggs, you're first."

Trystan busied himself with tying up the horses as the old man lumbered toward the far side of the clearing and revealed his own sigil. He reached into his pocket and pulled his crystal free. Closing his eyes, he held it above the ground and mumbled something under his breath. His voice grew louder. "Chaos. Disorder. Darkness. Your magic is here." Light shot from his crystal, striking the ground. A cloud of dust encompassed Briggs. When it drifted away, he was left standing on top of his sigil that had been carved into the ground.

Lonara nodded and stepped forward, performing the same movements as Briggs. "Light. Fate. Harmony. Your magic is here."

Instead of moving forward to complete the triangle, Ramsey jerked his head up. "Someone's here." Light broke free of his crystal and he directed it toward the trees behind them.

Trystan spun.

Standing in the light with his sword at the ready was Davi.

"Ramsey," Lonara yelled. "Hurry. Trystan, deal with him. We must complete the ceremony."

Trystan's eyes met Davi's across the span.

"Looking for this?" Davi asked, extending the hilt of his sword in front of his chest. Even at the distance, Trystan knew he was holding the Toha sword, the one belonging to the king of Dreach-Sciene. The very weapon with Ramsey Kane's sigil carved into the hilt. The first clue of his mother's true identity. Calis' guards had taken it when Trystan was captured.

"Trystan," Rissa yelled.

His eyes found her with Lonara's discarded sword in her hand. Her hard eyes bore into him as she ran forward.

"I can't fight him, Ri," he whispered.

"You have to." She glanced back at the Tri-Gard, their only hope. "It isn't Davi anymore. Not our Davi. He died months ago."

Trystan shook his head to rid it of Lorelai's words that crept in every time he thought of Davi's death.

Someone you love will sacrifice their life for yours. Davi had done that without even blinking.

Someone you love will forsake your name. Had that meant Davi as well?

Someone you love will die by your hand. Trystan stumbled back. A part of him hadn't wanted to believe her words when she first said them. But she'd seen all of this. Davi's transformation. The fight that was to come.

"No," he said to himself. "I won't kill him."

"Then don't." Her eyes pleaded with him. "You were always the better swordsman. Injure him. Knock him unconscious. Something, anything, to keep him away from them." She flicked her eyes to the ongoing ceremony as she pressed the sword into Trystan's hands.

"No." He dropped the sword. "I won't do it. I won't kill him." He pulled at his hair. "It won't come true. I refuse to be controlled."

"What are you talking about?" Rissa picked up the sword and forced him to close his fingers around the hilt.

Davi advanced, grim determination on his face. He didn't once look toward the Tri-Gard, instead focusing solely on Trystan.

"You can't stop them," Trystan said.

"I didn't come for them." Davi raised his sword. "I came for you."

"I won't fight you, Brathair."

"Then you will die." Davi's words were as cold as the night air, but his face didn't hold the same harshness. Did he truly want them to die?

Davi covered the span between them at a run, yelling at the top of his lungs. His scream echoed in Trystan's ears as his sword slashed down in a clean sweep, aiming to sever Trystan's head from his body. Trystan blocked the blade with his own, grimacing as the tip scored his temple, blood mingling with sweat. Trystan retracted his blade allowing the other to slide off, causing Davi to stumble with the change in momentum. Trystan moved fast to the right to a better fighting position, but Davi recovered from his stumble quicker than anticipated and unleashed a barrage of attacks and strikes that forced Trystan to back up on the defensive. Sweat poured from his brow and down his face and he could taste it along with blood. Davi would not give up until Trystan was dead. He realized that now with crushing clarity.

"Davi, stop fighting me." He grunted as he parried another volley of blows, each more powerful than the one before.

"Not until you die under my blade." Eyes that were once filled with laughter now stared into Trystan's with pure madness.

Davi was always a good fighter, but Trystan could feel the power mixed with hatred radiating off him as he swung with relentless fury. Trystan struggled to absorb the impact of the attacks while desperately searching for a way to end the battle with both of them still very much alive.

In an attempt to best his attacker, he swerved his body, feigning a low attack, but his effort proved ineffective as Davi uppercut Trystan's sword with his own and sent Trystan stumbling backward. He lost his balance and tried to catch himself from falling, even as he saw Davi approaching out of the corner of his eye, sword raised to strike.

"Davi, no!" Rissa screamed as she jumped in front of her brother, ready to take the blow meant for him. Davi paused for a split second before a roar of anger bellowed from him and he swung the blade Rissa's way. Trystan leapt without thought, pushing Rissa out of the way and barreling into Davi's side. A grunt fell from Davi's lips at the impact as his sword flew out of his hand. They fell backwards, Trystan landing on Davi's chest, nose to nose with his old friend. Both of them gasping for breath, Trystan tried to quell the sudden nausea rising from the pit of his stomach. Davi had tried to kill Rissa. Would have run her clean through if he hadn't stopped him. Their Davi would never have tried something so horrendous. Their Davi no longer existed.

"You tried to kill my sister, you bastard," Trystan hissed as he held his sword to the vulnerable hollow of his opponent's throat. "I ought to kill you right now for that."

"Trystan, stop."

His sister's voice cut through his fury.

"Trystan, please," Rissa sobbed.

Trystan strained against the impulse to bring his sword down, cutting off the other man's life. Davi's face was hauntingly familiar.

Someone you love will die by your hand.

"I can't." A single tear collected in the corner of Trystan's eye and he blinked it away. "I can't." His eyes ran down the sword he'd taken from Davi. His sword. Davi had been there when he'd been given it. He was supposed to have served as Trystan's second in command.

Davi's chest rose and fell rapidly, but he pushed Trystan off.

"Do it," he croaked. "Come on, King. End my life like you've wanted to since I was a prisoner in your palace."

"You were never a prisoner, you idiot." Trystan kept one hand braced him against Davi's chest as the other continued to hold his sword against the Dreach-Dhoun prince's throat.

Davi swallowed and his skin grazed the blade. "Your lies won't work on me."

Everything inside of Trystan screamed for him to do it. To take this life. It would fulfill the curse. It would take something from Calis Bearne.

The Tri-Gard's chanting grew louder in the background.

"Agh!" Trystan grit his teeth and used his remaining strength to pull the sword back. "No! I won't do it."

Someone you love will die by your hand.

"No!" He threw himself to the side, away from Davi, his sword clattering onto the ground beside him.

Davi rolled with a quickness Trystan didn't know he had. He ran for Lonara's sword, picking it up without stopping his forward movement. Before Rissa could escape Davi, he yanked her tight against his body and placed the blade across her neck. Her hands grabbed at his forearm in defense trying to remove the sword, even as her wild eyes begged Trystan for help.

"Davi! You don't want to do this." Trystan leapt to his feet, his hands held out in pleading. "Let her go."

"Let her go? Like you let me go, Renauld? You showed me no mercy by holding me prisoner for years." The Davi glaring at Trystan was so unfamiliar, so unlike the Davi he knew that Trystan's heart sank.

There was no reckoning with this man.

"Why should I do as you ask? You stole my life from me. You and your father kept me away from my home. My family. You stole my childhood. Why shouldn't I take something from you that you hold dear?"

"None of that was real," Trystan growled in frustration as he swallowed the lump of fear in his throat. "Davi, please, you need to understand. Those were false memories planted in your head by Ramsey and your father. You're my brother, Dav. We're your family, me and Ri. We stole nothing from you. You have to remember. Please."

"Stop your lies!" Davi's angry scream was tinged with desperation. "I don't want to hear any more lies."

"Davi, remember when we were on the ship to Sona?" Rissa's voice was calm and collected. "You were so seasick? And you told me the story of how you never felt the palace was your home when we were growing up?"

"Stop talking," he growled as he dug the blade harder into her neck. Trystan started forward, but Rissa held up her hands, holding him off.

"I remember. I told you the palace *was* your home, and we were your family and that the next time I heard you say that I would kick your ass. I still mean it. So if you don't want a severe fight coming your way, Davion, you will let me go right this moment."

Trystan sucked in a breath as the blade at his sister's throat trembled a little before nicking her skin.

"Ri," Trystan yelled and leapt their way just as a loud groan erupted from the very earth around them and the land under their feet began to shake. The Tri-Gard's chanting reached a crescendo.

Leaves rained down as the trees swayed with the movement of the earth and Trystan was thrown to his knees.

He pushed himself to his feet, shaking his head to clear away the noise of sliding rocks and rupturing earth. Avery and Alixa came running from the trees, both halting in shock at the sight of Davi holding Rissa, his sword hanging loosely at his side.

"Trystan!" Alixa pointed to the Tri-Gard. Their crystals rose in the air of their own accord as the sorcerers were lost in a trance.

The crystals flew toward the earth and slammed into the ground in a cloud of dust, disappearing. The ground undulated, throwing them all off balance.

Rissa let out an ear-piercing scream and a blast of power released from her, striking Davi square in the chest. He shot into the air before slamming back into the wide base of a tree and sliding down into an unconscious heap.

Rissa stared at her hands in horror.

Magic filled the air with its thickness, zipping along Trystan's limbs, infusing strength into him. He no longer felt as if he'd traveled all day or even been in a fight. He felt as if he could do anything.

He stepped in front of Rissa. Her eyes shone as she looked around him to Davi's form.

"I... I... Trystan." She buried her face in her hands. "I couldn't control it. The magic entered me and fought for release." Her back shook. "I think I killed him."

Trystan pulled her against his chest. He'd blamed himself for Davi's death before, but he hadn't actually wielded the sword. Rissa was never going to forgive herself. He rested his chin on her head and sucked in a quivering breath.

"It's over," he whispered. "The Davi we knew has been gone a long time."

He looked toward the Tri-Gard who were all picking themselves up from the ground. They'd done it. The impossible.

Magic. He'd grown up seeing it as no more than a fairytale. Now it was back. Dreach-Sciene was as it should be.

Lonara and Ramsey's lights were gone now, throwing them all at the mercy of the night. Why weren't they recreating it?

A commotion started from their direction and when Trystan pushed Rissa forward, he caught sight of Ramsey lunging for Briggs.

"I've been waiting twenty years to get my hands on you," Ramsey growled.

Lonara didn't stop him this time.

When Briggs spoke, his voice held none of the craziness they knew him for, only clarity and a cold aloofness.

"But I was better than you, Kane."

Ramsey knocked Briggs to the ground.

Briggs laughed as the air rushed out of him. "It's been a long time since I've had a good old brawl. Where's your magic, Ramsey?"

Ramsey pulled his hand back and light shot toward Briggs. He rolled away and deflected it with a wave of his hand. "That's more like it."

Lonara grabbed Ramsey's arm before he could try again. "We have him now. Let's take him back to the palace of Dreach-Sciene. He's our only source of information on Calis."

"Twenty years!" Ramsey jumped to his feet. "I have been doing Calis' bidding for twenty years because his loyal dog, Briggs Villard, was close enough to my grandchildren to strike."

Trystan shook his head. "No, we found him in Sona." Briggs couldn't be the enemy, could he?

Ramsey turned on him, but before he could speak, Rissa's scream reached their ears.

Trystan had run to Ramsey as Rissa approached Davi's prone form. He looked so still, lifeless. Rissa hadn't gotten a chance to examine Davi the first time he died. She hadn't seen the way his face softened with an innocence he'd long lost. It had kept her from grieving properly.

When Davi died, it hardened her and she couldn't ever go back to the girl she was before.

It was a funny thing, loss. From the moment she'd seen Davi in Dreach-Dhoun, she'd imagined she could have him back. Even when he didn't recognize her, there was still a chance. While he was standing at his father's side, there was breath in his lungs and therefore she was alive as well.

Magic flowed into her effortlessly. Briggs once told her magic had to be drawn upon, controlled. It took practice and skill. But it entered her veins of its own will as if the earth was giving her a gift instead of making her take it.

The Tenelach allowed her to feel the earth trying to thrive before magic was returned, but it hadn't prepared her for the hum vibrating through her body now that it had.

It was all she heard as she stared down into Davi's face. Tears welled in her eyes. There was yelling across the clearing. She glanced up briefly. Something was happening with Ramsey and Briggs, but her mind was to full to process their struggle.

She lowered herself beside Davi in a crouch and for a moment, wished she too could bring him back as Calis had. That she had the power of the Dreach-Dhoun king. It was hard to reconcile the man before her with the one who'd come to Dreach-Sciene to kill Trystan.

Yet, he was no longer the boy she'd known.

She stroked his cheek and was so focused on his closed eyes, she almost didn't notice it.

His chest moved.

A whimper caught in the back of her throat. "Dav." She felt frantically for a pulse, her eyes widening when it beat strong against her finger. "Davi." She gripped his shoulder and shook him. What if her magic had broken his neck?

Her hands ran over his chest looking for any open wounds and finding none.

"Davi," she cried. "Please, wake up. You can't do this to me. Not again. I barely survived it the first time." She bent forward and pressed her face to his chest. The tears broke free. "Please. Please."

She lifted her head in time to see Davi's eyes shoot open.

"Dav?"

His arms flew up, and he grabbed her by the shoulders before launching himself at her and pinning her to the ground. Her scream pierced the night air.

"Davi," she wheezed, trying to breathe as she was crushed. Her magic warmed her skin, but she refused to use it. Not on him. "It's me." She squeezed her eyes shut, waiting for him to make his final move. "It's Rissa. It's me. It's me. It's me. I love you."

"Ri," Trystan called, running toward them. He was too far. Davi could end her before he reached them.

She waited for him to fulfill his mission for his father. Kill the king and princess of Dreach-Sciene.

But the moment didn't come, and she opened her eyes. A dark gaze held hers, confusion clouding over his face.

"Davi." She reached up to touch his cheek. He didn't stop her.

The confusion faded away.

"Ri." His voice was hoarse as if not used to saying her name.

She swallowed a sob.

Trystan reached them and ripped Davi off Rissa, pushing him to the ground beside her. He held his Toha sword, angling it down towards Davi.

"Trystan." Rissa sat up and bent forward to bury her face in her hands. "It's him."

"What do you mean?" Trystan snapped.

Rissa looked up with tears streaming down her face. "Our Davi is back."

Understanding flashed across Trystan's face and he stumbled back, dropping his sword to the ground.

Davi laid on his back breathing heavily, his eyes drifting to the stars above.

Ramsey joined them. "He's gone."

"Who?" Rissa pushed herself to her feet.

"Briggs. We'll explain later, but he got away." His eyes found Davi. "But it seems someone else has returned to us."

Rissa wiped her face. Davi was here. Their Davi. She turned to him and extended a hand. The minute he took it, warmth enveloped her. The earth too was rejoicing in his return.

As soon as he was on his feet, Rissa stepped toward him wordlessly. He moved back, but she caught him. "Davion, you're infuriating."

As if his full name on her lips cracked the wall standing between them, he pulled her against him. She wrapped her arms around his back and held on as if it would keep them together forever.

"I didn't remember you." His entire body shook, and he buried his face in her neck. "I can't believe I forgot you. I held a sword at your throat."

"It wasn't your fault." She breathed him in. "I remembered enough for both of us."

His tears dampened her skin and she couldn't remember ever seeing Davi cry, even as a child.

"I'm so sorry." He squeezed her tighter and rested his chin on her shoulder.

"Me too. I gave up on you."

He pulled back and wiped his thumbs under her eyes.

Trystan approached them, his own eyes shining. He put a hand on Davi's shoulder, but Davi flinched away and released Rissa.

His eyes darkened when they found Ramsey. "I sense magic. It's returned? What have you done?"

"What do you mean?" Trystan asked but Davi shook his head and stepped away from Trystan. "I... I'm sorry. I need to..." Without an explanation, he took off into the trees.

Trystan and Rissa both looked to Ramsey, desperate for answers.

Ramsey sighed. "That boy." He shook his head. "You don't know what he's been through. He may have his memories returned, but that doesn't mean he's the same young man you lost. I'm afraid he never will be again. Do not forget, whether he remembers his life with you and your father or not, he is still the son of Calis Bearne."

Lonara spoke up for the first time since Briggs escaped. "None of you are to attempt using the magic you now have access to. Sleep tonight. Tomorrow is a new day with new challenges. We have brought power back to Dreach-Sciene this day, but it is only the beginning."

CHAPTER 26

Davi pulled magic from the earth, using it to protect himself from the cold morning air. Now that Dreach-Sciene had their magic back, the cold would stretch out for months. He'd experienced seasons in Dreach-Dhoun. The power kept the weather in balance. It would allow crops to thrive and the people to be fed.

If they survived what was to come.

The voice in his head reminded him just who he was, as if he could forget. His memories were recovered days ago, but the ones of the past few months were also there.

Growing up, he'd longed for a family name. He'd always just been Davion. Now he was Davion Bearne. He wanted to hate the name and the man it came from, but he couldn't.

His father was not a good man.

And yet he loved him.

He was the only family Davi had. Well, not the only family.

Lorelai. What was happening to her? She'd chosen to help Ramsey and Trystan.

The crunch of grass alerted him to someone's presence just moments before Trystan dropped down beside him. It wouldn't be long before they reached the far edge of Aldorwood and the forests grew thicker the closer they got.

But the trees didn't provide him with the solitude he needed, the peace he'd sought since waking up to remember everything he'd done to the people he loved.

Trystan extended a wooden bowl toward him. Rabbit stew again, no doubt.

"Thought you could use some breakfast."

Davi took the bowl, doing his best not to shrink away from Trystan's voice. He could see the two of them in his mind, sparring and laughing and fighting side by side. But what he hadn't told anyone was that the memories Calis and Ramsey planted in him were still there as well. One moment, he saw flashes of stumbling through the palace with Trystan after too much wine. The next, it was Trystan standing on the opposite side of the bars of a cell, taunting him.

With Rissa, it was better. Ramsey had taken everything of her so all he had was the truth.

He couldn't even look at Ramsey Kane.

"Eat," Trystan said.

"Are you going to force me?" Davi looked to the sky, ashamed at the harshness of his voice. "I'm sorry. I just can't always tell what's real."

"I'm real, Dav. You and I are real. You're my brother."

Davi breathed in deeply. "Truwa, Brathair."

A grin spread across Trystan's face. "Trust, brother." He nodded toward the bowl. "Now eat. We have a long day ahead of us."

Red hair shining in the sunlight caught Davi's gaze and Trystan followed his line of sight. Rissa stood at a distance with Avery and Alixa, sword in hand. She danced around them with quick feet.

"Since when is she training with a sword?" Davi raised an eyebrow.

"You know Ri. She finally annoyed Avery enough to teach her. She's fast, but not really any good at actually handling the blade."

Davi laughed, the first genuine laugh since coming to Dreach-

Sciene. "She's good at everything else. She has to leave some things to the rest of us who are rather useless without a sword in our hands."

Trystan looked sideways at him. "I missed this."

"I'm going to try, Trystan. Do you think they'll welcome me back at court now that my parentage is known?"

"They're coming around on Alixa."

"Duke Eisner is not the same as Calis Bearne and you know it."

"Then it's a good thing I'm the king now."

Davi stared into his stew as he took another bite. "That's going to take some getting used to."

Trystan laughed, but when Davi looked at him again, all humor was gone.

"Can I make a first request of the king?"

"Dav." Trystan gripped his arm and when Davi tried to flinch away, he held it tighter. "Anything."

"I need to go back to Dreach-Dhoun."

Trystan's hand dropped. "I wasn't expecting that."

"It's not what you think." Davi rubbed his neck. "My cousin, Lorelai. I need to get her away from my father."

"No. Absolutely not. I am not letting you risk your life for the woman who killed my father." Trystan jumped to his feet and Davi followed him.

"She didn't do it."

"That's bull, Dav. Don't lie to me."

"It's true. Lorelai couldn't kill him. A man my father sent to watch her finished the job."

"I don't believe you."

"Do you want to know how I know?" Davi growled. "Thom was blackmailing Lorelai. Using her. Her body. Her mind. She almost let him destroy her just to keep her secret from Calis." He stepped close to Trystan. "And you know what I did? I killed him."

Trystan's jaw unclenched. "This Thom killed my father?"

Davi nodded.

"And he is dead? By your hand?"

"I'm glad he is." Davi pounded on the side of his own head. "My feelings about Marcus may be messed up because of what Calis put in here, but I know what he was to me. He has been avenged, Brathair."

Trystan leaned back against a tree and slid down until he was sitting again. "My father's killer is dead."

"I have a lot to tell you, Trystan, but I'm not going to tell you everything. You're going to have to be okay with that. You have to give me time."

"Now that we've completed our mission, time is something we finally have."

"I wouldn't be so sure of that." Davi knelt in front of Trystan. "All we've done is exactly what my father wanted." He paused for a long moment to study Trystan's face. "My orders were to allow you to escape and then follow you. Once magic was returned to Dreach-Sciene, I was to kill you."

"I'm not an idiot, Davi. As soon as I learned who Lorelai truly was, I started putting the pieces together. I assumed Calis wanted the Tri-Gard in his possession. We knew he'd sent us to find Briggs in Sona. Lorelai set us on that path. I even suspected there was something we didn't know about you. But, after we got the magic back?" Trystan shook his head. "That doesn't make sense. Why would he want us to have our power?"

"Because everything you've done, every action you've taken was orchestrated, planned. You've been playing his game since before you knew it."

"More than just finding Briggs?"

Davi met his gaze. "Lorelai was first sent to your father when we were five-years-old. She told him a man would rise to defeat the darkness. He took that to mean you. Lorelai also placed me in your household at that same meeting. For the next fifteen years, my father used blood magic to watch you through my eyes.

Davi scratched the back of his neck. "This is where Briggs Villard comes in. He's always worked for my father. His job was to stay close to the palace. He lived in the village. His proximity to you and Rissa is the reason Ramsey did many of the things he did. When the time came, Briggs relocated to the swamps of Sona where he released a bit of his magic, suddenly making him traceable by all seers."

Davi paused, but when Trystan didn't say anything, he continued, "So, Lorelai reappeared. She told us of feeling the magic."

"What about the curse?" Trystan leaned forward. "The one she placed on me. Was that Calis' doing?"

Davi shook his head. "It wasn't a curse that was placed on you. Lorelai saw it come to pass. Those words were a reading of the future." He smiled slightly. "But you were able to change it."

"I had to," Trystan said.

"So, Briggs joined you and he was able to lead you to Lonara. The unit of soldiers who attacked when I... died." He gulped in air. "They were supposed to capture us all and take us to Dreach-Dhoun. Briggs released too much magic. He'd never been good at controlling it. One of the guards told me my father was livid with him. Then Eisner went after you, and I've never seen my father so angry. You weren't supposed to die yet. Not until you were reunited with Ramsey. You had to reunite all the Tri- Gard. Only you could get them to willingly do what Calis has wanted them to do for years. Once you were captured in Dreach-Dhoun and Ramsey had his crystal, he allowed you all to think you escaped."

"But why? Davi, why does Calis want us to have our magic?"

"Think about it." Davi ran a hand nervously through his dark hair. "The people of Dreach-Sciene have their magic back, but they're untrained and weak from years of suffering. They don't know what to do with the magic they now have. If Calis had brought his army across the border before, then he wouldn't have magic either. Calis' army wouldn't have stood a chance in hand-to-hand combat with Dreach-Sciene's massive army. Now that the magic is back, Calis' army has the upper hand. They know what to do with it. Your people do not."

Davi sat back on his heels as Trystan's expression grew angrier with each passing moment. For a second, he allowed his mind to retreat into the false memories of Trystan and his father. Their treatment of him. Their scorn. It hadn't seemed any different from the questions before him now.

But it was different. He pushed out a breath. It hadn't been real. This was real. He couldn't fear the man who'd been more like family to him than his own father.

"Everything we've done." Trystan shook his head in disbelief. "This quest. Finding the Tri-Gard. Why me, Dav? Why did Calis choose me?"

Davi rocked back and pushed himself to his feet, his eyes finding Rissa once again. She blocked Avery's sword as Alixa cheered her on. He'd never seen her fight with a sword, only her bow. His father had been right. Women like her were dangerous. Once you loved them, you'd do anything they needed you to do. Anything.

The answer was so simple. His father hadn't told him why Trystan was important or why it had to be him, but it didn't take much to figure it out.

He looked back down at his friend. "Because my father loved your mother, and she chose someone else. Because Ramsey loved his daughter and spent the past twenty years doing everything he could, everything he was against, to keep my father from going after you. Because Lonara loved the girl she trained, and only for that girl's children would she come out of hiding. Everything comes back to you, Trystan. You and Rissa."

"Me and Rissa. He's coming for us."

"Not just you this time, Brathair. He's coming for Dreach-Sciene."

Davi turned without another word and walked toward the three women. When he stepped up beside Alixa, he motioned to the sword in her hand. "Mind if I borrow that?"

She raised one dark eyebrow. "I still don't trust that you're not evil Davi."

"Evil Davi?"

She shrugged. "That's what I've been calling you in my head. Evil Davi and annoying Davi."

"What about ridiculously handsome Davi?" He smiled.

Alixa smirked. "Guess that answers that question. Evil Davi was a dick, but he didn't have the ego of annoying Davi."

Neither noticed Trystan joining them until he spoke. "Say it again, Dav."

"Say what?" He didn't take his eyes off Rissa and Avery's fight as he spoke. Even as she got her butt kicked, Rissa was beautiful. Her hair flew out behind her as she spun and then ducked under Avery's blade, holding hers high to block it.

"The ridiculously handsome thing."

Davi finally tore his eyes away from Ri to look at her brother in amusement. "That's kind of an odd request from a fancy king... or from anyone, really."

Trystan shook his head with a laugh. "It's just... that was the first time you sounded like yourself. We get that you need time. We all do. It's only been a few days, but before this morning, you've barely spoken to us and when you have, there was a formality to it."

Davi understood what he meant. He'd separated himself from them through their days of travel and their nights among the trees.

He shrugged. "Admit it, you've just missed seeing this ridiculously handsome face."

Trystan slapped him on the back. "Thank you."

Alixa held out her sword to Davi hilt first, and he wrapped his hand around it before stepping forward. Rissa and Avery ceased sparring immediately and looked to him in question.

"You're gripping the sword too tightly, Ri." He reached her and Avery joined the others.

Rissa stared at him, distrust in her eyes. He'd put it there. She'd been through hell and he'd avoided her. Offering her a smile, he reached forward and touched her sword hand. "Loosen your fingers. The sword should be an extension of yourself, and if you use too much strength just to hold it, you'll tire quickly. Let it swing freely."

He put distance between them and demonstrated with Alixa's sword, letting it fly in a controlled arc.

Rissa watched him for a moment longer. "Sometimes you have to hold on to things to keep them from flying out of your grasp."

She wasn't talking about swordplay.

He froze. "Every battle is different, but they all come down to one thing. Not strength. Not power. Endurance. You can't give every part of yourself in the beginning because there'll be nothing left when it really matters."

She swung her sword, and it met his in a crash of steel. "I should have fought harder for you."

"You didn't know I was alive." He advanced, and she met his movement with more ease than he'd been expecting.

"But then when I did, I gave up on you."

"If you'd tried to fight for me in Dreach-Dhoun, I would have destroyed you."

She flinched, but he wouldn't hide the truth from her.

"Endurance is key, Rissa. You'd have given everything to save me. No one is worth that."

She lowered her sword, chest rising and falling rapidly. "You are."

"And then where would Dreach-Sciene be? They need their princess. You did the right thing."

Her chin quivered, but she stopped it by hardening her jaw. "I left you."

"That wasn't me. It was…" He glanced at Alixa. "Evil Davi."

Rissa closed her eyes, trying to even her breath. "Not evil. Never evil. Confused. Broken." Her eyes snapped open and trapped him. "Lost."

Davi's sword slipped from his fingers and fell to the ground. "I was so lost." His shoulders shook.

Rissa discarded her blade and stepped in front of Davi. Raising her hand, she paused as if asking for permission.

He nodded, and she cupped his cheek. He leaned into her.

"You're not lost anymore."

Her words permeated his skin, seeping into him and sending warmth throughout his body.

"Blood doesn't matter. You're one of us. Family. And you're finally home."

He crushed her to him and took her lips as if he needed them for survival. She wound her hands around the back of his head and kissed him back.

"I never thought I'd get to do that again," she whispered, resting her forehead against his.

He leaned in for another kiss when Trystan cleared his throat. Davi had forgotten they were there.

Rissa laughed and pulled her face away, but remained in his arms.

Trystan moved toward them and wrapped his arms around them both. It had always been the three of them since they were children. Marcus was gone, but he'd raised them to follow in his footsteps.

Lonara's voice drifted out to them as she and Ramsey appeared. "Are you all ready to start the day? We should reach Aldorwood by nightfall and then the palace by early next week."

The palace. Home.

Davi released Rissa and studied the faces surrounding him. It wasn't just the three of them this time. He clasped Trystan's shoulder.

"We did it, didn't we?"

"Did what?" Trystan asked.

"We set out to do the impossible, bring magic back to our dying kingdom."

"It wasn't impossible. You said it yourself, Calis planned this."

"Trystan." Davi shook his head. "That doesn't change the fact that you united the ancient Tri-Gard and brought back the power you once told me you didn't believe in."

Trystan's smile spread across his face. "Yeah, then I guess we did. I only wish my father could have been here to see it."

"Me too."

Alixa spoke up. "The only reason you boys accomplished anything is because Rissa and I forced you to take us along."

Trystan was about to argue, but he met Davi's eye and laughed. "Probably true."

Davi bumped Trystan's shoulder with his own. "He'd be proud."

"Yeah, I think he would. For a moment. Then he'd tell me to get back to work because this was the easy part."

Davi arched a brow. "Easy? You think me dying and coming back to life while you were chased across Dreach-Sciene was easy?"

Davi's words were lighthearted but Trystan heard the underlying fear. "I think, my friend, that this is only the beginning."

There's more!! The story continues in A War For Love!!

ABOUT M. LYNN

M. Lynn has a brain that won't seem to quiet down, forcing her into many different genres to suit her various sides. Under the name Michelle Lynn, she writes romance and dystopian as well as upcoming fantasies. Running on Diet Coke and toddler hugs, she sleeps little - not due to overworking or important tasks - but only because she refuses to come back from the worlds in the books she reads. Reading, writing, aunting ... repeat.

See more from M. Lynn
www.michellelynnauthor.com

ALSO BY M. LYNN

FANTASY AND FAIRYTALES

Golden Curse

Golden Chains

Golden Crown

Glass Kingdom

Glass Princess

Noble Thief

Cursed Beauty

THE HIDDEN WARRIOR

Dragon Rising

Dragon Rebellion

QUEENS OF THE FAE

Fae's Deception

Fae's Defiance

Fae's Destruction

Fae's Prisoner

Fae's Power

Fae's Promise

LEGACY OF LIGHT

A War for Magic
A War for Truth
A War for Love

ABOUT MICHELLE BRYAN

Michelle Bryan lives in Nova Scotia, Canada, with her three favorite guys; her husband, her son and her crazy fur baby. Besides her family, her other passions in life consist of chocolate, coffee and writing. When she is not busy being a chocolate store manager or spending the day at her computer, she can be found with her nose stuck in any sort of apocalypse book.

See more from Michelle Bryan
https://www.michellebryanauthor.com

ALSO BY MICHELLE BRYAN

THE CRIMSON LEGACY TRILOGY

Crimson Legacy

Scarlet Oath

Blood Destiny

The Waystation - a Crimson Legacy novella

THE BIXBY SERIES

Grand Escape (Strain of Resistance Prequel)

Strain of Resistance

Strain of Defiance

Strain of Vengeance

THE LEGACY OF LIGHT SERIES

A War For Magic

A War For Truth

A War For Love

POWER OF FAE SERIES

The Lost Link

The Lost Magic

The Lost Prince

STANDALONE

Clash of Queens

ACKNOWLEDGMENTS

A War for Truth was the most emotional book we've ever written, and the amount of support and love we've received has been amazing.

First and foremost, the people who made us feel we were writing a story worth telling. Our advanced reader team who badgered us with questions about when this would be ready and talked across the internet about Prophecy of Darkness. You, readers, are why we do what we do. The stories are for you.

Our brilliant content and line editor, Melissa Craven, who never held back opinions and made our manuscript shine.

Angela Campbell, our wonderful proof editor. I'm sorry we can't be friends anymore, but I don't control what my characters do. <;

Linda Higgins, our talented sketch artist. Your artwork for the cover continues to amaze me.

Maria Spada for creating this awesome cover.

Bethany, Genevieve, Patrick. Your opinions are invaluable.

To everyone who pre-ordered or waited with bated breath for this book, THANK YOU.

Let me put it this way, Davi wouldn't exist without you <;